THE GREEN HELMET

THE

1958 NEW YORK

GREEN HELMET

a novel by Jon Cleary

WILLIAM MORROW & COMPANY

THE GREEN HELMET

c.1

1

The car, anonymous in the early morning darkness, its colour dawn-grey like that of all the other cars, hit an oil slick as it came through the bends of the Esses. Its driver fought the skid as the car hurtled down toward Tertre Rouge, the car's headlights slashing a berserk pattern across the track ahead of it. For one moment it seemed that the driver had won the battle; then the car slewed suddenly and hit the wattle fence. It seemed to rebound, as if the fence had been of concrete instead of thin pickets, then abruptly it halted right across the middle of the track. Almost instantly, back at the pits, a yellow light began to flash a warning to the other cars coming at full speed up the straightaway. The race slowed, and the cars went cautiously through the Esses and past the wrecked car. A minute later the wreck, recognised now as a blue French Gordini, had been pushed from the track.

3

In the stands a thin, elderly man turned as the girl beside him, wrapped in a rug, sat up and stretched. "Another one out. That's seventeen gone now. Did you sleep?"

The girl shook her head, and a lock of black hair fell down over her face. She found a comb and began to arrange her hair. "I slept, I guess. But it was like being out there in the middle of the track."

Joseph Bartell grinned. "You kept twitching all the time."

"I was dodging cars." Sophie Bartell smiled back at her father. "I don't know how you could sit there all night and not get a headache from all the noise."

Bartell tapped his pocket and smiled again. His smile, to a stranger, might not have appeared pleasant; but his daughter saw affection in it and was both surprised and warmed. "I turned off my hearing aid. Best comfort yet invented for watching auto races. Better even than a soft pillow for a bony tail—sorry, girl!" The long, thin face seemed to crumble with embarrassment. "That's the way we talk around the plant. I keep forgetting I'm not there now."

"You've spent too long around the plant," Sophie said.

"Your mother said that, too," said Bartell, and Sophie knew that she had hurt him.

She put her hand on his. "I'm sorry, Dad. I didn't mean it like that."

"I know, girl," he said and turned his hand over under hers. He pressed her fingers, the first physical sign of affection that had passed between them in four years. Sophie wanted to lean forward and kiss him, but she was held back by more than the fact that they were surrounded by hundreds of people. She was not sure what her father's reaction would be; she had a dim memory as a child of once seeing him break into tears when her mother had stolen up and kissed him. She had not seen her father weep in years, not even at her mother's funeral, but the tears could still be there. And she did not want to see him weep before a crowd of strangers.

4

She turned away from him, breaking the moment as gently as she could, and searched for a flask in the small basket at their feet. "Coffee?"

"You wouldn't like to go down to one of the restaurants and have a good breakfast?"

She had noticed the hesitation before his question. "Would you?"

"I—well, not just yet awhile. Do you mind?" He fidgeted a little, looking down at the track and not at her. She wondered if he was sometimes like this with the men who had worked for him, but she couldn't imagine it. At the plant she knew her father was the boss, and he never had to ask anyone if they minded anything. "Ham Rafferty should be coming out again soon. I want to watch him."

"You've been watching him every minute he's been on the track."

"I know. But it looks as if it might rain soon. I want to see what he's like in the wet."

"It's dangerous when it's wet, isn't it?"

"Could be. Depends on the driver. Depends, too, on the tires he's got under him."

Bartell was staring across the pits toward the lightening sky in the east; his lips moved soundlessly, almost as if he were praying for rain. Sophie looked at him and felt another quiver of the fear she had known as a youngster, in those years when she had begun to realise that there was a part of her father that she could not understand. It was in those years that her father had become dedicated to his plant, when he had begun to forget about being a husband and father, when her mother had slowly begun to die.

"When are you going to speak to Rafferty?"

"When this race is over," Bartell said. "He's the man I want, if I can get him. A driver who's been racing long enough now not to be reckless but who'll still take a risk if the money is big enough. And I'll pay him well."

5

"Is he the sort of man who's interested in money?"

"They're all interested in money," said Bartell. "The pros, I mean. I'm not talking about these rich amateurs. Rafferty is a pro, and so was his old man. I can't see him turning his nose up at what I'll offer him."

"Was Rafferty's father good, too?"

"One of the best ever. He was killed in the Mille Miglia in 1947. Rafferty was right on his tail and saw his old man go off the road."

Sophie shuddered. "You seem to know a lot about the Raffertys."

"I've been looking them up, girl. I don't hire pigs in a poke."

"And Rafferty has gone on racing, even after seeing his father die like that? He *must* be interested in money."

"Who isn't?" Bartell said, then happened to glance at his daughter. "No, I shouldn't have said that, Sophie. Your mother never was."

"Neither were you, once," she said.

"I'm still not," he said.

"But you believe other people are?"

He nodded. "Most people. People like those fellers out there." He nodded at the track and the cars hurtling by. "Otherwise they wouldn't be out there, risking their necks season after season."

Sophie stood up. "I think I'll go find a place where I can wash up. Then I'll try for some breakfast."

"You want me to come with you?"

"No," she said, and tried to make her tone as gentle as possible. "You stay and watch your Mr. Rafferty."

He smiled gratefully at her, and she thought: this is my father, and he is almost a stranger to me. She smiled back at him, brightly and warmly, stricken by her conscience; then she made her way out of the row of seats and went down behind the stands. As she walked she was aware of the cars

6

screaming by on her left, like juggernauts on a treadmill that had run amuck; across the track two cars had pulled in at their pits and the mechanics there had begun their stylised drill that was almost like a swift, short ballet movement. The air was heavy with the acrid smell of oil and fuel and rubber; would rain, she wondered, do something to clear the air? Even Manhattan, at rush hour on an August evening, had smelt better than this.

Her head ached from the broken sleep she had had and the constant noise of the cars that now seemed as if it had been going on forever in her ears. Indeed, the sound seemed to have gone beyond her ears; the noise was in her brain, drilling away at her very sanity, she thought. She smiled to herself at her own exaggeration; but she wondered how some people, especially the drivers, could endure this din for twenty-four hours. To begin with, she had been fascinated by the atmosphere of the race; she had never seen a motor-racing meet before, not even a stock-car meet back home in the States. She had caught the infectious excitement of the crowd, and for the first hour or two her interest had been as enthusiastic as that of her father. Then gradually she had become bored by it all and now she was downright sick of it.

What other sport goes on as long as this, she wondered. Maybe a game of chess; but that was quiet, and not hard on the nerves. Her bottom and back ached from constant sitting, and she had a crick in her neck from the position in which she had slept. She had once sat through two hours of sleet to watch a football game in the Yale Bowl; she had been broiled in the deep pan of Forest Hills, watching a Davis Cup match. She had never felt as uncomfortable, dirty, weary and bored as she felt now after watching a race that was still only half over.

Yesterday afternoon at four o'clock, while the June sun blazed on the Circuit Permanent de la Sarthe and the sud-

7

den hush of a quarter of a million spectators had become something almost tangible, sixty sports cars, of all shapes and power, had been lined up at an angle to the road in front of the pits. The cars—British green, French blue, Italian red, German white, Dutch orange, Belgian yellow, the white and blue of the Americans, the blue and yellow of the two Argentinians, the red and white of the Swiss—dazzled like a metal rainbow. Across the road from the cars had been their drivers, each standing in a small numbered circle, like slaves ready for some huge auction; some of them trying to look unconcerned, some of them prancing about as if the hot surface of the track were burning their feet, each one of them conscious of his stomach puffing and contracting like a trapped octopus. A loud-speaker, nasally French, sardonic, almost insulting in its calm recital, had been counting off the minutes. Then the flag had fallen, a nervous tic in the vast glare of the scene. There had been a loud gasp from the crowds in the grandstands, and the drivers, feet hissing and whispering on the tarmac, had hurled themselves across the track and into their cars. A moment later the first car, its tires screaming at the sudden torture, its engine moaning, then rising to an angry whine, had been away; the rest of the field followed at once, weaving itself into a many-coloured pattern that, as the race went on, was to turn itself into a long, twisting streamer from which odd snippets would occasionally fall away, sometimes dramatically and suddenly. Now, twelve hours later, the Le Mans Grand Prix d'Endurance, the twenty-four-hour race, was half over, and the huge sleeping crowd had begun to stir again, coming awake like a giant animal thirsting for excitement and, perhaps, hoping for blood.

Not all of the crowd had been asleep. Many had been saving their energy and waking hours for the past week, determined to enjoy every moment of their twenty-four hours' stay at Le Mans, like lovers on some sort of annual honeymoon. Behind the six grandstands, where many people dozed uncomfortably in their seats, the coffee and liquor bars were doing good business. Across the track, behind the concrete pits where no one slept at all except the relief drivers trying to shut their ears and minds to the din only yards from their stretchers, here was the area known as Le Village. Here were rows and rows of display kiosks, manned by red-eyed, crow-throated salesmen: would monsieur like a new car, an electric lawn mower, an engagement ring for the girl he had just met? In another area was the carnival: circuses, music halls, shooting galleries, snake charmers. Girls stood on platforms smiling with tired eyes and through cracked make-up at the suckers in the crowd; one twitched a muscle in her thigh, and it was hard to tell whether it was supposed to be provocative or whether it had been a nervous reflex from sheer weariness; sex appeal was not something that would ever merit a Grand Prix d'Endurance. The Fattest Woman in the World sat on her stool losing weight by the hour; next door the Thinnest Man was a crumpled line of shadow. The Strongest Man in the World couldn't find the weakest link in the chain round his neck; the Two-headed Woman had a double headache. Beyond the grandstands the early morning light sought dim reflection in the windshields of an enormous shoal of parked cars.

Dawn began to break through low-hanging clouds. The weather had cooled during the night and the sky had a cold forbidding look. A flight of sparrows burst from the trees around Arnage and swept across the paling sky; a hawk, swift as the cars below but silent, plunged out of a cloud, and the sparrows swept down to the trees again. From the stands one could only guess at what was going on along the rest of the course, from the Dunlop bridge right round to the White House, six miles of track where anything, from comedy to tragedy, could happen. From down on the Mulsanne straight came the whining tornado of cars accelerating to top speed;

the chain lightning of their headlights flickered through the trees. Along the straight the higher-powered cars were doing 180 miles an hour; on each side of the road dark pines stood like disapproving peasants halted on their way to early Mass. Tires squealed, engines whined and roared, cars switched off their lights and began to take on colour, becoming individual again, and the sleeping crowd stirred, sat up, stretched and found the taste of excitement still there in their dry, sleep-lined mouths.

Sophie crossed the footbridge and walked down behind the pits. She was hungry and thirsty, but all at once she now had a compelling desire to see at close range some of the racing drivers. She particularly wanted to see Ham Rafferty.

She recognised him from his photographs when she was still twenty or thirty yards from him. He was standing at the back of the pits, talking to a grey-haired woman and a younger, slimmer man who looked as if he could be his brother. A spot of rain fell, then another, and Rafferty looked up. With his head raised and the light from the pits striking slantwise across his features, his face had a hard, cruel look: he looked a man suited to his profession, one where death was part of the wages. Then he looked down at the grey-haired woman and smiled, and his face seemed to soften.

A moment later the grey-haired woman and the younger man turned away from Rafferty and came past Sophie. "We must get some tea," said the grey-haired woman. "I can never begin my day till I've had my cup of tea."

Sophie knew at once that this must be Ham Rafferty's mother, and she wondered how the grey-haired woman could go off for a cup of tea so casually, just a little something with which to begin her day, while her son was drawing on his helmet and gloves and getting ready to go out and begin *his* day, the end of which he might not live to see.

Sophie looked back at the pits, but Rafferty had already

turned away and was talking to a short, plump, bald-headed mechanic. He looked relaxed, a little bored and almost too sure of himself. He looked like a man who would have no time for anyone but himself, on or off the track, and before she had even met him, Sophie began to dislike him.

She turned away and began to walk back toward the foot-bridge. She did not like motor racing and she knew she never would, and she began to regret now that she had come to Europe with her father. She had been here at Le Mans only since yesterday at lunchtime and already she had had enough of the sport to last her a lifetime. Yet she knew that if her father asked her to go with him to a motor race every day of their stay in Europe, she would have to go with him. She was not just at the beginning of a new day but starting her life all over again.

The grey-haired woman, who had been here at Le Mans since Friday evening, who had been coming here every year the race had been held since its first meeting in 1923, said, "I don't like the look of that sky. It looks like rain."

Taz Rafferty patted his mother's hand. "Don't worry. Ham can handle a wet track as well as anyone. You know that."

Janet Rafferty nodded and tried not to let her worry show on her good-humoured, unlined face. She had been a beautiful young girl, and the beauty was still there, if only like that of a rose left too long under glass. "I know. But rain is like—well, a memory. I can't forget what it did to your father."

"I don't think Ham forgets it, either. That's why he's made himself so good in the wet. He's got it down to a fine art."

Janet smiled, letting him know she was putting her fear behind her, and drew the yellow cardigan she wore a little tighter about her. "It's a little chilly, isn't it?" Born and reared in India, she felt every northern breeze was a personal attack on her; she read the weather reports in *The Times*

11

the way other people read horoscopes. "I wish they'd hurry with that tea."

Taz laughed, glad that the moment of fear and worry was past, even if it had not gone completely beyond recall. Each year at Le Mans and in the various Grands Prix, at Monza, Monaco, Spa, wherever they were held, it was always like this when Ham drove; their mother could take the shorter races on the British tracks, the bread-and-butter events, but the longer races always taxed to the limit her capacity for self-control. Taz knew that his mother thought her fear didn't show, and he took care to be as offhand and casual as he could be in his reassurance of her. His brother Ham, he was sure, the man who caused the fear and worry, knew nothing of what it cost their mother each time he drove in the big races. But even while he felt resentment of his brother's indifference, Taz was already dreaming of the day when he, too, would drive in the Grands Prix.

"I'm going to six o'clock Mass," Janet said, searching in her handbag for her rosary beads. "Are you coming?"

"I'll leave it till later," Taz said. "There's nine o'clock and eleven. Ham's due out again soon."

"That's why I'm going now," Janet said, laughing a little, taking the edge of fear out of her voice. "Now is when he wants the prayers. Not when he's resting."

"It's a little early to start praying for him to win, isn't it?" Taz asked this same question every year and every year he got the same answer.

"I never pray for him to win. I just pray for him to finish."

"Here's the tea," said Taz and silently thanked the waiter, who appeared every year at just this right moment.

"I'd better hurry, otherwise I'll be late for Mass," Janet said.

"It's begun to drizzle," said Taz, looking out the door of the restaurant. "Did you bring an umbrella?"

12

"Of course," said Janet and produced an umbrella from the back of her chair. "I don't relish standing out in the open hearing Mass with rain water trickling down the back of my neck. There's a limit to my devotion. Unfortunately."

Taz helped her move her chair out from the table. "You aren't so vague after all, are you? You think of practically everything."

"Practically everything," his mother said and didn't look at him, looking instead out at the falling rain and knowing that the worry had begun to show again on her face.

Taz watched his mother walk away through the drizzle that was now turning to steady rain. He loved her and never wanted her to be hurt again as she had been when his father had been killed; and yet lately he had begun almost to resent her for the promise she had extracted from him five years ago, when he had been only sixteen. She hadn't asked the same promise of Ham, his elder brother, and lately Taz had begun to resent him, too.

He turned up the collar of his jacket and stepped out into the rain. He walked round in front of the stands and stood behind the low fence for a moment, staring across the safety bank and the track at the pits opposite. He saw the works car that his brother drove flash by with Harper, the codriver, at the wheel, and saw him acknowledge the signal board held up to him by one of the mechanics in the pit.

Two more laps, and then his brother Ham, the one he resented, the one who had everything, would take over the car. He would take it out onto the track and drive it in the race that Taz, standing there in the cold beaded curtain of rain, oblivious of it, ached and hungered in every part of his body that he, too, might some day drive in.

The moment he was out in the middle of the track Ham Rafferty knew that it was a long time since he had driven through rain like this. Even before he had reached the end of the pits his goggles were smeared with water; a silver Mercedes, hurling spray, went past him while he was still gathering speed, and it was like driving into a waterfall. He drove through the wide sweep under the Dunlop bridge almost by instinct; when he could see properly again he was coming down into the Esse bends. He changed down to second, keeping his tail right for each section of the bend, then he was out of them, changing up to third, then swiftly down again as he came into Tertre Rouge.

This was a tricky corner even in dry conditions. Because of the cambering of the road you had to take the corner later than seemed wise. The lift of the car's tail over the hump of the road as it joined the main road to Tours could take him in a spin into the protecting sandbank beyond. He judged the moment carefully, holding his line, feeling the adhesion beneath him, then he was through, and the corner was behind him. Ahead of him, a dim grey strip running up into the flooding sky above, was a four-mile stretch of fast road.

He went up through the gears, confident now, and began to overhaul three smaller cars ahead of him. At 170 he went past a Panhard crawling along at 105, and a moment later, like a horizontal waterspout, whooshed by an M.G. and an Osca. At this speed the rain was being deflected over his head by the pressure of the car as it swept through it; his goggles were clear now but the road ahead was still lost in the thick fog of rain. But this was his seventh Le Mans, and he knew the road as well as he knew the instrument panel in front of him. He had driven round the course innumerable times in practice; in the six races he had completed he had done more than 1200 laps. He knew this section of the Department of Sarthe probably better than he knew his home county of Buckinghamshire back in England: the stern dark pine forests, the grey farmlands, the French provincial houses with their buttoned-up look; and he knew the sometimes grey, sometimes blue, sometimes black road better than he knew any road in the whole of the British Isles. All he had to worry about was the possibility of wrecks across the track, but they were always a possibility even on the driest of days. If you thought about such things, you would never drive. So you didn't think about them, but left it to your reflexes to get you out of trouble when they suddenly appeared in front of you.

He saw the hump in the road ahead of him and immediately he began to slow. As he came over the hump he saw the right-angled bend of Mulsanne four hundred metres ahead of him down the road. He began to brake, changing down opposite the 300, 200 and 100-metre signs that marked the right-hand side of the road like numbered tombstones, and went into the corner in bottom gear. Out of the corner of his eye he saw a car coming back up the road that led to Tours; its driver must have come down to the corner too fast and rather than risk going into the sandbank and having to dig himself out, had taken the safer if less spectacular way of the escape road. In the 1952 race Ham had gone that way himself and been glad of it. Only fools and men who didn't live long sneered at escape roads.

He accelerated, changing swiftly up, and went over the next rise at close to 150. The road began to curve right and he began to slow as he came down into the corner at Indianapolis. He went through the first bend in third at eighty and changed down to take the next bend in second. Then he was into another right-angled bend, this time Arnage. A car had gone into the sandbank here and its driver was furiously digging it out. Ham came out of Arnage in low gear, and on acceleration passed four cars whose drivers didn't trust the slippery surface. He went over the brow of the hill halfway between the eleven and twelve-kilometer stones at close to 120 and went down toward the White House corner. This was the worst corner of all, the part of the track with the highest record of casualties. There had been some famous smashes here; twice there had been pile-ups involving no less than six cars. One cynical driver had once suggested that the name of the place should be changed to the Blood House.

Ham went into the corner in third at around 110. The rain seemed suddenly to thicken as he was halfway through the bend; for a moment he had an impression of sitting in a cockpit full of water. The rain whipped his face and slashed across his goggles; he drove blind but kept his wheels on the line he had chosen. He came out of the bend and the blinding rain, pleased with the way he had driven through it.

And there was the red car right across the track in front of him.

Reflexes, developed through experience, took control of him. He saw the gap between the car and the outside of the road and he aimed the green car toward it. He went through with inches to spare, the red car suddenly bursting into flame right beside him, and then found himself heading for the bank. He twisted the wheel round, got back on the road; then felt the rear wheels going from beneath him in a wild sliding skid. He careened up the road, working desperately on the wheel, fighting the car and yet coaxing it at the same time, but the road had turned to glass beneath him and the tires were oiled silk. He saw the bank loom up ahead of him, saw people running away in terror, saw the grey implacable sky as the car hurtled up toward it, felt the daggers of rain against his face, then everything had spun away from him, the ground was rushing up to meet him, and a moment later he saw and felt nothing.

Up the road at the pits the flags came out and the yellow light began to blink its warning.

2

The blue Jensen sports car came slowly up Park Lane and turned right into the forecourt of the Dorchester Hotel. Over in Hyde Park the trees had begun to droop, like great green balloons out of which the summer air had begun to leak. Nannies wheeled perambulators with fussy dignity, as if they were pushing royal broughams. Children played, dogs ran, birds pecked, lovers fondled; summer had gone, and the days were running out. September was slowly turning gold, autumn had come over the crest of the world and was moving south, and another year had begun to die. Ham Rafferty, in the Jensen, had no use for autumn.

He backed the car into a space between a shining black Rolls-Royce and a yellow Cadillac with CD plates. Once he had passed here and seen an Austin Seven parked in the forecourt, like a waif on the doorstep of Buckingham Palace;

an hour later when he passed this way again, it had been gone, and the Dorchester, a little paler perhaps, had settled back on its foundations. He sat for a while, easing the stiffness in his left leg. A commissionaire came from the doorway of the hotel and hurried across toward the Jensen, leaning into the wind that blew across from the Park so that his top hat wouldn't be whisked away into the rich creek beds of Mayfair. Ham looked at the tall, burly man walking toward him with the crooked neck, one eye cocked up toward the teetering hat, and wondered if London hotels dressed their commissionaires for the benefit of American tourists. He had by now become completely unconscious of the fact that he himself was given to eccentricity in his dress.

He wore a yellow bow tie, a green checked shirt, a tan waistcoat with brass buttons, a green large-checked hacking jacket, tan cavalry twill trousers, yellow suède boots and a brown-and-white-checked cap. Right after the war, when he had first started racing, the effort to be conspicuous had been conscious; for a while he had also sported a huge moustache, a relic of the RAF, but too many girls had complained that it tickled them. He had felt the shadow of his father, who had still been racing then, and he had set about building his own reputation and personality. For a time he had been something of a joke, he knew; but being such a big man, no one had ever risked joking about him to his face. Then people had begun to take his eccentricity for granted; by the time of his father's death, the eccentricity had become habit for him. He had become a bird of paradise unaware of the drab plumage of the other birds in the jungle.

Ham got out of the car, reached in for his stick, then limped across the path after the commissionaire. "I want to see Mr. Bartell. What is his room number?"

"Mr. Bartell has a suite, sir," said the commissionaire, and Ham felt he had slighted Mr. Bartell. "The lift will take you up, sir."

Ham felt in his pocket, but all he had was sixpence. He never had any small change, often even forgot to carry money with him at all, that was part of his father that he had inherited, anyway. But you didn't tip top-hatted commissionaires with a sixpence. Ham smiled gratefully, trying to give it the value of a two-shilling piece, went into the reception lounge and across to the lift.

"Mr. Bartell's suite," he said.

The liftman didn't give Ham a second look; celebrities had made him blasé toward the oddly dressed characters who sometimes came to the Dorchester. He stared at the wall of the lift and dreamed of Thelma and the Hammersmith Palais. "Mr. Bartell's floor, sir."

The stiffness had begun to ease out of Ham's leg now, but he still leaned on the stick; he hadn't yet learned to trust the leg again. He knocked on the door of the suite and stood waiting. He was looking forward to meeting Mr. Joseph Bartell, if only out of curiosity.

He took off his cap and ran a hand over his thick, dark hair. He needed a haircut: he would call in at the barber's downstairs when he was leaving. A woman went by, looking at him out of the corner of his eye; he was aware of her scrutiny and he grinned to himself. He was not vain about his attraction for women; it was something he took for granted, just like his skill at driving. You either had it or you didn't, and if you were sensible you accepted it. He had never looked a gift horse in the mouth; least of all, Nature.

He was a big man, some said too big for a racing driver; he had never been successful in small cars and he had given up driving anything below the 1500 c.c. class. Before his accident at Le Mans he had been in perfect condition; like several other drivers, he had trained as assiduously as any boxer. Now, after the six weeks in hospital and the ensuing convalescence, there was a little fat on him around the middle. His face was handsome only to those who admired strength; it was too broad for those who looked for the aesthetic. There was a hint of cruelty in the features, the hooked nose and the big, determined mouth; but the dark blue eyes under the thick black brows had a balancing hint of humour and kindness. The cheekbones were high and broad, the jawbone square and with a decided sweep to the chin. A Milan newspaper had once featured a cartoon of him, emphasising the hooked nose and the strong chin, and christened him L'Aquila, the eagle; with the Continental penchant for romanticism, the name had stuck to him on all the European circuits.

The door was opened by a girl. Even against the light of the big windows behind her, Ham could see that she was attractive. He had heard that American executives always went in for attractive secretaries.

"Won't you come in, Mr. Rafferty?" She was a well-trained secretary: she had been expecting him. She stood aside, letting the light fall on her face, and he saw now that she was more than just attractive: she was downright beautiful. "My father called up to say he has been delayed. He asked me to look after you."

"Your father?"

"I am Sophia Bartell." She closed the door behind him and turned round so that the light from the window was now full on her. He looked carefully at her, trying not to stare; beautiful women fascinated him, and he would not want to live in a world where there was none. He had seen plenty of American women and known a few: in London, in Paris, in Rome, and once in Florida when he had gone there to drive in the Sebring 12-Hour. He had felt that they had all come from the one mould, at least the ones he had known: hair style, dress, even their manners and opinions had been the same. Their individuality had been lost in the pages of the glossy magazines they bought and studied; they had become the

20

American Woman, born of *Vogue* and the *Ladies' Home Journal.* He had for some years idly studied a beer advertisement in American magazines that he would pick up in his travels: each year it featured a different girl, Miss Beer of the Year, and yet except for the colour of their hair, you couldn't tell this year's girl from last year's or the nominee for next year; healthy baby-faced college beauties who looked as if they had never had a beer in their lives. Sophia Bartell came from no common mould, and she looked as if she might drink beer or even vodka.

"Will your father be long?" he said. "Would you rather I came back later?"

"He expects to be only ten minutes or so," she said. "Do you mind waiting? Would you care for a drink?"

"Yes. A beer, if you have one. Do you drink beer?"

"Occasionally," she said and looked a little puzzled. "I like your English beer, when it is iced. Usually, though, they serve it lukewarm."

"It's the sensitive English stomach. It needs coddling."

"Have you a sensitive stomach?"

"No," he said and returned her smile; at least American women were always easy to meet and become friendly with. "I'll take it iced."

"We'll sit over there by the window." She poured the drinks and followed him across the room to the chairs by the window that looked out across to the Park. "Is your cane a legacy from your accident at Le Mans?"

"Yes. How did you know about that?"

"I was there. I didn't see you go off the track, but I saw the ambulance bringing you in." She looked down at her glass; he noticed the extraordinary length of her eyelashes and wondered if they were false. "A lot of people thought you were dead."

"So did I," he said and tasted his beer. "I would have been if a couple of spectators hadn't dragged me out of the car just

21

as it caught fire. I never knew who they were, but they saved my life."

"Were you burnt at all?"

"Just down my left arm."

"Badly?" Then she flushed and made a quick little gesture with her hand. A thick gold bracelet winked in the September sun; he was glad to see there was no gold or diamonds on her fingers. "I'm sorry. You mustn't want to talk about it."

"It's all right," he said. "You get over it. You have to, if you want to go on driving. It doesn't pay to brood or indulge in self-sympathy."

"It must be like bull fighting. Or test piloting."

"In a way," he said and changed the subject. He had met too many women fascinated by only the glamour of motor racing: he found himself hoping that Miss Bartell was different. "What does your father want to see me about?"

"Didn't he say in his letter?"

"No. He just introduced himself and asked me to come and see him. I made a few enquiries about him—" He smiled. "Perhaps I should have known of him, or at least heard of his tires. But frankly, I hadn't."

"The Bartell tire is not one of the big ones back home in the States. I even have friends who have never heard of it."

"But I gathered your father was a big man. Big by our standards, I mean."

"You mean someone told you he was a millionaire?" She smiled, but there was no derision in the smile, only a gentle amusement. "He is, I guess. But millionaires don't necessarily have to be well known."

"Obviously," he said. "I'm told that down in Texas there is one perched on every oil derrick."

The smile died. "You've got something against millionaires, Mr. Rafferty?"

He saw that he had made a mistake: he was forever finding

that not everyone appreciated the Irish humour he had inherited from his father. "I didn't mean any offence. But we English do joke about American millionaires. It is probably just plain envy. Luck is always something to be envied. There are lords and dukes in this country who envy the dustman who wins the pools."

"I don't know how much luck had to do with my father's being rich. He started with nothing. Every cent he has he's made himself."

"Then I admire him, too. All out of tires?"

"All out of tires," she said, and he wasn't sure that she didn't sound faintly bitter.

Then the door opened and Joseph Bartell came in. As he came across the room toward them Sophie saw his hand go to his pocket. He never had his hearing aid turned on unless he wanted to listen to people; he had lived so long with himself that he had come to treasure silence. "Mr. Rafferty. Sorry I'm late. My daughter looked after you?"

"Very well." Ham stood up, moving stiffly. He saw Miss Bartell look at his leg, then at her father. But Bartell had turned away to get a chair.

"Don't get up, Mr. Rafferty," Bartell said, bringing his chair to the window. His voice was a rough rasp, some of the words slurred and chopped before they had reached his lips; he had come a long way from New York's lower East Side, but part of it had followed him. "Get us a drink, will you, Sophie? Ask Mr. Rafferty what he likes."

"He likes cold beer," Sophie said and went to get the drinks.

Bartell looked after her for a moment, and to Ham it seemed that he was looking at his daughter with the pleasantly surprised approval of a stranger. Then Bartell turned back. "Suppose you're wondering why I asked you here, eh?"

"I've wondered, Mr. Bartell. But I haven't made any guesses."

Bartell sat back in his chair, locking together a pair of hands that seemed too big for the lean wrists. Ham, sitting across from him, saw a man almost as tall as himself, a thin camel of a man who sat awkwardly in his chair with his legs flung out as if they were not controlled by him. His face was thin and dark, with a mouth that once might have been soft and gentle but now had tightened into something resembling a closed slot. The black eyes once might have been lighter; they looked as if they had turned black with contempt of the world. The stiff grey hair was close-cut, the veins in the temple showing clearly, like worms beneath the skin. His clothes hung on him as if they had been bought for another, stouter man. It takes all types to make a world, Ham thought, all types of millionaires. He sat and waited for Bartell to speak.

Sophie came back with a beer and a glass of something colourless. "Vichy water," said Bartell, taking it. "It's all I drink."

"Secretly, I think he loves to burp," said Sophie. She smiled at both of them and went out of the room.

Bartell looked after her again, smiling: it was a strange smile, ugly as a leer and yet tender. "You married, Mr. Rafferty?"

"No." He was not the marrying type; but he didn't have to tell Bartell that.

Bartell suddenly decided there had been enough small talk. "Mr. Rafferty, what do you know about tires?"

"No more than any other driver whose life depends on a good set of them. I'm no technical expert, Mr. Bartell."

"You ever hear of the Bartell tires before I wrote to you, Mr. Rafferty?"

"Yes," said Ham.

24

"You're lying," said Bartell, as if he were no more than telling Ham that his bootlace was undone. "Don't butter me up, Mr. Rafferty. I have three thousand employees working for me who get paid to butter me up."

"Righto," said Ham and grinned; it was possible that he might come to like this man. "I'd never heard of them."

"And that's one of the reasons why I wanted to see you. A man in the auto business, a professional driver, and he never heard of the Bartell tire. And I'll bet there are hundreds, maybe thousands like you."

"It could be, Mr. Bartell. There are a lot of American things that we haven't heard of on this side of the Atlantic."

"You've heard of Firestone, Goodrich, Royal, haven't you?" Bartell said, and Ham nodded. "All good tires, American ones. But none of them better than a Bartell. And none of them producing one as good as the one I've got back home waiting to be tested."

Ham put the question that was expected of him. "Is that why you asked me to come? You've got a tire you want me to test?"

"Exactly." The big hands slapped together: it was like two handfuls of bones meeting. "You said something a minute ago, Mr. Rafferty. A driver whose life depends on his tires. All drivers' lives depend on their tires, the Sunday drivers as well as professionals like you. A car is only as good as the tires on its wheels, as far as safety goes. Right?"

It was an argument that had several points, but Ham hadn't come to argue. And Mr. Bartell didn't look the type of man who would tolerate an argument, even from men he didn't pay to butter him up. "Right."

"Okay." Bartell took a sip of Vichy water, burped behind his hand and went on, "I've designed a tire that's got twice as much durability as anything now on the market. But that isn't all. My tire reduces the chances of skid by close to fifty

25

per cent. You went off the track at Le Mans because of a skid. You'd be a man who'd appreciate a tire that wouldn't skid. Am I right?"

Ham paused for a moment, then he said, "Are you offering me a job to test your tire on the track? In a race?"

Bartell had another sip of Vichy water and another burp, this time without bothering to muffle it behind his hand. "Mr. Rafferty, I know a lot about you. I knew a lot about you before I came over here from the States. I know that you've been runner-up in the World Championship and that you aren't as good as you used to be. You know all the tracks in Europe, and everyone who goes to the tracks knows you. You're a character, Mr. Rafferty," said Bartell and wasn't apologetic about the description. "You get your name in the papers, advertising gasoline, chewing gum, maybe even laxatives, I don't know. You haven't ever advertised tires. I checked on that. You are reckoned to be one of the best drivers in the world on a wet track. You've been driving long enough now not to try to beat your brains out, but you can still win. You've got brains—I checked on that, too—and you've got guts. You're the man I want, Mr. Rafferty."

Ham sat saying nothing for a minute or two. He had never had himself so succinctly catalogued before; Bartell had summarised him better than he had ever seen himself described in race programs. "Maybe I am the man you want. I don't want to be rude, Mr. Bartell. But what if yours is the job I *don't* want?"

"I haven't finished yet," said Bartell. "You haven't got a job now, Mr. Rafferty. I know you aren't signing up with the works team again, the one you drove for this last season. I don't know why you aren't signing up—" he didn't wait for an explanation and Ham was glad of that "—but I know you haven't signed with anyone else. I'll give you twenty thousand dollars to work for me for one year. That's just over

26

seven thousand pounds. And you won't have to drive in more than two races."

"What do I do the rest of the time?"

"You test my tires. You test them till we know we've done everything we can do to get the bugs out of them."

"And what races do I drive in?"

"The Mille Miglia and the Le Mans."

The race that killed Dad and the one that almost killed me. And right then Ham knew that Bartell's proposition had suddenly become a problem. All at once his leg seemed to burn with pain, and he shifted in his chair, trying to ease it. "The seven thousand quid sounds attractive. But why am I worth that much money to you?"

"I see it this way." The dark bony fingers stuck up like rusty spikes. "First, I've got to do something spectacular to show up my tires against those of the big fellers. I could spend a million dollars on advertising and it wouldn't mean a damn thing unless I've got something to really boast about. Second, something to boast about would be a couple of big races that were won on my tires, and there aren't any really big races in the States. Oh sure, there's the Indianapolis five hundred, but a lot of people don't reckon that's a fair test of a tire. So I've come over here to try to win a couple of European races. Third, all the works teams on this side are signed up already with the big tire manufacturers over here. So I buy a good car, one you choose yourself, I get you to drive it, and that's it. If the whole deal costs me fifty thousand, seventy thousand dollars, it's still cheap. When I go back home and start my advertising campaign, I'll really have something to boast about."

"I could choose my own car?"

"Anything you like. Jaguar, Mercedes, Ferrari, Maserati, Aston-Martin, anything you like. All I want is you to have a car you can win with."

"Do you want my answer today?"

"No, no." Bartell drained the last of his Vichy water and burped like a man who had been shot in the solar plexus. "Tomorrow will do. Take your time."

"Thank you," said Ham, but Bartell missed the irony.

Sophie Bartell came back into the room as Ham stood up. His leg had begun to ache and had stiffened; he slowly bent the knee-joint before he put his weight on the leg. Only when Sophie came forward with Ham's walking stick did Bartell notice it for the first time.

"You have to walk with a stick?" he asked with surprise. "They didn't tell me that. Neither did you."

"You didn't ask me, Mr. Bartell. Matter of fact, you didn't once ask me how I'd come out of the Le Mans crack-up. Oh, I'm all right, and so will the leg be, too, in another month or so. You don't have to worry. If I decide to take your offer, you'll be getting a driver whose every part works."

"I'm sorry I didn't ask how you were," Bartell said. "I guess all I wanted to talk about was my tire. I'm sorry, Mr. Rafferty."

Sophie looked at her father, then at Ham. "I'll see you to the door, Mr. Rafferty."

"I'll ring you Monday, Mr. Bartell," Ham said, leaning on his stick. "You'll know my answer then, one way or the other."

"I hope it'll be yes," said Bartell and put out his hand. The fistful of bones had surprising strength. "As I said, you're the man I want."

At the door Sophie turned back to speak to her father. "I'm going down to the beauty parlour." But Bartell was standing with his back to them, gazing out of the window, and he didn't turn round. Sophie closed the door as she and Ham stepped out into the corridor. "He's got his hearing aid turned off. He turns it off when he wants to dream about his tire."

Again Ham thought he detected a note of bitterness, but he said nothing. As they walked along the corridor toward the lift, Sophie said, "Will you take the job?"

"I'll have to think about it," he said and smiled down at her, boldly and frankly. "How much time do you spend with your father and his tires?"

"Very little." Sophie was aware of his physical presence beside her and could feel it working on her. She had never been a girl who was ashamed of the physical attraction men had for her; she had never been promiscuous, but she was honest in her admission to herself that what attracted her first to any man was his looks and the physical power and strength that his looks might suggest. This man beside her suggested power and strength, even half crippled as he now appeared to be, and it was useless to deny that she could feel the effect of him. But he was a stranger to her, and it would be best if he remained one. His world was one that she did not know and had no desire to know. Her mother had never known her father's world and Sophie had seen the effect it had had on her. All at once, without knowing why, she said, "Do you drive just for the money, Mr. Rafferty?"

He had been smiling at her, but now the smile was lost in the puzzled look that creased his face. "If there were no money in it, I shouldn't be driving, if that's what you mean."

"Is that all you can do?" she said. "Drive a car?"

"Yes," he said and felt annoyance seeping through him. "I've got only the one trade. How many have you?"

She flushed. "I'm sorry. I—I just wondered what the future held for men like you. I noticed at Le Mans that most of the drivers seemed to be young men."

He pressed the button for the lift. "You don't think much about the future in our game."

No, she thought. And that would be one good reason why I shouldn't want to get to know you any better than I do right now.

29

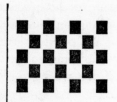

3

Clouds had begun to develop, and by the time Ham had reached Chiswick the sky was grey and full of rain. He turned onto the Great West Road and opened up the Jensen. He had gone past London Airport and was doing eighty down the long stretch to Colnbrook when the rain began to fall. Before he had realised what he was doing, his foot had eased on the accelerator and his speed had dropped to fifty.

He was amused at first, then a little shocked. His hands had tightened on the wheel, and he was aware of a tenseness in his stomach that he usually got only in races at the worst moments. He had had it at Le Mans when he knew, in the last moment before the car lost all adhesion, that he was going off the track. Now suddenly his palms were sweating, and that was something that had not happened in years.

He eased his foot still further and reached into his pocket

for a stick of gum. It was an almost automatic action, the way other men would reach for a cigarette in a moment of stress. He had never smoked, not even as a schoolboy. His father had advised him to chew gum, mainly to keep his mouth from becoming dry during the long hours of a race; as time had gone on he had found that it was almost a sedative too, something that helped him to relax while driving. Up to now he had never felt the need of it while driving away from the track.

By the time he reached Stoke Poges it had stopped raining. The clouds had broken, to show streaks of silver sun, but the evening had turned cold. He ran the Jensen into the double garage, parked it beside his brother's ancient silver Amilcar, got out and limped across the gravel drive to the house.

The house was one of the few solid legacies Pat Rafferty had left to his wife and family. He had bought it against his own inclination and on the unwanted advice of his father-in-law; he had never liked it and had rarely lived in it himself. Part of the house had originally been a sixteenth-century cottage; in the seventeenth century it had been added to and converted into an inn. There was nothing wrong with the house, neither as a thing of beauty nor as a place to live in; Pat Rafferty just didn't like anything that resembled a home, a word that seemed to frighten him. "That racing Irish tinker," his father-in-law had called him; and the jibe had never been meant as a joke.

As Ham came round the corner of the house he saw that his grandfather's car, a Rover, was parked before the front door. He grimaced, found his key and let himself into the house. The house was warm, but already he could feel the chill of his grandfather.

"Is that you, Ham?" his mother called from the living-room. "Grandfather's here."

His mother never overlooked the obvious, nor did she allow anyone else to overlook it. He threw his cap on the stand in the hall, propped his stick in the umbrella stand, took the gum from his mouth and dropped it into a flowerpot after debating whether he should keep it and shock his grandfather by chewing it in front of him, and went into the living-room.

"Hello, Granddad." He knew his grandfather hated being called Granddad. Brigadier Allday stiffened in his seat but said nothing. If he had had his way his grandsons would have called him Sir, but his son-in-law, Irish and rebellious and out of the bogs, had never been one to teach his sons anything as conventional as that. "How are the stocks and shares?"

Brigadier Allday stroked his hooked nose, the one thing he had in common with his elder grandson. He had been a soldier all his life, the son and grandson of soldiers, he no longer wore uniform, but he dressed each morning as if for inspection. It had taken him a long time to accustom himself to the eccentricities of his grandson's dress; he accomplished it by looking at Hamilton with a distant stare, as if the latter were just a speck on an Indian plain.

"Hamilton, your mother has been telling me you are not going to drive for the works team next season. Are you retiring from racing?"

"I don't know," Ham said, trying to swallow a scone; his grandfather was the impatient type who didn't like to have to wait for an answer: the men in the regiment had always had their mouths empty when he spoke to them. "I hadn't got as far as planning *that* definitely."

"You never were a planner," said his grandfather. "Neither was your father."

"Neither was I," said Janet, silently defending her dead husband.

"That was your mother coming out in you," said her father. "I had to run the house as well as the regiment. It has been fortunate that someone in this family has done some planning."

32

Ham felt a sudden spasm of resentment, but he said nothing. He had never been able to get on with his grandfather; yet he knew that his grandfather's intentions were the best. Brigadier Allday was basically a kind man, but he saw the rest of the world as incompetent junior subalterns and ignorant lance-corporals. He lived in nearby Iver and ran the local bazaars and fetes as if they were gymkhana days in Peshawar.

Allday glanced round the room. The bookcase had only books on motoring; there were also bound copies of all the principal motoring magazines. One entire wall was almost obliterated by the trophies won by Pat Rafferty and his two sons: the room shone with the triumphs of the past. Both Ham and Taz had been diffident about exhibiting their trophies in such a prominent room in the house, but Janet had been insistent that they add their cups and shields to those won by their father. They were cleaned regularly once a week, by a grumbling cleaning woman who had never seen a motor race in her life and had no desire to, and the room burned with their cold fire. They were not admired by Brigadier Allday, whose own study walls were covered with muskets, swords and the horns of animals that had run the wrong way and not fast enough.

"I hope you do retire," Allday said. "Give up sport and settle down to acting like an adult. England needs workers at a time like this, Hamilton. Not playboys."

"Are you offering me advice, Granddad?"

"That's right. I'd like to see you settled down to some sort of career. What are you now—thirty-two?"

"Thirty-three," said Ham. "Old for a playboy."

Allday smiled slightly: he had a sense of humour, but it was wintry. "I have a few contacts in the City. If you wish I can get you some introductions. What would you like to do?"

"I'd like to drive cars. What sort of cars do they have in the City?" Ham asked, then forced himself to smile at his grandfather. "No, I'll give it serious thought, Granddad. Really."

"You don't want to waste too much time. You're not earning any money now, are you? If you don't mind my asking."

"A little," said Ham. "I endorsed a hair cream last week."

"That's a contribution to the country's production effort," said Allday and stood up. "Who uses the hair cream? Teddy boys?"

"You speak with the bitterness of a bald-headed man," said Janet, rising and following her father to the door. "Go home, Father, and Ham and Taz and I will come over at the weekend to see you. By then, Ham may have decided to go into the City. I'll buy him some striped pants and a briefcase, just in case."

"Goodbye, Hamilton," Allday said, setting his bowler hat carefully on his head and picking up his stick. "And remember: You can't go on driving racing cars forever."

When his mother and grandfather had gone out of the room, Ham sat staring into the glowing crystal ball of the fire. The red coals told him nothing he didn't already know; the tongues of flame spoke no new wisdom. And his grandfather had, like his mother, just stated the obvious.

You couldn't go on driving racing cars forever. You couldn't go on driving them past your own middle age, not unless you wanted to reduce the chances of your living to old age. Every meeting had its casualties; every season had its deaths. The programs stated the message as clearly as any: Motor Racing Is Dangerous. The cars got them all in the end if they went on long enough: you didn't have to be a tyro and lacking in skill to die. Ascari had gone, even while only practising, Pierre Levegh, Varzi, Dick Seaman, his own father: they had all gone out to drive once too often. The cars had even caught the greatest of them all in the end: they had never been able to take Tazio Nuvolari off the road and kill him, so they had killed him with their exhaust fumes. The Flying Mantuan had driven till he was well past middle age, still The Master; but he had coughed blood for the last two years of his life and had been in a paralytic coma when he died. And it was the cars that had killed him.

Ham's leg had begun to ache again, and he got up and began to move about the room. Something was stirring inside him, and only memory told him that it was fear; he hadn't been afraid since he was a child, and then only in the dark. He had not been afraid even during the war, although he had had his sudden moments of sweating doubt; he had flown a plane with the same skill and confidence with which he was later to drive a car. He had never despised men who were afraid, not even cowards. Fear was there in every man, even himself; it was a part of man as much as blood and bone and intestines. He remembered what Taz had once said about courage when they had been talking about the daring of some drivers: Plato or Aristotle—one of the Greeks, he could never remember which—had placed courage in the last degree of virtue. And another thing Taz had said: St. Exupéry, one of the few writers who had appealed to both of them, had called it a concoction of feelings, a touch of anger, a spice of vanity, a lot of obstinacy, a tawdry, sporting thrill, above all a stimulus of one's physical energies. Well, maybe the Greeks and the Frenchman had it right. Up to now he had never analysed what it was that made him drive as he did, day after day through the long summer, and why, when each season was finished, he had looked forward impatiently to the next. *Had* looked forward to. But not to next season, the one that was now only six months away.

His mother came back into the room, buttoning her cardigan to the throat. "It's chilly." She went to the fire and threw more coal on it and stood for a moment warming her hands. "We really must get central heating in this house."

She had never asked him for money directly, nor had she ever expected him to keep her in any sort of luxury. But she had no idea of the value of money nor of the cost of things;

35

central heating was only another item, like butter, meat, a pair of shoes. If she had been the type who could organise herself into finding a central-heating engineer and having the heating installed, it would have been in the house long ago, and Ham or the Devil would have been left to look after the bill. But anything to do with the house or garden had always been left to Ham, and she had gone on year after year mentioning that they must get central heating but never querying why Ham didn't have it installed. It would have been too involved to explain to her that it was a question of money, and why he didn't have the money for central heating. And so he had never prolonged the discussion after her initial comment.

"The place will warm up, now Granddad's gone," he said.

"You shouldn't talk about him like that," she said. "I know he's a bit of a trial, but he does try to be helpful."

"I know, Mum. But I wish to hell he'd get off the parade ground once in a while. If ever I do something that pleases him, I expect him to pin a medal on my chest."

She began to gather up the tea things. "Taz rang up from the office this afternoon. He's going to drive in the Formula Two races next season. And in the Ulster this month."

Ham had walked to the window, but now he turned slowly back. "He's going to *what?*"

"I thought it would surprise you. It surprised me."

"Who's he driving for?"

"For the Bourne End team." The Bourne End team was a private team financed by a wealthy spark-plug manufacturer. "Evidently he's been in touch with them for some time."

"How long?"

She bent her head over the tray, arranging the cups." He told me he'd written to them the week after Le Mans."

Out in the hall the tall grandfather clock struck six; the chimes were cracked, and time had a harsh sound. The room was dark now, lighted only by the glow from the fire; Janet's

36

shadow danced on the wall, skipped over the glimmering trophies. "He waited till I regained consciousness, then."

"Ham, don't talk like that!" The cups rattled on the tray. "Look, I don't like this any more than you do. I haven't minded his driving in the small-car races—there's less danger in those, and we both know he is a good driver. You've said so yourself. I've never wanted him to drive in the big cars, and that was why I made him promise never to try to become a Grand Prix driver while you were still racing. I—I don't want to lose another of you, as I lost your father. But you've both got his blood in you and I knew you wanted to race. I couldn't stop you from that. All I wanted was to have one of you with me while the other was racing. You were the elder and so you were the first on the track. We can't blame Taz for wanting to have his chance, now that you have retired."

"He didn't know I had retired. Not a week after Le Mans. I was still in splints and bandages."

"You looked as if you would *have* to retire."

"That's not the point," he said angrily. He turned sharply away from her, on his bad leg, and had a sudden spasm of pain shoot up into his groin. He groped for a chair in the gloom and sat down.

He heard the teacups rattle again. "Are you all right, Ham?" She put down the tray and came and stood beside his chair. "Is your leg hurting?"

"Yes." And that wasn't all that was hurting.

"You see, then?" she said, and he realised she was trying to be gentle; but he couldn't help resenting the fact that she seemed to be taking Taz's side. "It may be ages before you can drive again. A racing driver needs two good legs."

There was the sound of a key in the front door, then the lights were switched on in the hall. "Where are you, Mother?" Taz called, and came into the living-room, switching on the lights. "Hello, what's this? A secret meeting or something? I got a lift from the station with Joe Grimble. Phew, it's turned cold all of a sudden! I was going for a run up to Aylesbury, too. Pamela's up there at her aunt's."

"Who's Pamela?" asked his mother and crossed the room for his kiss.

He kissed her cheek. "I brought her in here a month or two ago. One Sunday afternoon. A blonde."

"I'm always expected to remember them by the colour of their hair. Why don't you bring home a girl with a wooden leg or something?" She picked up the tray and went out to the kitchen.

Taz dropped into a chair and began to pull off his shoes. He was a handsome boy; both the strength and the touch of the aesthetic were there in his face. His voice was higher and quicker than Ham's: he had been to a public school and he had the quick, light, public-school accent. Everything about him was quick and light: he was that much more like their father than Ham was. He undid his tie and threw it over the back of his chair.

"I've had a busy day," he said and lay back in his chair.

"Mum tells me you're going to drive in the Formula Twos."

The caution dropped like a veil over Taz's face. "Yes. I'm having a go in a Cooper-Climax."

"It's going to be different from the five hundred stuff."

"You've told me that before." Taz wasn't looking at him but staring down into the fire. Looking at his own future, Ham wondered? "But I've got to start sometime."

"I suppose so," Ham said, and there was the bitterness spilled out between them: it was almost as if he had spat bile on the carpet between their chairs.

"You don't have to be like that." Taz's voice was higher still, a stranger's voice. He sat in his stockinged feet and collarless, and tried to look proud and defiant. His face was flushed, but the fire had died down; he reached over and threw more coal on it. "You've retired."

"Who said so?"

"Well, you have, haven't you?" Outside in the kitchen the teacups ceased to rattle: was their mother listening, waiting on his answer, too?

Ham leaned back in his chair, straightening his left leg out in front of him, and closed his eyes. He had left the Dorchester and Bartell with a simple decision to make, one that he had expected to make by tomorrow morning; and yet every minute since, beginning with the rain on the Great West Road and the sweat in the palms of his hands, the decision had become more complex until now his head ached with the problems of it. He had never had to make a major decision before, and now suddenly he felt another sort of fear, the one of responsibility. He had been a man for years, fought in a war, got drunk, loved women, looked death in the face and been old enough to recognise it for his own. And now all at once, and only now, he felt old and grown up. Lesser, more staid men had reached this stage long before he had; their humdrum existence had strangled youth before it could go on too long. But he had avoided the humdrum existence up till now. Now it loomed before him, like the possibility of cancer.

"I don't know," he said. "I'm still making up my mind."

"I took it for granted," Taz said, suddenly hesitant, and looked at the stiffened leg.

And that's been the trouble, Ham thought, but without bitterness this time. You and Mum have taken so much for granted since Dad was killed. When Pat Rafferty died, he had left behind him only the house, the trophies he had won and 622 pounds. Robert Allday had offered to help, but Janet, knowing how her father had been against her marriage and how he had never completely reconciled himself to it, but not knowing how they were going to fare, had refused his help. She hadn't asked Ham to assume the responsibilities of head of the family; he had taken them on himself without discussion and almost automatically. It was he who had signed the cheques for all the bills, maintained the house, put Taz through school, even got Taz the job with the firm for which he sold cars. For the first four years after his father's death he had been in debt, borrowing from the bank without his mother's knowledge; then he had reached the top bracket as a driver and his income had begun to swell. He was able to command bigger appearance money, he had got into the big prize money, firms had paid him to endorse their products in advertisements. He had signed with a works team at a guaranteed figure, had appeared on Television and doubled for a film star in a picture about motor racing. For two years his income had topped ten thousand pounds; but all he had in the bank now was a little over two thousand. Taz might understand where it had all gone, but his mother wouldn't; she couldn't understand taxes, high or low, nor the rising cost of living, the expense of sending a boy to a public school, nor the high expenses that were part and parcel of the profession of a racing driver. True, he hadn't thought much about saving, reckoning on at least another five years of racing before he would have to think about retiring. He had bought the Jensen, when he might have had a cheaper car, and all the women he had known had known him for a generous lover, in more ways than one. The money had come in and gone out, a tide of currency, and Taz and his mother had taken it all for granted. They were grateful, he was sure of that, but that didn't alter the fact that they had taken it all for granted.

"What else can I do?" he said suddenly, and it was like a cry of anguish. "Granddad was here awhile ago. He wants me to go into the City!"

"I don't like my job any more than you'd like the City," Taz said, and made selling cars sound like a job in the salt mines. He got up and began to stalk about the room, a quick, lithe figure, quick with energy and ambition and the secret urges of all young men who still have to open the door into the world they desire.

Ham looked with sudden sympathy at his brother, but all he could say was, "I want another season at least."

Taz spun round. "God Almighty, why must you be so bloody selfish? When will you have had enough?"

Then Janet came back into the room. "What's going on here?" But she knew what had been going on, and her face told it plainly: in this moment she couldn't disguise the fear she felt.

"We've been talking about my retiring," Ham said, trying to keep his rising anger under control. "Only I haven't made up my mind yet."

"How long do you want to make up your mind?" Taz demanded. "Four months—"

"Are you going to sign again with the works team?" Janet asked.

Ham shook his head. "I've had an offer from an American tire manufacturer."

"Oh, then you're not going to race?" Taz looked suddenly relieved. "You're going to sign as a test driver or something?"

"In a way," Ham said. "But he wants me to drive in races. Two of them. The Mille Miglia and the Le Mans."

"Only two?" Janet said. "Why?"

"That's the way this American wants it." Ham then explained who Bartell was and what he wanted. As he talked he realised that that was what he had become, a test driver. He was still a racing driver, and racing drivers were, in a way, advanced test drivers; but he was a racing driver who was on his way out. He was like the matinee idol who had at last been asked to play someone else's father. If he hadn't yet completely retired, he had at least begun. He hoped that made both his mother and Taz a little happier.

But it hadn't; at least not Taz. "Then you haven't really retired?"

"No," Ham said bluntly. "I haven't."

Taz thumped the sideboard; the cups and trophies rattled. "How long do you want the bloody limelight?"

"Taz!"

"I'm sorry, Mother. But it isn't fair! He's had ten years of it now. Not the limelight—I didn't mean that. I apologise for that. But doing what he wants to do, doing what *I* want to do! Driving cars. How long can you expect me to sit around and wait?"

"You're only twenty-one," Janet said. "Fangio was twenty-three before he had his first race. You've been racing for two years."

"In small stuff," Taz said, as if the 500 c.c. cars were no more than pushcarts.

"Fangio's first car was an old Ford that broke down under him," Janet said. "I remember his telling me one day at Silverstone. He was twenty-seven before he drove in his first Grand Prix."

"Dad drove in *his* first Grand Prix at twenty."

"Your father was different," said Janet and closed that line of argument. She turned to Ham. "The Bourne End team were going to take Taz on full time."

"I'm sorry about that," Ham said. "Unless you'll let him drive?"

Janet shook her head. "Not while you're driving. I made him promise me that and I'm keeping him to it. I told you—" Her voice rose a little, tight with fear and remembered grief and anger at her sons for making her ask this promise of them: "I don't want to be left alone. I want to be sure that at least one of you will always be with me."

42

"But this is different, Mother." Taz turned his attack on his mother: *she* was the one who was holding him back. "Ham will be driving in only two races. The rest of the season he'll only be watching, a spectator like yourself. Won't you?" He looked at Ham for confirmation, and Ham nodded; he wanted to help Taz if he could.

"It isn't different," Janet said stubbornly; she was in a jungle of doubt and fear, but she wasn't lost. "If—if something happened to you early in the season, say at Monaco—" she stopped for a moment, as if she had just tasted the horror of her own words. "Ham would still have to drive at Le Mans. There would still be time for something to happen to him, too."

"Something happening! You're always expecting something to happen." Taz went back to the window, staring out at the last pale light of the day.

"I was always expecting it to happen when your father was driving." It was the first time she had ever told them that: she offered them small secrets, like gold sovereigns hidden in the cupboards of the years. "And eventually it did."

Taz continued to stare out of the window, his head slightly tilted. High in the cold blue there were a plane's vapour trails, like chalk marks across a vast blue wall; someone had escaped and was doing what he wanted to do. "How long have I got to wait, then?" he said, and the question was directed at Ham, not his mother.

Suddenly Ham was all anger. He stood up, twisting away from his chair, hurting his leg but ignoring it. The other hurt was too great; he flung out his own secrets: "Christ Almighty, who are you to talk about things being unfair? Who paid to put you through school? Who got you your job, paid for your entries in your first races, bought you your car, kept this house going, let you use the flat in London? What do you think has paid for all that? I've got only two thousand quid left in the bank. It's more than a lot of people

43

have, I know. But it won't buy me a business or a career that will bring me the money to let us go on living the way we have been. I've been offered seven thousand quid for this job. Just to drive in two races, and I'll have nothing like the expenses I've had in the past. I haven't accepted it yet, but I haven't turned it down, either. You can bloody well sit and wait till I'm good and ready to retire!"

"Ham!"

But he didn't turn back as his mother called after him. He stamped out of the house into the cold evening, and was glad of its coldness: it was like water on the fire of his anger. He got into the Jensen, stamped too hard on the pedal as he backed out of the garage, spun gravel back at the house like stony spittle and drove furiously away. He didn't know where he was going, he just drove, and then he found himself heading back to London, to the flat in Cromwell Road.

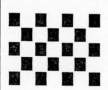

4

The flat in Cromwell Road, near Earl's Court, was a small one, a *pied-à-terre*, a love nest, call it what you liked: it had served several purposes in the past, including that of hideout for another racing driver desperately trying to avoid the attentions of a wealthy middle-aged admirer. Now it became something of an ivory tower, with dirty dishes in the sink, an unmade bed, a carpet of copies of *Motor Sport*, and a lavatory cistern that dribbled monotonously. It was not an ideal place for cogitation, but it was better than the atmosphere at Stoke Poges. And Ham, after storming out of the house, had plenty to think about.

He had an almost sleepless night and when he rose in the morning his thoughts were no more ordered than the bed in which he had tossed and turned. There was no food in the flat and he breakfasted on a cup of black coffee. Then he rang the Dorchester.

Sophie Bartell answered. "You've made up your mind, Mr. Rafferty?"

"Well, not quite," he said and wanted to prolong the conversation; she had a pleasant voice, even over the phone. "But you're going to be in London for a while, aren't you?"

"You mean me or my father?" She had caught his inference.

"Both."

"I'll put you on to my father," she said, and he was left with the soft crackle of the line in his ear.

Then Bartell's voice, rough as a rusted exhaust, said, "Morning, Mr. Rafferty. You made up your mind, eh? Frankly, I always thought you British needed more time. You're not ones for quick decisions, are you?"

Bartell had given him a ready-made excuse: blame it on the so-called national characteristic. "No, I suppose we're not. I'd like a little more time, if that's all right?"

"It's not your leg?" Bartell had obviously been thinking about that. "Your leg is fine? You're not stalling for time?"

"The leg is going to be all right," he said, a little irritably: the leg seemed to have become some sort of symbol to everyone. "It's just that your offer was so unexpected, there are so many things to consider—well, I'd just like a little more time."

There was silence at the other end of the line; a radio was playing faintly, some housewife's choice in the Dorchester. Then: "All right, Mr. Rafferty. My daughter and I are going over to Italy for a few weeks. We'll be back early next month —I want to see your motor show. We'll leave it until then. But I want your answer when we get back. You understand?"

"I understand," he said, sarcastically servile: he was not going to enjoy working for Mr. Butter-me-up Bartell.

46

"And Mr. Rafferty." Ham waited. "In the meantime look around for a car to drive in the race. Pick a good one. Goodbye."

The phone went dead, and Ham put it down. *In the meantime look around for a car to drive.* Well, there was one man who had no doubt what his decision would be. Ham wondered how many major decisions Bartell had had to make; then, remembering the man's face, knew there had been many. Every year, every problem, every decision had been there in Bartell's face: it was as chipped and worn as a tire that had spent its life on a rough and rocky road.

Ham did spend the next few weeks looking about for a car. He looked at all the cars he thought would stand a chance of winning the Mille Miglia; and couldn't make up his mind about any of them. He had his preferences, but he had never before been forced to choose a car for just one particular race and had the onus thrown on him of spending the money for it. It was different when two or three manufacturers bid for your services: you just chose the car you liked and the cost didn't worry you. For sheer speed he liked the Ferrari, but for some time Ferrari had been having trouble with their brakes and you never used your brakes so much as you did in the Mille Miglia. The Jaguar had speed and good brakes, but for some reason its record in the Mille Miglia was not as good as in other races. He had never driven a Mercedes and he would prefer an easier race in which to make his debut in it; he had heard some drivers say that its power could get away from you, and you had to watch it all the way. He liked the Maserati, but he had never had any luck in one of them; like all drivers, he had his superstitions, and he had come to believe that he and a Maserati were not a successful combination. The Aston-Martin was a good car, fast on the straights and good on the corners, but it, too, had to prove itself in the Mille Miglia.

47

But before he went looking for a car, he went back home to Stoke Poges. Nothing was said about the argument, but for a few days the three of them acted like guests at a British seaside hotel, polite but distant. Gradually they fitted back into the regular pattern of their life before the row; but in the week before Taz went across to drive in the Ulster Tourist Trophy, the atmosphere became strained again. Janet was going with him, but Taz didn't ask Ham if he wanted to go till two days before they were to leave.

"I wondered if I was going to be asked," Ham said.

"I didn't know if you would want to come," Taz said, making a great pretence of finding something wrong under the bonnet of his old Amilcar. "Considering the way you feel about things."

Then Ham realised how churlish he had been in not saying a week or two ago that he would be coming. Taz had always come to watch him race, whenever he could get away, and he knew now that he would have been hurt if Taz hadn't come. He had been taking a few things for granted, himself.

"Of course I want to come," he said, and Taz straightened up from beneath the bonnet of the Amilcar, looking as if he had found the source of his trouble and was no longer worried about it. "I'll go round the course with you at practice, if you like. Maybe I can give you some hints."

"Thanks," said Taz and looked genuinely pleased. "I wish you would. I want to do well in this race."

Ham grinned, not unkindly. "Think you might win?"

Taz grinned back. "No. But I'd like to finish, that's all."

"That's all I want, too," said Janet from the open doorway of the garage behind them. "Shall we have some tea now?"

So the three of them went across to Dundrod and Taz drove a very creditable fourth behind three hard-bitten and experienced professionals. The newspapers heralded the entry of another Rafferty into the racing world. The Irish papers were particularly ecstatic. Pat Rafferty, though he had done most of his racing in England and on the Continent and had gone back to Ireland only once a year to race, had been a national hero. The fact that his younger son, this boy who had the beginnings of another hero, had been born in England of an English mother and brought up in England, was something that the papers brushed aside. The boy had Irish blood in him, didn't he, and wasn't Irish blood thicker and better than any other?

Immediately after the race Taz was elated at what he had achieved; he bubbled over with as much excitement as if he had won. But going back on the plane he had quieted down, and he remained like that after they had reached home. He was waiting for Ham to say whether he was retiring or not.

Ham's leg got better, he went to the specialist who had been treating him and was told he was now completely recovered and he put the stick away in a closet. Then he came to his decision.

At the end of the first week in October he rang the Dorchester again. Again it was Sophie Bartell who answered the phone. "My father is out at Earl's Court at the motor show. Have you made up your mind?"

"Yes," he said. "Look, would you care to come to the motor show with me? Maybe we can pick up your father there. It'll be as good a place as any to tell him what I've decided."

"You're going to take the job, then?"

"I'll pick you up in twenty minutes," he said, avoiding the question. It had been a big decision to make and somehow to give his answer over the phone reduced it to something unimportant.

He picked her up at the Dorchester and they drove out to

Earl's Court. "A snappy car," she said, admiring the sleek lines of the Jensen. "But then, you racing drivers can't go about in something sedate-looking, can you?"

"You'd be surprised," he said. "Stirling Moss even drives a small Standard."

"But you don't," she said and looked at him quizzically; he was wearing a tan shirt, a bright green bow tie, a plaid waist-coat in which the predominant colour was yellow, and a jacket that looked as if it would have been more at home on a horse. She thought she had seen better-dressed men in the chorus of "Guys and Dolls."

He smiled, suddenly catching the meaning of her look. "No," he said and for the first time in years became a little embarrassed by his eccentricity of dress. "I'm the type who has to carry his atmosphere with him."

"I've never heard it put that way before," she said. "I guess there are people like that."

"What's your atmosphere?"

"I haven't any," she said, feeling suddenly lonely again, and looked out of the window of the car. "Is it far to Earl's Court?"

At Earl's Court in the big exhibition hall they walked among the shine and glitter of the new cars on display. They looked at poems of design; and at creations that hurt the eyes. They looked at cars that were almost sexual in their conveyed impression of sensual luxury: Casanova would have ridden in these, had there been cars in his day. They saw cars that had no pretensions to aesthetic looks but had been built for the man whose pleasure lay in speed and the sensa-tion of power given by a car that responded totally to every-thing its driver asked of it. They were approached by gen-tlemanly salesmen in public-school or regimental ties; Ham wondered if there were any car salesmen who had gone to council schools or had been conscientious objectors. Chrome glittered like so much captive silver flame; paint reflected faces like so many varicoloured mirrors; luxurious interiors beckoned like so many bedrooms. This was the year when the manufacturers were making their cars with an eye on the woman in the family; and as always when women were appealed to by men, taste had gone out like smoke from the exhaust. Wives who would have shot their husbands if those men had dared to come home in a pair of two-toned shoes, swooned rapturously over cars in combinations of caramel, violet and black. Other women, who wouldn't have bought an electric kettle until it had been taken apart and demonstrated to them, urged their husbands to buy a car that had a vanity case under one of the seats; when the husbands asked the salesmen for particulars of what was under the bonnet of the car, they were told by their wives not to waste time over unimportant things ("all engines are the same") and to get out their chequebooks in a hurry. Ham wandered among the cars and wondered what men like W. O. Bentley and Ettore Bugatti would have thought of cars produced solely for women. The next step would be powder puffs in the tool kit.

They met Richie Launder standing in front of the Jaguar stand admiring the latest XK150. He stood there, a short, fat figure as elegantly dressed as Ham was garishly so; but his elegance ended at his cuffs, where his hands betrayed his trade. The hands and nails had been scrubbed, but the grease had become part of the skin. He had been claimed and branded by the things he loved.

"G'day," he said in his flat gravelly voice: his throat always sounded as if it were lined with sand. He waited for Ham to introduce Sophie and then gave her a smile that winked gold. "An American? Waddia think of the lousy climate here?"

"Richie is an Australian," Ham explained. "He does nothing but complain about the English weather."

"Why don't you go home, then?" Sophie asked.

51

"That's what all the English say," said Richie, still grinning. "Don't you start."

"How's business?" Ham said. Richie had come to see him in the hospital at Le Mans and had called him a couple of times since he had come back to England. He knew that Richie, the best mechanic in the game, had left the works team and was now working full-time in his garage at Chalfont St. Giles. It was only five or six miles from Stoke Poges, and he had been going to drive up there several times, but somehow he had never got around to it. He felt a twinge of conscience now: he and Richie had been good pals when they had belonged to the works team. He had never developed a close friendship with any particular man, spending most of his free time with women; but he felt that the friendship with Richie could have developed into something more than the camaraderie of two men engaged in a job they both loved.

Richie's bald head shone under the bright lights: the scar on it was dark like a lizard on a rock. "Today is the first day I've taken off since I came back."

"Business as good as that?"

Richie spread a plump, strong hand and ducked his head, almost as if in embarrassment. "The garage is doing all right. It's something else." He looked up at Ham, squinting at him. "I've been working on my car."

"Your car?" Ham said, and then remembered: Richie had once or twice talked about it, but Ham had never taken much notice of what he had said: every man in the motor-racing game had some sort of dream. His own dream had been to be World Champion and he had almost achieved it.

"Yeah," Richie said and looked at Sophie. "In this country every second garage has a man in it who wants to make a car of his own. Something he reckons none of the others has got."

"A racing car?" Sophie said.

"No. A sports car. One that could be raced, but a sports car." He jerked a thumb at the XK150 behind them. "Like this."

"And how's it going?" Ham said.

"Ah, all right." Richie shrugged. "I got the chassis done, and a mock-up done of the body. But money is the thing. I need to win the football pools or something. I wanna build a car that'll compete with these jobs." Another jerk of the thumb at the Jaguar. "And where'll I get an engine to put into it? There are some, but they all cost money. I don't wanna build a car that looks like a streak of lightning but's got no guts under the bonnet."

Then Bartell said behind them, "Mr. Rafferty. You got my daughter here. I tried to get her to come, but she said she was sick of cars and anything to do with them."

Sophie said quickly, as if she was afraid she had hurt her father, "Mr. Rafferty's persuasive powers were stronger than yours, Dad."

"I guess they were." Bartell looked at her, and so did Ham. The latter tried to remember how persuasive he had been; he must be a better persuader than his past successes would have led him to believe. He looked at Sophie with new interest: he had begun to think she was not a girl who would have been an easy conquest. He smiled at her, trying out his persuasive powers, but she was looking at her father.

"This is Mr. Launder, Dad," she was saying.

Bartell gave Richie a perfunctory handshake; he wasted no time in being polite to strangers. "You made up your mind, Mr. Rafferty?"

"Yes."

Bartell had taken Sophie's arm and begun to walk away. Ham stopped for a moment to say good-bye to Richie. "I'll come up one day and have a look at the car."

"Who's that rude bastard?" Richie said.

53

"My new boss," said Ham, patted his shoulder and moved after Sophie and her father.

"Well?" said Bartell.

"I'll take the job, Mr. Bartell," Ham said, and Sophie smiled across at him, looking genuinely pleased.

"Swell! That's swell." There was no mistaking Bartell's pleasure; he put out his hand and crushed Ham's. "I knew right along that you would, Rafferty!"

"That's more than I did," said Ham.

"I'll get a lawyer, and we'll have some papers drawn up. I can't tell you how pleased I am, Rafferty." Ham noticed that he was no longer Mister Rafferty; he was working for Bartell now, one of the employees paid to butter him up. "I talked about it all the time we were in Italy, didn't I, Sophie?"

"Didn't you!" Sophie said and smiled affectionately at him; she seemed pleased for his sake that Ham had taken the job.

"You picked a car yet?" Bartell said, looking around at the cars displayed. They stood beside a big Daimler, a limousine built to carry diplomats to conferences and mourners to funerals, journeys where speed was not a necessity and the sober thoughts of the occupants were good enough as brakes.

"Not yet, Bartell," said Ham, staking out his independence before Bartell could ride roughshod over it. Both Bartell and Sophie looked at him, but he pretended not to notice. "It's your money I'm spending. I just want to be sure I spend it on the right car."

"I guess there's no rush about the car," Bartell said. "The important thing is, I've got you signed up. Now we've got to start testing my tires."

"Do I have to come to America for that?"

"That's up to you. You get more rain in this country and that's what I'm trying to sell. A tire that's good in the rain. It won't cost me any more to do the tests on this side than back home. I don't expect to have to do any alterations to the tires," he said confidently. "I think they're okay as they are."

Ham looked at Sophie and she read his thoughts. Despite herself, she had been thinking of him a lot while she had been in Italy. She had tried to analyse what attracted her to him and been angry because she couldn't name it. And now, feeling angry with herself even as she spoke, she said, "I'm staying in London for six months. Dad will be flying over to visit me once in a while. I hope," she said, looking at her father.

"Sure," said Bartell and made an awkward attempt to press her arm affectionately. "I'll come over often as you like, girl."

"I'll stay in England, then," Ham said. "Till we see how things go."

He drove them back to the Dorchester and Bartell asked him to have dinner with them. Bartell, drunk on Vichy water and the vision of his own dream coming true, monopolised the conversation. He told Ham how he had gone to the States as a child of five with his parents. Lived on Mulberry Street on the lower East Side of New York—"my old man, our name was Bartelli then, he played the hurdy-gurdy for pennies. I don't think he'd believe it if he saw me here now—" and he looked around the glittering dining-room. "Then I went to work when I was twelve—" moved to Akron, Ohio, when he was sixteen, and took a job in a tire factory. Started his own plant at the depths of the Depression— "had six men working for me and they all made more money than I did"—and got his chance during the war. And now here he was, dining at the Dorchester with his daughter, "isn't she beautiful, Rafferty? That's the Italian in her"— and a famous racing driver. And with the most revolutionary development in tires, with his name Bartell stamped on every goddam one, all but ready to go on the market. "And now I think I'll go to bed, Rafferty."

55

"What time tomorrow shall I come in?" Ham asked, but Bartell was getting to his feet and didn't answer.

"He's had his hearing aid switched off all the time," said Sophie, and tapped her father's pocket. "That wasn't fair, Dad. Making Mr. Rafferty listen to you all through dinner, and you tuned out."

Bartell looked at them, saw they were both smiling, then laughed out loud. He said good night, elaborately tuning in his hearing aid again, and went across the room, still chuckling at the joke. Sophie looked after him. "That's the first time I've ever heard him laugh like that. Not since I was a kid. He's happy."

"Is there any reason why he shouldn't be?" Ham said.

She clutched gently at the gold bracelet on her wrist, as if it were hurting her. "You wouldn't be interested."

"You mean it's none of my concern? Not if you don't want to talk about it, it isn't."

She was still working the bracelet on her wrist: Ham didn't know it, but it was the first present her father had given her after their reunion. "Are you a good listener?"

"I listened to your father, didn't I? He told me his life story."

"He told you only part of it." She spun the bracelet on her wrist and looked up quickly. "Don't get me wrong. I don't hate my father or anything like that. Oh, you think all we Americans are the same, don't you? If we haven't got ulcers, then we're all crazy, mixed-up kids." She looked about the dining-room. "I'll bet there are just as many ulcers in this room as you'd find in any hotel in New York. And just as many neurotic women."

"You don't have to talk to me as if I'm your psychiatrist," he said. "I'd like to hear all about you. But I'm not prying and I'm not judging. You don't have to make excuses to me or tell me what's wrong with the English."

"Thanks," she said drily, and looked about the room again as if to make sure no one else could hear her. Then she looked down into the black eye of her coffee cup. "All right. We were a perfectly normal family until I was about, oh, seven or eight. When America came into the war. Then success, as it does to so many men in the Land of Opportunity, came to my father." She looked up at him, but he didn't smile. He didn't read *Time* nor any parodies of it. "The plant became his second home. Then it became his home altogether, or just about, and it was his family that came second. My mother and I. Have you ever seen a woman wither and die, like some flower in the ground where the water doesn't run any more? That happened to my mother. We moved from Akron back to New York—my mother had come from there, but I was born and raised in Akron. I doubt if my father knew we had gone. No, that's a lie. He knew, all right. The night before we were to go, he came home, to our real home, and pleaded with my mother to stay. But she wouldn't, and then he got angry. They had a terrible argument, and I crouched under the bed, waiting for the lightning to strike. But the lightning didn't strike, and next day Momma and I left for New York. I've never been back to Akron. I once saw a picture of the plant in *Fortune*, but that's all."

"And your mother?"

"She never went back, either. Dad kept us well supplied with money, but he never came near us. My mother just sort of faded away. Then one winter she got pneumonia. I wasn't there in New York, I'd gone up to Vassar."

"What's Vassar?" he said.

"Vassar? It's a girls' college. One of *the* colleges."

"I'm learning," he said. "Go on."

"Maybe if I'd been there when she first got ill, she might have been all right. But the doctors said she didn't seem to want to live. You've got to understand," she leaned forward,

57

"she *loved* my father, really loved him. She was Italian. A lot of American women, maybe English women, too—they just can't love like that."

"My mother could," he said. "She really loved my father. She almost died of grief when he was killed."

"Then you do understand about my mother. Well, Dad came East for the funeral. He stayed three days, and we hardly had a word to say to each other. We were strangers with the same name. He went back to Akron, and I went back to Vassar. Twice a year we exchanged letters, and occasionally he'd call me long-distance. Then I came out of college and got a job in the research department of a magazine. I'm good at history. That's why I'm enjoying London so much, why I'm going to stay on here in England for another six months."

"You're going back to the magazine?"

"I don't know. They gave me leave of absence. Early this year Dad came to New York, told me he was coming to Europe this summer and asked me to come with him. I couldn't refuse him. I didn't want to," she said. "Suddenly I didn't hate him any more. I was sorry for him."

"But you're still getting used to him?"

"You'd be surprised just how hard it is to get to know your father again. You have to undo all your memories and start all over again. That is, if you want to love him. And I want to love him." She tried to hold back the tears, but she knew her eyes must be glistening. "I'm an Italian, too. At least that way."

"You mean if you love anyone, it has to be all the way?"

"I don't know if it's a good thing, not being able to love just to a degree, the way some women can. And yet I'm glad I'm not like them."

"So am I," he said.

5

Ham had come back to Stoke Poges the night before, driving back with a mixture of light-heartedness and foreboding. Now he had made his decision he felt better; and he didn't want to put off telling it to Taz and his mother. Yet he knew that Taz wasn't going to like what he had to tell him, nor perhaps even his mother. Just before he had gone to sleep he had had an abrupt moment of anger and resentment; he had felt that his mother was on Taz's side and wanted him to retire. Then sleep had come, quickly as it always did with him, and the bitterness had been lost somewhere in the night.

Now Taz, at the other end of the breakfast table, was reading from *The Times*. The car salesrooms required him to work only every second Saturday: it was a high-class firm that sold only high-priced cars: very few people bought

Bentleys and Lagondas on Saturday mornings. The people with money for such cars were hunting foxes or golf balls or chorus girls at the weekend. Saturday is the day for selling secondhand cars: the impoverished middle classes and the workers who had won a little something in the pools came and inspected what richer folk no longer wanted: salesmen with sincerity as false as their educated accents extolled the virtues of the ancient wrecks. In odd, frightening moments, Ham had sometimes wondered if he might finish up in the same sort of job himself. There were few more precarious professions than that of a secondhand car salesman.

Taz was saying, "We've all been expecting Lamott to retire, but not to start the season and then suddenly chuck it up. He must suddenly have felt his age." Lamott was an international Rugger winger; he had been playing for England since the end of the war and was known as Old Man Lamott. And yet he's younger than I am, Ham thought. "That leaves the wing place wide open now."

"Do you think you might get it?" Janet said.

In the winters Taz played Rugger and last season had distinguished himself in inter-counties matches as an exceptionally fast winger. "Oh, I don't know," he said, and Ham knew that his modesty wasn't feigned; Taz really didn't care about Rugger and looked on it only as something to fill in the autumn and winter Saturday afternoons. He was the sort of boy who always had to be doing something active, and he had no interest whatsoever in any of the other winter games. And, as he had once confided to Ham when their mother wasn't there, you couldn't bundle up with a popsie *every* Saturday afternoon.

"There are at least four of us with a chance," he said.

"It would be nice if you got an International cap," Janet said.

"We could hang it up there on the wall above Dad's helmet," Ham said.

"We should not," said Janet. "We don't want the wall cluttered up with headgear."

Despite her tone and remark, Ham knew how she felt about his father's helmet. It meant more to her than all the trophies Pat Rafferty had won: to her it was her knight's helmet, the only thing of his she had asked to be brought back from Italy. Ham changed the subject and spoke to Taz. "How old would Lamott be?"

"Thirty-one or two," Taz said. "Time he retired."

"Speaking of retiring," Ham said, and both Taz and Janet looked up. They've been waiting for this, he suddenly knew; all these weeks they've been waiting for just this. Again he felt the anger flare in him, and he said a little more sharply than he had intended, "I'm not retiring. I told Bartell last night I'd take up his offer."

Taz said nothing for a moment. His young, thin face seemed to crumble and his hand shook as he put down the cup he had been holding. Then abruptly he stood up, flung *The Times* savagely across the room, and strode, almost ran out and upstairs to his room. A moment later they heard his bedroom door slammed shut.

"A schoolboy," Ham said. "I thought he'd grown up."

Janet began to butter some toast, deliberately and delicately, as if afraid of breaking the toast into small pieces. "I wonder how you would react if you happened to be denied something you'd always wanted? You never have been denied anything, you know." She looked up and saw the hurt and angry look on his face. "You are acting like a schoolboy now. You think I'm taking his side. I'm not, you know. And I wish you'd both get that into your heads. In this, I'm on nobody's side but my own."

The anger died at once. "I'm sorry, Mum. Would *you* like me to retire? I mean, for your sake?"

The toast broke under her knife. "Don't ask me to make your decisions for you, Ham. No woman should ever have to do that for a man. Perhaps it's just as well you never married. One woman to worry about you is enough."

He thought about that as he drove up to Chalfont St. Giles later in the morning. He had decided, coming back from London last night after meeting Richie Launder at the Motor Show, to ask Richie to help him choose a car. No one knew cars better than Richie, and Ham knew he would feel better if he had someone to back his judgment when he finally made his choice.

But as he drove along the winding country road, between the hedges that were already beginning to thin and under trees whose leaves fell on him in a dry golden rain, he was not thinking about the car he was to buy. He was thinking about the women he had known, the ones he had loved without loving, and for the first time he wondered if any of them had ever worried about him. Then he began to think about Sophie Bartell, to wonder if she had ever worried about a man. He didn't know whether she ever had, but he was certain that she *could*. She was a girl capable of the sort of love that included worry for her man as part of the emotion. It was the sort of love his mother had had for his father.

Chalfont St. Giles was cupped in a fold of the hills: a line of cottages dribbled down the side of the cup from the brow of a hill. In the heart of the village, around the small green, houses leaned together in the gregariousness of old age, seeking support from each other. Farther up the hill the village thinned out: stucco cottages stood in a shabby primness of their own. The main road to Aylesbury bypassed the village, and it had a certain peace and serenity that were fast dying in other villages as close as this to London.

Richie was there at the garage, and his wife and two small sons. "I'm asking him what he'd like for tomorrow," Kitty Launder said. "If he had his way and we could afford it, he'd live on steak. Steak and eggs. These Australian gourmets."

"Any nation that boils cabbage the way the English do,"

said Richie, "has no right to sling off at the tastes of other nations."

Richie had come to England with the Royal Australian Air Force in 1940 as a bomber pilot. He had met and married Kitty, a girl from Lincolnshire, in 1943 and six months later had crashed on the way back from a raid on Berlin. He had spent the rest of the war in hospitals and in a prisoner-of-war camp; he had the scar on his head and several other larger scars on his body as relics of the crash. He had never gone back home to Australia, but he still wrote regularly once a week to his father, mother and brothers on the small farm outside Camden in New South Wales. He had never stopped being an Australian.

"How's your mother, Ham?" Kitty Launder was a girl who missed being pretty, but the humour and kindness in her face made it a near-miss. She was full of love and good will toward all men but appreciated the irony that if it hadn't been for a war she wouldn't have met the one man she had ever loved. "And Taz?"

"They're both well," Ham said.

"That's nice," Kitty said. "Your mother bears up wonderfully, doesn't she?"

Then she took the two children and went off to do her shopping, and Ham, who knew women but had never understood them, was left wondering what she had meant. He turned to Richie. "I've come up to look at the car."

"Out the back," Richie said and led the way. Two young mechanics were working at a bench in the garage; they nodded shyly as Ham went past. It wasn't every day that a famous racing driver came into the garage; they'd have something to tell their girls tonight.

Richie led the way across a small yard, cluttered with the skeletons and steel bones of cars, and into a long galvanised shed. "There it is, sport. We put the body on the chassis this morning. Just to see how it looked."

Ham walked slowly round the car. As always when he was with cars, particularly new ones, other things dropped out of his mind; the row at home was abruptly forgotten, if only for the moment.

"We'd do the body in Fiberglas," Richie said. "Like the Jensen."

"Who designed this?" Ham asked.

Richie looked at him in surprise. "I did, of course," he said and sounded a little hurt. "The whole bloody kit and boodle. Chassis, body, the works. All I want's an engine."

Ham stood back from the car, admiration growing inside him. He had always known that Richie was a good engineer, as good as they came; he had never realised that the bald little fat man was also an artist. Even allowing for the roughness of the mock-up, the car was a thing of beauty. All its lines flowed strongly and evenly toward the rear; there was not a weak curve in the whole conception of the body styling. Nothing projected above the smooth line of the car other than the low windshield; even the door handles had been recessed. The car *looked* swift, even standing still.

"What's the chassis?" he asked.

"I modelled it on the Maserati, with a few adjustments of my own. Independent front suspension, and the rear is de Dion. If I can get them, it'll have disc brakes. We mounted an engine in it one day last week, an old Austin A70 I'd worked on, and took it out to see how she went. She went all right," he said, his plump face bright with pride. "I'd like to try it with an engine with more power." He patted the plaster moulding of the body. "I got a car here, sport. A real car. But stone the crows, wouldn't I like a bloody engine!"

"What sort have you got in mind?"

"Let's go and have a beer." Richie could drink beer like no other man Ham had ever met, and yet it never seemed to have the slightest effect on him. No matter where the works

64

team had gone to race, France, Italy, Spain, Belgium, he would never drink wine but would order the local beer. When they had gone to Germany he had been as happy as a Greek knee-deep in nectar.

"I can't understand why you never get drunk," Ham said, "the amount of beer you drain into you."

"I used to get drunk on Aussie beer," Richie said. "Beer on this side of the world is just hog wash. Yeah, about the engine. I'd like something like the XK150. But I can't afford to buy one—I dunno if Jaguar would even sell me one. But they're selling 'em to put in the Allard Palm Beach model and maybe they'd sell 'em to me if I could convince 'em I had a car that was good enough. But I'm not gunna get anywhere designing and selling just one car. I gotta have orders for at least half a dozen to warrant totaling up. And I ain't gunna get people to put up their money in advance, just on spec. And the bank won't increase my overdraft."

"So what are you going to do?"

Richie shrugged, finished his beer and ordered another. "I dunno. What I gotta find is enough dough to buy me one XK150, try it out and show how good my car is, maybe at Oulton Park or Goodwood, and have enough still left in the bank to put in an order for another five or six engines if the orders came in. Ah, I wish my old man had run sheep instead of bloody dairy cattle. I'd have the cash for whatever I wanted. Right now all I can afford is a hotted-up A70."

Ham sat thinking for a while, sipping at his beer. Behind him two farm labourers were looking at him, in his orange turtle-neck sweater and green corduroy trousers, as if about to offer him a job scaring away the crows in their fields.

"Must be one of them actors," one of them gurbled in his beer.

"Moight be a furriner," said the other and shook his head at how England was being invaded.

65

At last Ham said, "If you got the right engine, do you think your car could stand up to the Mille Miglia and then the Le Mans?"

Richie looked at him over the top of his glass. "You fair dinkum, sport? You're not pulling my leg?"

"I'm fair dinkum," Ham said.

"He be a furriner," said one of the farm labourers, and his companion nodded.

"I'm not building that car to race it," Richie said. "Not in something as tough as the Mille Miglia."

"No, but could you?" Ham persisted.

"I reckon I could," Richie said with quiet confidence. "The strength is there in the chassis and frame. It might need strengthening in one or two places, but I built it to take punishment. We'd have to build another body for it. Use another material than the one I had in mind, I mean. I'm not keen on Fiberglas for a race like that. Why?"

"I've just signed to drive in the Mille Miglia and the Le Mans next year," Ham said and told Richie about Bartell.

"I've been told to choose my own car."

Richie's face lighted up, and he stood up straight; then slowly he relaxed and took another sip of his beer. He rubbed the scar on his head with a greasy finger, leaving a shadow beside the lizard on the rock. "Ah, you don't want a car that's never been proved. You want a job you *know* is good. A Maserati, something like that."

"How do you know your car isn't good?"

"What class are you going in? You wanna win the big prize in both, don't you? You're not interested in just going in for the class stuff, like up to two thousand c.c.'s or something like that, are you? You gotta have a big car to win the big prizes, Ham. You know that."

"In the Le Mans, yes. But I'll worry about that one later. In the Mille Miglia it's the driver who wins the race, not the car. In 1947, the last time I drove in it, Nuvolari would have won it in a little Cisitalia if his engine hadn't flooded on the run between Turin and Milan."

"You're not Nuvolari, sport. I only saw him race twice, but even I know that. No offence."

"Nobody compares himself to Nuvolari. You know that."

"Okay. But look: When Moss won the Mille Miglia in 1955, he did it at an average of just under a hundred an hour. He was doing a 180 on some of the stretches. Try that in your little Cisitalia."

"You're talking about the record drive," Ham said. "The Millie Miglia is different every year. You never know what the conditions are going to be like, and nobody will take bets on who's going to win. A car with a top speed of 150 has just as much chance as anything over that. You don't win the Mille Miglia on the stretches. You win it on the bends, the two or three thousand of them, and in the mountains. You build me a car that can stand up to that thousand miles, with good brakes and good suspension. I'll buy you a Jaguar D-type engine and take my chances on winning."

Richie stared at him for a moment, then he said quietly, "I thought you were never gunna drive in the Mille Miglia again?"

"So did I," said Ham. "But we all have the bait we can't resist."

Richie drew patterns in the beer slopped on the counter from his glass. "It'd be something, wouldn't it, if we could do it? A car out of a backyard shed and a bloke that everyone had written off after Le Mans." He looked sideways at Ham, his finger, broken-nailed, grease-stained, the finger of an artist and an engineer, stabbing at a car sketched in the beer slops. "They had, you know."

"I know," Ham said. "But everyone made a mistake."

"Come a gutser, we call it in Australia," said Richie, and put out his hand. "We'll show 'em, sport. When do I meet this Mr. Joseph Bloody Bartell?"

6

When Ham got back home, Taz had left, to lunch with some girl and then go on to his club Rugger match.

"A Mrs. Picton phoned," Janet said. "She wanted you to ring her back. Who is she?"

"Just a girl I know."

"A Mrs.?"

"It's all right, Mum. She's divorced."

Louisa Picton had been his last interest, and fleeting at that. He had met her one night in a dimly lighted club in Notting Hill, dressed in black and acting like a *femme fatale;* later, in the daylight, he had discovered that she always wore black, with dandruff accessories, and she was more *fatale*-looking than *femme.* He had made some mistakes in his choice of women, and he had never intended that any of his affairs should be permanent; yet he never liked to hurt them, and it had always been a problem how to break off relations with those women who couldn't read the signs.

"I'll give her a call," he said and then forgot all about Mrs. Picton. Instead, he put through a call to Bartell: "I've got a proposition to put to you regarding the car I'm going to drive."

"Proposition?" Bartell had the businessman's suspicion of propositions; his voice tightened up over the wire. "What do you mean, Rafferty?"

"I'm not trying to make anything on the side, Mr. Bartell," Ham said, surrendering his independence: I may as well get used to the idea that he is my boss now. "I just have an idea that may help you more, publicity-wise, and that may also help a man who has designed what looks to me like a good car."

"Publicity-wise? Where'd you learn that, Rafferty? You sound like some advertising men who work for me. In this country, at least, I thought people would talk the King's English."

"It slipped out," Ham said, smiling into the phone. "Some sort of reflex."

"Keep your reflexes for the track, if they sound like that," said Bartell. "All right, what's the deal on this car?"

"Are you free this afternoon?" Ham asked, and Bartell said he was. "Righto, I'll come up and pick you up and bring you down here and show you the car." He hesitated. "Perhaps your daughter would like to come, too?"

Bartell must have turned away from the phone, putting his hand over it. There were distorted sounds at the other end of the phone, as if someone were being throttled to death, then Bartell said suddenly, "She'd love to come. Those are her words, not mine."

Ham smiled again into the phone; he was beginning to like this rude, abrupt American. "I'll pick you up at two-thirty."

He then called Richie and told him he was bringing Bartell to see him and to have all his facts straight and on the tip of his tongue. "I read somewhere that Americans like facts. That's all they want. The facts."

"You been looking at *Dragnet*, sport."

He said something rude to Richie, then put down the phone and went into the living-room. His mother was making out a shopping list, something she did every Saturday and which she always lost before she got to the shops. "Is there anything you want, Ham?"

"Get me some gum," he said. "A dozen packets."

She looked up and smiled gently. "That's the first time I've ever had to buy you chewing gum at this time of year."

"I think I'll become an habitual gum chewer," he said, smiling back at her. "Not only in races."

"It's such a disgusting habit."

"So's smoking. At least gum chewers don't blow their smoke in other people's faces. Or leave soggy cigarette butts in saucers."

"There are other things you are going to need," she said. "Somebody stole your helmet when they were lifting you into the ambulance at Le Mans. And your goggles were smashed to smithereens. It's a wonder you didn't get some of the glass in your eyes."

"I remember flicking them down just before the car landed. Some of the chaps like to keep them on, but somehow I can never trust the glass in front of my eyes. Dad was the same, remember?"

It had only struck him now that this was the first time he had given a thought to his racing gear since the accident. Perhaps it was an indication that, subconsciously, he had already made up his mind to retire. But that was before Bartell had appeared on the scene. "What did you say?" His mother had said something.

"I said, I don't know if Taz will come home tonight. He went out this morning without even saying good-bye."

"Is he taking it out on you, then? Look, what's he got to complain about? He's had a good life—"

"You told him all that a few weeks ago, Ham." The mildness of her tone made him calm down before he could become angry again. "I know Taz went to a good school, had a better time than a lot of less fortunate boys have. But you had a good life as a youngster, too. And I think that's what Taz envies. He envies what you had and what you've got. You were fortunate, Ham. In being born first, I mean."

He realised that his mother, in her gentle way, was trying to tell him that he, too, had taken a lot for granted. He had indeed had a good life as a boy. He had seemed to spend more time travelling with his mother and father than he had spent at school; he could remember his grandfather once telling Janet that she was ruining the boy's life. Somehow he had picked up an education, although he had never sat for examinations and it was impossible to know what grades he would have got. But experience had proved that he rated high in his knowledge of cars, foreign places, languages and the sensibilities of people in other lands. By the time Taz was old enough to be taken round Europe from track to track, the war had begun. He had been at school when their father had been killed and had never actually seen him race.

"I hadn't thought much about it that way," Ham said. "But he seems to think that I want to stick with racing just for the glory and the excitement. He doesn't seem to realise that, with me, it's a job as well. If I were in a bank, would he want me to move over and make room for him?"

"If you were in a bank, there would be room for both of you," said Janet. "There is no danger in working in a bank."

Ham sat down, looking at his mother as he couldn't remember having looked at her before. The years had gone for

71

her, he realised: she had more memories than hopes. Her hair was immaculate, as always; but it was grey, not a young woman's hair any more. The cold autumn light came through the window, falling on an autumn face; he remembered she had once been beautiful, but the beauty had begun to fade now. And for the first time since his father's death, he saw the pain in her eyes.

"Do you worry much about me, Mum? When I'm racing?"

She nodded, knowing she no longer had any secrets from him. "All the time, Ham. I've said more prayers—" She made a little gesture; her Englishness corsetted her, making her afraid of sentiment in front of her son. Pat Rafferty had been all sentiment, and she had never felt restrained with him. She had laughed and wept with him, at victories and defeats, at a flag, a shrivelled shamrock, an English rose in an Italian garden. But Pat Rafferty was not her son. "I'm sorry you should know, Ham. But one can't help worrying."

"And when I retire and Taz takes up racing, you'll go on worrying?"

"Of course. Sometimes I wish I'd married someone other than a racing driver." Then abruptly: "No, no I don't. Your father couldn't have been anything but what he was. And I couldn't have married anyone but him," she said, and for the moment wasn't afraid of her sentiment. Nor her love.

She had married Pat Rafferty the day after her twenty-first birthday, when she had been legally old enough to defy her father's wishes. She had told her father what she was going to do, and then had gone to Germany and she and Pat had been been married in Nürburg. After the wedding, at which all the guests had been racing drivers and their wives and girl friends, Pat had gone out and driven in the German Grand Prix. Before even her wedding night, Janet Rafferty had known what it was like to sit for hours while her husband went out to see if that was the day Death had chosen for him.

But she could not deny that she had also enjoyed the life.

72

It had glamour and excitement, and for nine months of the year they followed the sun. There had been parties and invitations to grand houses; once she and Pat and Tazio Nuvolari had dined with King Alfonso in Madrid. Tazio Nuvolari had been Pat's one and only idol, and Taz had been named after him.

Ham stood up and walked across and kissed the top of his mother's head. "I promise you," he said. "This will be the last season for me."

She looked up at him. "Is that a promise to Taz, too?"

He hesitated, then he said, "All right. It's a promise to Taz, too."

She stood up beside him. "It will be a relief when you're both retired. I just hope I'm not too old to enjoy the comfort and peace of it." Then she looked across at the photograph of the laughing, carefree man who had been her husband and lover. She stared at it for a moment, then she looked back up at Ham. "And yet I'm going to miss the tracks and the cars. They were your father's only real background."

He pressed her shoulder. "I know. That's one thing we've both got, seeing Dad at work in a race. I could understand if Taz envied me *that*."

After lunch he drove up to London to the Dorchester. Bartell and Sophie were waiting for him. "You're late," said Bartell, looking at the enormous gold watch he wore; his wrist was manacled by time.

"So were you," said Ham, "the first day you asked me to call."

Bartell looked at him. "You're not going to butter me up, eh, Rafferty? Is that it?"

"Being late was not intentional," Ham said. "But I'm not used to buttering people up, either."

"Atta boy," said Sophie, and her father looked at her. But she was smiling, and after a moment he smiled, too. Father and daughter were coming to know each other. "Mr. Raf-

73

ferty's in a different category from the others back in Akron, Dad."

"Does he butter you up?" said Bartell bluntly, still smiling at her.

But Sophie wasn't embarrassed; she wanted to know what Ham's reaction to her had been. "Do you, Mr. Rafferty?"

"I don't butter up women," Ham said, joining in the joke, part of their circle. "Only the foolish ones."

"Let's go," said Bartell. "I don't want to get into a discussion on the foolishness of women."

"And men," said Sophie, unable to forget completely the past, but her father had gone out of the room and was heading for the elevator. She looked up at Ham, at the soft, battered hat he had put on as some concession to formality. "You look better in a cap."

"I might have known it," Ham said. "The hat was part of buttering you up."

"I'm not a girl who responds to buttering up," she said and looked at him from the corners of her eyes. Her eyes had a slightly Oriental slant, as if sometime in the past a Chinese had dallied for a night in a bosom of the family. She had a mouth that was perhaps a little too wide and full for real beauty; at first glance the lips were almost sullen and petulant-looking. Her teeth were white and perfect, and when she smiled her cheeks shadowed into dimples. She was a girl whose looks had brought her a lot of flattery, but none of it had turned her head nor done much to help the men who had flattered her.

"Will you have dinner with me tonight?" Ham said.

"I was hoping you'd ask me," she said and walked ahead of him out the door and down toward the elevator where Bartell stood waiting impatiently for them.

At Chalfont St. Giles Richie was waiting for them outside the garage. Perhaps to impress the American millionaire, he was wearing a brand-new pair of white coveralls. He was

74

introduced again to Bartell, who remembered him from the night at the motor show, then he led the three of them through the garage and out to the shed at the back.

"It isn't much of a place to come and look at a car," Richie said; Ham had never heard him sound apologetic before. "But this isn't Detroit."

"I started off myself in a place no bigger then this," Bartell said. "Every good car that's been made started out in a small barn some place, eh, Rafferty?"

Ham knew of a few that hadn't, but he was learning early that it was better to agree with Bartell on the small things. "This one of Richie's is a good car," was all he said.

"Me and the boys worked all morning," Richie said. "We put the A70 engine back into it. Afterwards, we'll take the body mock-up off it, Ham, and you might like to try it out. See what you think of the steering and the way she holds the road."

Bartell walked round the car, chewing on his empty cigarette-holder, making no comment at all. Sophie had gasped at her first sight of the car and clasped her hands together; and Ham had been pleased. She appreciates beauty, he thought, even if she doesn't realise that this looks as if it might also be a good piece of mechanical design. At last Bartell said, "It looks all right to me. Now what's the proposition, Rafferty?"

He has some patience, Ham thought; all the way down here he's held off asking me what I had in mind. "I still have to test this car, Mr. Bartell. But I know Richie's worth as an engineer—or anyway, as a mechanic—and I'm willing to take him at his word that this is a good car. I like the body design very much. I had a look at the chassis and I like what he's done there, too. But it wants an engine, a good, powerful one. Now if we could interest one of the big companies, Jaguar, for instance, in letting us have one of their engines, with an option for further orders of them, I think we might have a car here that could win us the Mille Miglia."

"I want to win the Le Mans 24-Hour, too," said Bartell, and Richie looked at him sharply, then ran a hand over his bald head as if tilting an invisible cap over his skeptical eyes.

"We'll worry about the Le Mans later, if you don't mind," Ham said. "A driver prepares for one race at a time, Mr. Bartell. He never thinks beyond the one that's immediately in front of him."

"I see what you mean." Bartell was not completely insensitive. "But why can't we put an American engine in this? A Cadillac, for instance? Briggs Cunningham used a Cadillac engine in his cars at Le Mans. Or a Chrysler."

"The Cunningham was a big car, designed to take those engines," Richie said. "I'd have to tear this down and completely redesign it to fit a V-8 as big as the Cadillac into it."

"So what's your idea?" Bartell said to Ham.

"Well, if a brand-new car with a brand-new tire won the Mille Miglia, wouldn't the publicity be double?"

"I'd want to know more about this car before I'd go risking my tires on it," Bartell said.

"Would you mind risking a little money?" Ham said. "Look, Mr. Bartell: The Mille Miglia isn't until next April. If we don't get a car till two months before then, we're all right. That gives us nearly five months for Richie to build his car and for us to find out if it's good enough to put in the Mille Miglia. He'll need staking, but whatever it costs, it'll cost less than if I chose, say, a Ferrari. That is, if the car turns out to be a good 'un. If it doesn't—"

Richie said suddenly, "If it doesn't turn out to be any good, Mr. Bartell, I'll sell my garage to repay what you spend on it. I been thinking about it ever since Ham rang me to say he was bringing you out here. I know now I don't wanna be a garageman for the rest of my life. This is what I wanna do." He patted the car with a loving hand." I reckon I can risk what I got, just for the chance to prove I got a good car."

"Go on, Dad," said Sophie. "It's worth the risk. You won't miss the money."

"It isn't the money," Bartell said, looking around at the three of them arrayed against him. "I just don't like to get my name tied up with something that mightn't come off. I've never backed a failure yet."

"You shouldn't judge the car till it's had a chance." Ham was surprised at how Sophie was backing him and Richie; he looked gratefully at her, but she was looking at her father. "And it needs money to have a chance."

"How come you're so interested in this, Sophie?" Bartell's voice was good-humoured.

Sophie shrugged, smiling at him. "Oh, I don't know. Maybe it's because I'm a little fed up with big business. You don't get this sort of thing in America any more." She waved a hand at the cramped shed, at the car standing sleekly close by their legs. "Oh, I know about the kids out in California with the hot-rods and their specials. But they're just built for speed trials. Not like this. The small-time stuff, the little man starting out to compete against the big fellers on their own grounds. I remember you telling Momma once, it was that sort of thing had made America." She stopped, as if she felt that, indirectly, she had called her mother in on her side. "I should think you'd want to back Mr. Launder, if only for old times' sake."

"I've got to think about it," Bartell said cautiously. "I'd want some facts."

Richie looked at a sparrow that had just flown into the shed. Before he looked back at Bartell he covertly winked at Ham. "Oh, I got all the facts, Mr. Bartell. I thought you might want 'em."

"While you tell him," Ham said, "I'll take the car out."

One of the mechanics came through from the garage and helped Ham and Richie lift the body from the chassis. The car had now lost all personality; it was just a skeleton and a heart. Ham had another close look at the chassis, checking suspension and the brakes, testing the strength of the tubular framing on which the body had been mounted; then he settled himself into one of the old bucket seats that had been fitted into it, and started up the engine. Then he looked up at Sophie. "Want to come? It'll be pretty blowy and uncomfortable."

But she had already clambered into the other seat beside him. "Let's go, mister."

"You'd better hold my hat," he said and gave it to her. He looked up at Bartell, standing like a tall camel beside the car, chewing the cud of skepticism. "This won't be much of a test of it as a racing car. But I'll do what I can with it with this engine in it."

"I'll talk to Mr. Launder while you're gone," Bartell said, looked down at Sophie, then back at Ham. "You have my daughter there, remember. Bring her back just the way she is now."

Ham nodded, seeing the bone melt for a moment in the older man's face; then he let in the gears and rolled the car across the yard and out through the garage into the street.

"Hang on," he said. "This'll be nothing like riding in a Cadillac."

The A70 engine was not a new one, but it was good; it was evident that Richie had done some work on it, and its response was gratifying. Ham took the car up along the Aylesbury road, and Sophie, sitting beside him, was amazed at the mixture of relaxation and concentration he showed. He drove in a most relaxed style, sitting well back from the wheel in what she was later to learn was the Italian style; yet he was studying every movement and reaction of the car to his work on the wheel and on the brakes. Like all women when they first see their men at work, she was fascinated; a man at work, doing what he knew and liked, was a different man from the one whose only concern up to now had been the social graces. Then Sophie could see nothing for the tears in her eyes; at eighty miles an hour they swept unprotected into the wind. I'm mad, she thought, crazy as some teen-ager. This is hot-rod stuff on a public highway; back home we'd be jailed for this.

Then Ham began to slow the car and for the first time looked at her. "Oh hell, I'm sorry. I should have got some goggles for you."

She smiled at him through her tears. "Is that all? If there's any more, I think I'll get out and catch a bus back. A nice, big, Cadillac bus."

"That's all," he said, grinning. "I'll want to try it out again, somewhere where I can put the pressure on it. But I think it's going to be all right. Let's go back and see what your father has decided."

As they drove back Sophie said, "Where are you going to take me to dinner? I'd like to have dinner out here in the country. In an old English inn with the ghosts of some Cavaliers."

"I don't know about the Cavaliers," he said, "but I know a good old inn. But what about your father? Tell you the truth, I wasn't counting on taking him to dinner, too."

But when they got back to Chalfont, that problem and the larger one of Bartell's financing Richie's car had been solved. "It's all set," Richie said. "Joe here has asked me to go up to London and have dinner with him. We got a few more facts to talk about." He grinned at Ham, his fat face bright as a sunflower; he slipped out of the tight, white pod of the overalls. "I'll ride back with you. I've rung Kitty that I won't be home for dinner."

"You won't ride back with me," Ham said. "You can take Mr. Bartell back to London in the Standard. I'm taking Sophie to dinner up at Amersham," he explained to Bartell. "She wants to meet some Cavaliers."

Richie went to get his jacket and the Standard; both fitted

79

him with almost equal snugness. Bartell jackknifed himself into the small car. "A kiddy car," he said. "That's what this would be back home in the States. A kiddy car." Then he ducked his head and looked out at Ham. "I'm beginning to think you might have had a good idea, Rafferty. It's almost like going back twenty-five years."

"And how does it feel, Dad?" Sophie said.

"Fine," he said and looked up at her. "And how do you feel?"

"Fine," she said and put her hand in Ham's.

As he and Richie drove away, they heard Bartell say, "You know, Richie, it would be a great thing, eh, if a couple little fellers like you and me put the big boys back on their asses, eh?"

"You fair dinkum, Joe? Little blokes like you and me? You with a million dollars and me—me with an overdraft I couldn't pole-vault over?" Richie's laughter floated back to them; there was more than just amusement to it; the cold evening dusk rang with his happiness.

"If you offered him a ticket back to Australia," Ham said. "I think Richie would refuse it today."

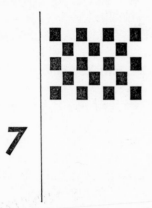

7

They went to the Griffin at Amersham for dinner. There were no ghosts of Cavaliers there, only the horseflesh-and-blood of a group who had come in from a point-to-point meeting. The Irish part of Ham sometimes asserted itself, and he could look at the English with the eye of an outsider: he never stopped being amazed at how the English, more than any other nation, could take on the look and atmosphere of whatever was their main interest. Men from the City often had the dry, dusty look of financial ledgers; their bowler hats were inverted inkwells and their furled umbrellas symbols of the pen. Antique dealers, even the young pansy ones in Kensington and Knightsbridge, were often hard to separate from their wares. And horsey crowds, especially in the illustrations in the society magazines, were sometimes hard to distinguish from the horses; the women had the nose-lifted, slightly startled expression of the thoroughbred mares, and the men wore overcoats and jackets that looked as if they had been made from horse rugs.

It was a generalisation, he knew, but then the English tended toward generalisation; they acted and talked in clichés that defined their classes as definitely as if they wore badges. It was possibly why, as a form of rebellion against the clichés of English life, England had produced more than its share of the world's eccentrics. He guessed that Sophie looked upon him as pure English, and he wondered in what group she classed him.

As Ham and Sophie walked into the bar, the horsey crowd looked at him and his clothes, branding *him* as an eccentric; but he was unaware of their stares and nudging elbows, and ushered Sophie on into the dining-room. "I'll give my mother a ring," he said. "Tell her I'll be staying up in London tonight."

When he came back to the table, Sophie was coming from the ladies' room. She had combed her hair and fixed her face; in the yellow light of the old dining-room she was excitingly beautiful. The horsey crowd came into the dining-room, and the men turned to admire her; they turned back sharply as they were kicked by their women, an old equestrian habit.

"This place is wonderful," Sophie said, sitting down and looking about her at the dark beams above her head. Shadows hung in the corners, but they were shadows from the years, not the lights. "We haven't been able to achieve this in the States. I mean something that is really antique. You go to old places in New England and Pennsylvania, but it's only like going back to yesterday."

"You mean there are no ghosts there?"

"There are ghosts everywhere. Even in the Dorchester."

She had these odd moments of seriousness, he had noticed; the women he had known had only been serious about lovemaking. Beyond her, the horsey crowd neighed at some joke; he had found himself hating them, wishing they'd eat their dinner and go. Then he knew he was wrong and tried to smile apologetically at one of the women as she happened to glance at him. The horsey crowd was no worse than the car-racing crowd he had gone about with. *Had* gone about with? When was the moment he had begun to think of them as part of the past?

Sophie was saying, "You must have ghosts of your own. Have you?"

He blinked, as if he had just come awake. "Yes. Yes, I suppose I have," he said and suddenly felt the ghosts of his father, of Ascari, Levegh, Keen, drivers who had waved and smiled at him as they stood by their cars, suggesting a drink when the race was over, but who hadn't lived to see the end of the race and had died thirsting for another few years of life.

"I tried to learn what I could about you," she said, smiling at him. "My experience as a researcher came in handy. But I couldn't learn everything there was to learn about you. Some things aren't in the records. Nor in people's gossip."

"I'm not a hard man to know. Nobody has ever complained."

"Maybe the people you knew didn't want to dig too deeply into you?"

"Do you?"

"I'm a researcher," she said lightly. "It's an occupational disease."

"You must be tough on the men you know back in New York."

She caught his unspoken question. "You mean, is there a man in New York? No. No special one, that is. I'm a careful girl. I don't want a career man. My mother married one. And New York is full of career men."

"I'm a career man," he said.

"I know," she said, looking at him and feeling the odd

physical attraction of him working on her again; she couldn't remember any man whose mere presence had ever had such an effect on her before. This is sex appeal, she thought, something the British are supposed to be lacking. And I'm falling for it. "That was something I didn't need the records to tell me. Nor the gossip."

"You don't like my sort of career?" he said. "Or any sort, for that matter? How do you expect a man to make a living these days if he hasn't got a career?"

"I don't know. Maybe I'm just being foolish. Maybe I remember my—my mother too much," she said, and suddenly found to her horror that the memory of her mother had grown dim. Had her father already won her back that far? "But I'd go home in the subway or walk about the streets, and I'd see men there who didn't look as if they needed careers to live. Maybe I've just been unlucky. I mean, in the men I knew. They all wore grey flannel suits."

"I don't get it," he said.

"It's a sort of uniform. Like striped pants and bowler hats over here. Like your coveralls and your green helmet."

The dining-room filled up as they ate. People came in, bringing with them the scent of the cold night air. The horsey crowd's hoarse laughter was lost in the chatter of the room; cigarette smoke thickened and everyone began to lose his identity. A feeling of relaxation and freedom filled the room; this was Saturday night the world over. Ham reached for a bread roll at the same time Sophie did, and for a moment his hand rested on hers.

"You're going to be here for six months," he said. "I shouldn't mind doing this every Saturday night. I know a lot of other old inns."

"I'm going back to Italy for three weeks," she said and was sorry now that she had accepted the invitation to go there. "To stay with my cousins. Next week, when Dad leaves to go back to the States. But when I come back—"

"Good," he said and pressed her hand. "Now what shall we do after dinner? I have a flat in Earl's Court. Would you like to go back there and listen to some records?"

"What sort of records?"

"Jazz. Erroll Garner, Joe Bushkin. I'm a piano man."

"I'm a jazz buff, too. But I like trumpet. Satchmo. In New York I go down to Eddie Condon's a lot to hear Wild Bill Davison. And there's an English trumpeter I like, too. Humphrey Lyttleton. Only an English jazz man could have a name like that."

"I have a few trumpet records."

She shook her head. "No, Ham. Not tonight. I'm still digging. What I've dug up, I like. But I wouldn't want to spoil it."

"How can you spoil it listening to some jazz records?"

"This wasn't in the records," she said, breaking the roll she had taken into small pieces. "The records about you, I mean. I got this from the gossip. You're a ladies' man. They gave you quite a reputation."

"I was no worse than a lot of others," he said and didn't try to explain why there had been so many women. "I just got talked about, I suppose. I never tried to hide it."

"I'm not annoyed or disgusted at you, Ham," she said and looked at him with that serious look again. "I'm no prude."

"Just careful?"

"Yes," she said. "Just careful."

They talked as they drove back to London, but now there was a barrier between them. The intimacy of the dinner table had gone; they could have been two strangers who had taken up a conversation in a bus. The road rushed at them along the beam of the headlights; trees fell in on them out of the night but they were past before the car could be crushed; behind them the trees reared back again, and the road spun out into the moonlight.

Ham saw the bend ahead and the reflection of the other

85

car's lights on the trees. He dipped his own lights and eased the speed of the Jensen. The other car came round the bend, its lights blazing, exactly in the middle of the road. Ham jammed on the brakes, jerked the wheel to the left, heard the savage sputter of gravel beneath the wheels, felt the beginning of the skid, heard Sophie cry out and the scream from the other car, then he had got the Jensen back on the road and was slowing it down. The other car had disappeared round the bend.

"That bloody fool!" He stopped the car and put his arm about Sophie. She was shivering, and for a moment he thought she was crying. "Clots like that shouldn't be given a licence."

"Well!" she said at last and sat back; she had regained control of herself. "I'm glad you're as good a driver as you are."

"I drive fast, but I drive on my own side of the road and I know how to handle a car. I'd take that cove's licence away from him if I had the authority." For the first time she saw the anger that was latent in him. "If you'd been hurt, I'd have killed him!"

For the first time, too, she was afraid of him; she realised suddenly that his threat to the vanished road-hog was a real one. "You find them everywhere," she said, trying to gentle him. "Fools who don't know any better."

He started up the car again and they drove on. "Every week, for six or seven months of the year, we go out and risk our necks, trying to make motoring safer for the ordinary driver." He looked at her in the reflected light from the dashboard. "We do, you know. Racing cars isn't only a sport. A lot of people look on it that way, including a lot of the drivers. But some of us don't. There's something more than that in it for me. All the time I was driving for the works team, four seasons of it, we were testing and developing things to go into the ordinary road car made by the factory. Brakes, for instance. And next year I'll be trying out

86

your father's tires. Everything we do on the track, in races on the road, adds up to something for the ordinary driver. Makes it safer for him when he takes the wife and kids for a Sunday drive. But clots like that—" He jerked his head back at the speeding driver who, if his car was still on the road, was now miles away. "On a track the boys would soon give him the works if he drove like that. He'd find himself edged into the fence before he'd done half a dozen laps."

"They really do that? I mean push other drivers off the track?"

"There aren't many who do it deliberately in a race. There are one or two, but we all know them and we watch them. We're all a bit ruthless, I suppose, but we have to be. Cream-puffs, as I heard one American driver call them, don't win races. But I don't think there would be one of us, the professionals, I mean, who'd hesitate about putting a man into the fence who was just a wild fool who didn't care about his own or anyone else's neck. We have to take enough risks as it is. You don't add to them unnecessarily."

When they drew up in front of the Dorchester he went to get out. "No, don't come up, Ham. Will you call me tomorrow?"

"If you'd like me to," he said. "You're not afraid of a ladies' man in the daytime?"

"I'm not afraid of you at all," she said and leaned forward and kissed him on the mouth. "There'll be other nights to listen to your piano players. Good night. And thanks for a lovely dinner and for bringing me back safe and sound."

She was out of the car before he had time to hold her to him and return her kiss. He watched her as she went in through the bright doors of the hotel, her cap held in her hand, her hair swinging loosely. She turned at the doors and waved to him, a gesture as warm and intimate as the kiss had been, then she had gone. He turned the car slowly out into the stream of Park Lane and drove out to Earl's Court, wondering what it was that made Sophie Bartell so different from the other women he had known.

He parked the car beneath the trees along Cromwell Road, locked it and went up the steps to the front door of the house in which the apartment was. It was ugly, part of a Victorian cliff of houses; but the landlord had painted it and put in a bright red front door. A tree, dusty-leafed but green, grew in front of it; and in the summer, window boxes brightened the face of it with their flowers. Now, in the autumn, the window boxes were bare and the street lights were clearly visible through the branches of the tree. Only the bright red door knew no season.

He let himself into the hall, and the tenant of the ground-floor apartment was standing at her door. "Oh, it's you, Mr. Rafferty. I always check who comes in. That is, if I haven't gone to bed. There are so many strange men about here now. One never knows if they might not come into the wrong house."

She stood there in the dim light of the hall, fully dressed, with her hat on, but with her hair in curlers; a thin, brittle slab of woman who was afraid of all men, white or coloured. She was about the same age as his mother, but the two women could have been born in different worlds and different centuries. She lived on a remittance sent her by some relatives in the North; he had seen her every Monday waiting almost desperately in the hall for the post to be delivered. The district was full of elderly women like her, who hadn't the money to live in Kensington itself but lived precariously on the fringes of it, clinging to their gentility and the disappearing past with fingers that were starved of strength. He was sure that his mother had more sense than to want to cling to a station in life that had passed her by, but he was determined that she would never be exposed to the chance of it. It was another reason why he had to race one more season.

"I don't think you have anything to fear," he said and did

his best to keep the irony from his voice; he felt sorry for her and wondered what she had ever got out of life but her petty prejudices.

"How is your leg, Mr. Rafferty? I notice you aren't using a stick now."

"It's fine, thanks."

"You lead such a dangerous life," she said, safe in the cocoon that she had never broken. "I don't know why you persist in it, Mr. Rafferty."

"Maybe I'll give it up," he said and began to climb the stairs, leaving her to the husk of her life. "Some day."

His flat was on the first floor: a bedroom, a combined living-dining-room, a kitchen, a bathroom. He put his key in the door and opened it. The standard lamp in one corner of the living-room was lighted, and in its shadowed light he saw a flash of movement from the couch. A girl stood up, adjusting her clothes, and slipped quickly into the bedroom. Taz, his face tribal-marked with lipstick, stood up and came across the room.

"I didn't think you'd be coming up to town." He brought out a handkerchief and began to wipe his mouth. "If I'd known—"

"It's all right. Were you staying the night?"

"I—" Then the girl came shyly out of the bedroom and Taz introduced her. "This is Pamela. My brother Ham."

All girls that age seemed to be named Pamela. Or Sally or Penelope. They had all been born just before the war and mothers in those days had all seemed to be reading the same library books. This Pamela was blonde and pretty and anonymous as a rose petal; she was still blushing at the situation in which she had been caught.

"How'd you go today?" Ham said, trying to relieve their embarrassment; he was fortunate in that his own lovemaking had never been interrupted. "You win?"

Taz nodded. "Too easily."

"He got two tires," said Pamela. "Absolutely fantastic ones. If they don't choose him for England this season, it'll be an absolutely scandalous crime."

Taz didn't blush; it was as if the girl hadn't spoken. "Have you ever seen Ham drive?"

"Of course," said Pamela. "Silly. I was going to car races before I met you. I saw you one day at Silverstone, Mr. Rafferty. You were absolutely marvelous. You had about three wins."

He had never driven more than twice a day in his life, but that wasn't important. She had called him *Mr.* Rafferty; she spoke with schoolgirl's exaggeration and looked on him as an old man. Yet she was old enough to go to a flat with a boy and take her chances. Ham wondered if the tenant below had checked on them as they had come in.

"Taz was telling me he hopes to be driving in the big cars next season," she said, prattling on with the thin drill of her voice, walking in her high heels across the eggshell tension that lay between the two brothers. "Wouldn't it be absolutely marvellous if the two of you had to fight out a Grand Prix or something? Your mother wouldn't know which one to cheer for."

"Perhaps she wouldn't want to cheer at all," Ham said.

"Perhaps not," said the girl, missing his point. "It could be awful having two sons in the one sport. Did you ever play Rugger, Mr. Rafferty?"

"No," Ham said, suddenly feeling vicious toward Taz: what right had he to tell the girl that he would be driving in the Grands Prix next season. "I've been driving cars ever since I was a little boy."

"You've been lucky, then. Will you be driving next season?" Pamela asked, her voice high and empty and senseless as a bird's; she was insensitive to atmosphere, a sparrow between sparring eagles. "Taz said you mightn't be. Something about your leg."

"The leg is all right," he said harshly. "And I'll be driving."

"That'll be marvellous, won't it? Where's my coat, Taz darling?" She looked about her, her pretty face more blank still as she looked for the missing coat. "I'll have to be going. It's been absolutely wonderful meeting you, Mr. Rafferty! I'll be looking forward to seeing you and Taz racing next season." Then as she went out of the door, she said, "I like your waistcoat. It's real snazzy. I wish Taz would brighten himself up."

"He's probably just waiting until he gets into the Grands Prix," Ham said, still vicious. "Eh, Taz?"

"I'll see you later," Taz said. "And I'm sorry about borrowing the flat without asking you."

"It's all right," Ham said, hating the boy and yet hating himself for the feeling that was burning in him. "You've borrowed it before, haven't you? Why ask me now? Are you coming back to sleep?"

"No," said Taz, going down the stairs, not looking back. "I'll go home."

"Good night, Mr. Rafferty." The girl's voice floated up: her words hung like party balloons in the high hall. "We must meet again soon. I'd adore having you tell me what it's like to drive in a race. 'Byeeee!'"

Ham had a bath and got into his pyjamas. Then he walked to the window and looked down on Cromwell Road. The theatre traffic was on its way home, to Hammersmith and the west; the street was a dark, glittering stream from which there rose the occasional goose-honk of a horn. On the opposite side of the road a man and a girl stood in the thin, betraying shadow of a tree; they strained against each other, longing for a bed in which to love. A woman strolled by them, taking a dog for a walk; the dog cocked a leg against the tree and the three people stood stiffly, even the lovers standing together like strangers. Ham grinned: that dog had no more sensitivity than Pamela or whatever her name was.

He turned and went through into the bedroom and got into bed. He lay there in the darkness, listening to the creaking complaints of the furniture; or was it the atmosphere that had been left behind in the flat that was creaking? Once, as a boy, he had lain in a room like this, listening to the sounds of it; it was a night when his father had lain unconscious in the hospital at Spa in Belgium. His mother had come in to say good night to him, had kissed him, turned out the light and then in the darkness had begun to weep. He had not heard her weep, and she had turned away almost immediately and gone out of the room; but he had known as clearly as if she had sobbed aloud and in broad daylight that she had been crying. When she had gone he had heard her tears in the darkness, and he had been afraid. He had prayed that night, saying the Rosary on his fingers, and in the morning his father had regained consciousness and was out of danger. But he hadn't prayed in a long time, and what was there to pray for in this case?

He put Taz out of his mind and began to think about Sophie. He lay on the shifting edge of sleep, remembering the details of her face, feeling her lips on his, seeing the look in her eyes when she had told him she was not afraid of him.

In the moment before he fell off to sleep he knew why Sophie Bartell was different from all the other women he had known. He had begun to fall in love with her, something that had never happened with any of the others.

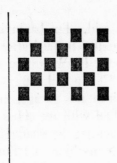

8

Bartell went home to Akron and Sophie went to visit her cousins in Italy. Ham stayed at Stoke Poges with his mother, and Taz, after asking if it was all right, stayed at the flat; the brothers were avoiding each other, and Ham was as agreeable to let Taz have the flat as Taz was to take it. There were no more questions on what was going to happen next season, either on Ham's or Taz's part. Janet lived in some silent purgatory of her own and went through her days in her same quiet, vague way. It was as if all of them had agreed to get through this year before thinking about next year.

Richie went to Coventry and saw the Jaguar people. Some of them knew him personally, and his reputation as a mechanic. They admired the sketches of his car he had taken with him, and listened with interest to his plans. Then they agreed to sell him two engines, with an option on another six if his car proved itself a success in the Mille Miglia. He came back from Coventry whistling "Waltzing Matilda" and that night, in the Merlin's Cave at Chalfont, drank more beer than Ham had ever seen him put away before. And still remained sober.

"It's in the bag, sport," he said. "I'm beginning to think maybe you weren't such a fanciful bastard after all. I think we'll be able to pull it off, sport. Have another grog."

"What about the car itself?" Ham said.

"I'm putting another kid into the garage, and bringing young George out into the shed with me. He's a good kid and he's tickled pink he's gunna get the chance to work on the car. I haven't promised him anything, but I'm hoping we might be able to take him to Italy with us. He's a bloody good worker, and we'll need some sorta team out there. And he's never seen anything but Southend on August Bank Holiday."

"You'll need more than just the two of you."

"I'm getting another bloke, Charlie Carter. He did his time at Mulliner's on panel-beating, and he knows something about welding, too. We won't be able to afford any steel presses, so we'll have to hammer out our bodywork. But we'll give you a car that'll stand up to anything you're likely to give it. Another grog?"

October was swallowed by November fog; the last of the leaves fell out of the grey skies. Bartell had opened a drawing account in Richie's name, and Richie went out and bought new equipment. It was too late to go looking for new quarters, and there was no room to enlarge the shed behind the garage. The shed became even more cramped as the new equipment was moved into it; a man with a welding torch had to be careful he didn't scorch the seats of his fellow-workers. Those who worked at the garage had been sworn to secrecy about what was going on; even Richie,

94

though still confident, wanted to be sure that, if the car failed, its failure wouldn't be too widely broadcast.

Sophie came back from Italy and took a flat in South Kensington. Ham took her out to dinner the night she arrived back, to a small place in Knightsbridge. They had walked to the restaurant, and after dinner they walked back to South Kensington. There had been no fog today and the night air was cold and sharp, like a rapier brushed softly against the cheek.

"The wonderful thing was," Sophie said, "they knew all about you. And your father. You're famous."

"Not really," he said, smiling down at her, holding her arm and feeling that *this* was the wonderful thing: having her back in London. He was aware of the city about them, like some giant room in which they were completely at home. He was not a lover of London as a whole, but he did like Knightsbridge; it had a reputation as a haven for soft men and mannish women, but its own atmosphere was stronger than that of the more notorious of its inhabitants. It had a gaiety and charm about it that you somehow associated with Continental cities; and yet it was and couldn't be anything but English. You could walk beneath the striped awnings of the *espresso* bars and stop to look into the self-conscious windows of the *boutique* shops, but all the time you were aware of the sober shadow of Harrods up the road and the shades of the dowagers alighting from their upright hearselike limousines. And, of course, the silent, never-barking, well-bred English dogs trotting contentedly at the end of their leashes.

"In Brescia everyone knows the drivers," Ham said. "It's because the Mille Miglia starts from there. It's just like at Newmarket, where everyone knows the jockeys. If you had gone to some other town in Italy, they'd have never heard of me."

95

"You're just being modest. But I like you modest. When I first met you, I thought you were conceited. Those outlandish clothes—How do you dress when you go to funerals?"

"The only funerals I've been to have been those of other drivers. I don't think their relatives have cared very much how I was dressed. What's wrong with the way I dress, anyway? Does it bother you?"

"Not at all. Only sometimes I feel I'd be less conspicuous if I were out with a couple of midgets."

When they reached the door of the building where her flat was, he looked at her. "Am I coming up? Or is my reputation still against me?"

She smiled. "Come up. I can always scream if you get out of hand."

In the flat, before she switched on the lights, he took her in his arms and kissed her. "I've never missed anyone before. And that's the truth."

"I know, Ham," she said softly. "I could tell by your kiss."

"Well?"

"I missed you, too. One of my cousins is engaged to be married, and her fiancé used to come to the house every night. Whenever I saw them together I used to start thinking about you. After a while they noticed it. They used to say, 'Sophia'—they always called me Sophia, my real name—'is dreaming about her driver.' "

She reached over his shoulder for the light switch, but he said, "Don't put on the light."

"Yes," she said and did. "I still haven't dug deep enough, Ham. I'm still careful. Do you mind?"

"No," he said and found that he didn't mind at all. "For the first time in my life, I feel there's all the time in the world."

The next night when he took her out he made some attempt at formality. He put on the only lounge suit he owned, a plain cream silk shirt, discarded his bow tie in favour of one of Taz's four-in-hands, and left off his fancy waistcoat. The effect was only spoiled by the yellow suède boots he wore.

Sophie took one look at him and shook her head. "It's my own fault. In future, stay just as you were. Maybe there's something to that about a leopard not being able to change his spots. Or maybe they meant he shouldn't. You're not Ham Rafferty any more."

"And it's Ham Rafferty you're in love with? Not me?"

"Who said I was in love with either of you?" she said and wondered how much she had given herself away.

Then in late November Bartell came back from the States with the first of his new tires. Ham borrowed a D-type Jaguar from a private driver he knew well, and they all went up to Silverstone to try out the tires. The Jaguar was taken up on the back of an old Leyland which Richie borrowed from a local coal dealer; and Bartell and Sophie went up with Ham in the Jensen.

"You're going to like these tires," Bartell said. "It might rain today, too. Give you a chance to see how good they are in the wet."

Ham was surprised at the lightness of the tires; they felt no heavier than those used on a small car. "That's another thing in their favour," said Bartell. "The normal tire averages around eighteen pounds in weight. This one weighs only fourteen, and all round it's a much easier tire to handle. You ever tried to take a tubeless tire off a rim? The Bartell Tubeless won't be any harder to get off than an ordinary tubed tire."

Ham was still skeptical. "I like a heavy tire; that's what I've been used to. You feel the car is sitting a little better on the road."

"You'll have to get used to a light tire, then," said Bartell, blunt as a tire mallet. "I've never yet made a heavy tire, except for trucks."

97

Richie and young George Hayes had rolled the Jaguar down from the back of the Leyland. They had taken off its wheels and were now fitting other wheels with Bartell tires. Ham stripped off his jacket and pulled on a pair of coveralls over his clothes; then he buckled the goggles round his neck and pulled on his helmet. Everything he wore was new: the bright green coveralls, the goggles, the white gloves and the green helmet, like a mildewed skull in the desolate grey of the day.

"It'll be raining soon," said Sophie, looking across the vast open space of the one-time aerodrome toward the ragged clouds racing in like dark vandals from the west. "Do you think you should go out now?"

"Of course," her father said. "That's what we want, rain. We couldn't have picked a better day. What's the matter, Sophie? You scared or something?"

"No," said Sophie, turning up the collar of her bright red raincoat. "But Ham knows how careful I am."

"She's ready, Ham," Richie said.

Ham climbed into the Jaguar and settled himself down in the seat. The D-type Jaguar has high sides to its cockpit that some drivers find confining; but Ham was a man who drove with a minimum of elbow flourish and never noticed the confinement. He tested each of the pedals, ran his hand over the gear lever and brake handle, felt the wheel to see if there was any play in it, then leaned his head back against the headrest. He breathed deeply, smelling the oil and fuel, the rubber and leather, even thinking he could smell the metal of the car. It was the first time he had been in a racing car since Le Mans, and it felt good. It was like some sort of homecoming.

"I'll take it slowly for a lap or two," he told Bartell. "Till I get the feel of it again."

"Do it your own way," said Bartell. "One thing I'm not going to tell you is how to drive a car."

Ham winked at Sophie, then started up the car and took it slowly out on the track. In his mirror, before he accelerated away, he saw the others come out through the gate and stand in front of the pits. Then the car was gathering speed, the wind became louder and harder as it pressed in on the long silver shape that was trying to defy it, and he was getting ready to go through Copse Corner.

In the cold grey day the car was a silver demon speeding round the flat, desolate countryside. Its sound rose and fell, a burring angry whine that produced its measure of fear in those who heard it and didn't understand it. The watchers at the pits followed it by its sound as it went round out of sight on the far side of the track; then they heard it coming up out of Abbey Curve and a moment later it shot into sight as it came down toward Woodcote past the gaunt, dark piles of the old hangars. It came through Woodcote with the tires squealing and went past with an angry roar and a vicious slap of wind.

Ham waved as he went past the pits. "Pretty soon," Richie said to young George Hayes, "you're gunna see a craftsman at work. Maybe even an artist. Anyhow, someone who does this job just a little better than most drivers and as good as anyone else in the world."

"Aw'll be watchin!" George's slow, thick, Buckinghamshire accent marked him as a farm boy, but he had already dedicated his life to cars. As he stood, thin as a flagpole and as straight, his coveralls flapped on him like a loosely furled flag.

Ham went round twice, getting the feel of the car again and the track, lapping at just under eighty, enjoying himself and feeling the pleasure growing in him all the time. The third time round he opened the car up. He went round at almost maximum speed, only steadying himself on the corners as he felt for the adhesion of the tires beneath him. The fourth time round he ran into rain as he went into Maggott's

Curve. By the time he passed the stands at Stowe Corner it was raining heavily. He didn't decrease his speed, but kept the Jaguar going at the same steady high rate. He changed down going into Club Corner, holding the car on the line he had chosen, feeling it move away a little under him on the wet track, then changed up, accelerating again and picked his line for Abbey Curve.

He was halfway through Abbey when the skid started. He jockeyed the wheel, working with all his old skill, quick and yet unhurried. It was a bad skid, and he knew it. The Jaguar snaked its way down the track, its spray now a curtain right across the track. It went right to the very edge of the tarmac, as if to plunge across the rough ground and bury itself in the dark, ugly hangars; Ham kicked the wheel, going against the skid now, and brought it back to the middle of the track. Then he felt the tires take hold beneath him, holding the car on the line he had chosen, and a moment later all danger was past. He took the car slowly down to Woodcote and rolled it to a stop at the pits.

"I thought you'd bought it then, sport," Richie said, as Ham cut the engine.

"It was my tires that got him out of it," said Bartell. "Isn't that so, Rafferty? You feel how they held you on the road?"

"That was nice drivin', Mr. Rafferty." Admiration was frank on George Hayes' thin, long-nosed face; he hadn't yet learned that he had to butter up Bartell. Richie was his boss and Ham was his hero. "You done a smashin' job, keepin' her on the track."

Only Sophie said nothing. Ham, still sitting in the car, wet through from the rain, glanced up at her. Her face was pale beneath the bright red hood she wore; in one hand she held a tattered handkerchief. The rain had gone as swiftly as it had come; but her cheeks were moist and something wet glittered on her lashes. Ham reached up and took her hand.

100

"It was all right," he said. "Even if I'd gone off the track, there'd have been no danger."

"Wouldn't there?" she said, but what he said didn't matter; she had had her moment when her heart had stopped and she had died.

The men were aware of how she had been affected. Richie and George turned away, making a pretence of checking the tires. Bartell took Sophie's arm and pressed it; he still didn't know his daughter well enough to have the words to comfort her. Ham clambered out of the car, pulling off his helmet. His clothes were sticking to him, but he had nothing else to change into. He took his overcoat from Richie and put it on, and hoped he wouldn't catch a chill.

"This sort of thing is part of the game," he said to Sophie. "You'll get used to it."

"Will I?" All she had was questions, but she didn't sound as if she wanted to learn. She had learned enough: that from now on she would ride every inch of every race with him. Every driver's wife or loved one has learned the same thing: the moment of truth comes to them long before it comes to the driver.

"He's a good driver, Sophie." Bartell was upset by the effect on Sophie. "He knew what he was doing. You've got to have confidence in him."

"With this wind the track will dry out soon," Ham said to him. "I'll go round again. I'm still undecided on the tires."

"What's the matter with 'em?" Bartell said sharply. "They went all right, didn't they?"

"I still want to test them some more," Ham said. "That's what you're paying me for, isn't it?"

Bartell backed down. "Okay. Test 'em all you want. You're the man who's got to ride on them."

"That's what I meant," Ham said and took Sophie's arm and began to walk along the track with her. The pits stood

101

empty beside them, caves from which the dwellers had fled, and across the track the wind blew a newspaper bird along the deserted seats of the stands. "Your father's not used to anyone arguing with him, is he?"

"Oh, Ham!" Her fingers dug into his hand; she hadn't heard his remark about her father. "Is it going to be like this all the time?"

"You mean going against your father?" Then he looked down at her and saw that wasn't what she meant at all. There was no rain on her face now; it was tears. He put his arm round her shoulders and felt the trembling of her. "Darling," he said, and it was the first time he had ever used the word. None of the others had ever been called "darling," not even jokingly. He had always held back from letting them take any hint that he was serious about them; he was honest to that extent, and most of them had recognised his honesty. He was honest now, more honest than he had ever been, because he was speaking with love, with nothing held back. "Darling, it's always like this. And I'm sorry for you. But it's the way it is. Every man has to do certain things. I don't think there's a man in the world who hasn't some danger in his life, always there. Mine's here." He nodded at the track, at the vast grey landscape, cold and empty as the frontier of death. Across the track, along the front of the stands, a faded sign said: The *Daily Express* will tell you all about it. "Some day I'll have to turn my back on it. But I can't just yet."

"Why not?" she said demandingly. "Why not?"

And he knew then that it was more than just a question of money in the bank, of working till he had something saved for his old age. He had known it for a long time, ever since he had sat behind a wheel and taken a car out onto a track; but he had never had to explain it to anyone and he couldn't now. It was the same driving compulsion that his father had had, and Pat Rafferty had never been able to nor had ever attempted to explain it to his son. There were questions some of the more introspective drivers asked themselves: what prompted a man to go on risking the only life he had? Why did a man, even when he had learned to fear death, go on courting it season after season? If any of the drivers had found the answers, none of them had ever told them to Ham. Because the drivers never spoke of these things among themselves. They all had whatever the compulsion was: a disease, a fire in the blood, a hunger for knowledge, a desire for escape. And they were glad they had it.

"Why not, Ham? Why can't you retire now?"

He looked down at her, knowing that she was earthbound and, in this at least, not of his world. She had never lived through the storms of a race; she had never known the excitement of speed, real speed. How could he tell her the thrill of taking your car through the same line on a corner time after time? It was artistry, but who had ever been able to explain the thrill of artistry? How could he tell her how satisfying it was to cheat death, and yet have the compelling urge to go back the next day and take the same risk? It was she who had compared motor racing to bull fighting and test piloting; and in her innocence she may have been right. She had experienced none of it and she would never know. It was like the test pilot trying to explain the purple loneliness of the stratosphere to the subway motormen.

"I shan't be racing forever," he said. "I'll have to retire some day."

She knew he had evaded her question. She turned round and began to walk back toward the car and the three men at the far end of the pits. He followed her, catching up with her, but saying nothing. He felt cold, but it wasn't all from the chill of his wet clothes.

103

"The tread was lifting on the back tires," Richie said. "We put on two new ones."

Ham looked at Bartell and the latter said, "Well, maybe they got rougher wear than we'd bargained on. It can be overcome."

"You've never made racing tires before, have you?" Ham said. "What's good enough for the road isn't halfway good enough for the track."

"We allowed for that. We got advice and we built you these tires."

"You haven't got my advice yet," Ham said. "In the end I'm the one who has the last say-so."

For a moment Bartell looked as if he were trying to grind his teeth to dust. His hand went to his pocket, as if to switch off the voice of this man who wouldn't accept his authority. Then abruptly he said, "Okay, Rafferty. You're the judge."

"I'll take it out again now," Ham said to Richie.

The rain clouds had gone. There was still no blue in the sky but the clouds had gone high and were turning silver. In the west the sun was trying to break through for a parting stab at the earth; a silver sword, pale gold at the hilt, was buried in the roof of one of the hangars beyond the Abbey Straight. The wind moaned through the pits, the ghost of a lost beast, and in the fields beyond the stands invisible crows cried their bleak winter song.

Ham caught a glimpse of Sophie's pale face as he accelerated away from the pits. Her raincoat was the one bright patch of colour in the fading silver of the day; she diminished to a red spot in his mirror and then she was gone.

The track had dried quickly under the wind. Ham opened the Jaguar right up. He took it into the corners at maximum safety speed. He was an expert at the four-wheel drift; only Fangio was considered to be better at holding the line

104

through a corner. He lapped once, having no more idea of his lap speed than that it was high; but one lap at high speed is no test for new tires. He went round four more times, drifting through the curves, taking the sharpest line on every bend, making the tires earn every mark he was going to give them.

On the sixth lap he put his foot down as he came out of Chapel Curve and went down Hangar Straight. He went into Stowe Corner faster than on any of the previous laps, holding the car on its line, taking the strain on his wrists and forearms, feeling the wheels beginning to slide outward; he kept his foot down, using the power in the rear wheels to push the car toward the corner and round it. The car was drifting, all four wheels in exact alignment, held on course now by the power of the engine. It was a perfect example of cornering at maximum speed, and he felt the elation well up inside him.

Then a bomb seemed to explode beneath the car. There was the loud, sharp crack as the offside rear tire went, and the back of the car seemed to lift for a moment. The car slewed violently, canting over; a piece of tire was flung high, like a dead bird, and steel scraped against the tarmac. Ham threw the car out of gear and crouched lower in the cockpit, unable to do anything, as the car hurtled backward off the track. Something hit him solidly in the middle of the back, his head snapped forward; then abruptly the car was still, its engine racing madly, both rear wheels twisted and splayed in the black, wet earth.

Ham switched off the engine. In the sudden silence every small sound was magnified; a sparrow whistled away with the scream of a hawk. Ham climbed slowly from the car, his neck stiff, his back paining where he had been jolted by the seat as the car had jammed to a stop. He dragged off his helmet and flipped the plugs from his ears; his goggles were already round his neck, as they had been when he had crashed at Le Mans. He stood there in the vast silence of the dying day, the stands rising starkly on his left like ancient ruins; he was alone and lonely and suddenly afraid. For he was trembling violently, in his limbs and in his stomach, and the vomit was already rising in him.

He turned quickly away and on unsteady legs walked some distance from the car and was sick. He stood there with his head bent, waiting for the trembling to cease and his stomach to settle, then he kicked dirt over the vomit. He walked slowly back to the Jaguar and sat on the side of the cockpit, willing the trembling to stop and feeling it slowly subside. He searched in his pocket for some gum and, luckily, found some. He was chewing when the Jensen came speeding down the straight and screeched to a stop beside the wrecked Jaguar.

Sophie was first out of the Jensen. She raced toward him and he straightened up and caught her as she flung herself against him. He kissed the top of her head.

"It's all right," he said. "I got out of it without a scratch."

Richie, followed by Bartell and George Hayes, came panting across. "We heard you go off! We couldn't see you. You all right, Ham?"

"I'm all right," Ham said, still holding Sophie to him, feeling her crying against him, but afraid to look down at her, holding himself stiff and straight in case his own trembling came back. "Even the car's not too badly cracked."

"What was it?" Bartell, too, was pale; the creases in his face were like streaks of charcoal. "What happened?"

"It was your tires," said Ham, bitter and angry. And yet knowing his anger was a stupid thing: it wasn't Bartell's tires that had at last made him absolutely afraid. "They're no bloody good for racing."

Far across the track some crows flapped across the fading sky with the mournful cry of birds that had seen their last sunset. Bartell looked toward them, but didn't see them. Nor had he seen the fear in the man standing beside the wrecked car. All he saw was the end of a dream.

"I don't believe it," he said, but his voice held no more hope than that of the crows.

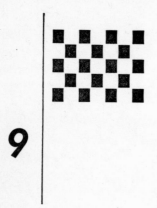

9

For the next two or three weeks there was depression in the camp. Bartell went back to the States, taking with him some samples of what Ham considered good racing tires. Richie continued to work on his car, but with the air of a man who expected it to burst into flames and be demolished forever. Sophie said nothing about the accident, but she had evidently been doing some more researching: she now knew exactly how many drivers had been killed in the last five seasons of racing. And Ham had his own private depression.

Then a cable arrived from Bartell, blunt and confident as the man himself had been when he had first come to England: *We can lick this. Keep working. Expect car ready for new year.* It didn't cheer Sophie, and Bartell's optimism about the tires could have little effect on what worried Ham. But Richie, at least, knew that he was to continue being backed and in the garage at Chalfont, if nowhere else, there was whistling and a great amount of enthusiastic activity.

Ham phoned Richie one day about a week before Christmas. "How's it coming?"

"The first engine arrives the day after tomorrow," Richie said. "And Charlie has just about got the body finished. I reckon we'll have a rough job for you to drive sometime between Christmas and New Year. That's if it's not snowing. Stone the crows, it's cold, isn't it? Now I know why there were so many convicts sent out to Australia in the early days. They stole loaves of bread, then gave themselves up, so they could escape this bloody climate. They weren't convicts or criminals. They were just the first migrants looking for assisted passages."

"Why don't you just throw up the car and ask Bartell for your fare home?"

"Ah, I guess I'm as silly as the English," Richie said. "I'm beginning to like it here."

Ham had begun to train again, getting back into condition and taking off some of the surplus weight he had picked up since the accident at Le Mans. Being as big as he was, he had to watch his weight; and hard flesh could soon turn soft. There were fat men driving racing cars, especially one or two of the Italians; but they were not big men, and there was room for their extra poundage in the cockpits of their cars. Ham began his training by going for long walks, testing his leg, and then he took to skipping. Close by the Rafferty home there was an old house that had once been a country club back in the thirties, and in its grounds there was a squash court, cobwebbed and dusty but still usable. Ham and Taz had cleaned it up and for several years had been going there regularly to play against each other. But Taz was still living up at the flat, and Ham went across every day and banged the ball against the walls on his own for half an hour or so.

He was working out there one day, in shorts and a thick sweater, when Janet knocked on the door in the back wall. "Sophie Bartell was on the phone."

"Did you tell her I'd ring her back?" He wiped his face with a towel.

"Yes. That Mrs. Picton still phones occasionally, too. What does she want? Mightn't it be important or something?"

"If it was important, she'd write me a letter," he said, smiling down at his mother. "I'm just a matinee idol, that's all. All us handsome devils have the same trouble with women. Didn't you chase Dad?"

"No. He chased me. Not that I tried to run away from him."

They began to walk back across the tangled grounds of the onetime country club. The house itself was now rented as a storage depot by a manufacturer from Slough; the rooms that had known gay parties were now stacked with baby chairs. The grass was knee-high, except for the path along which they walked; even the trees, bare-branched though they were, had a neglected look. In a bush lay a broken record, its label long since peeled off: Harry Roy, Lew Stone, some band of twenty years ago had played here under the stars: "Pennies from Heaven" had fallen on the wild grass that had once been well-kept lawns.

"I came here once with your father," Janet said. "It was a gay spot in those days. We left you with your grandfather in Iver and drove across here. That was when we had the old Bentley. There was a dance on, celebrating some meeting that had been held at Brooklands. I remember everyone who had been at the meeting came up here—it was nothing in those days to drive miles for a dance. It was when we first saw our house. Pat and I went for a walk between dances. It was moonlight, and there was the house standing there in the trees. I fell in love with it right away. But it was your grandfather who had to persuade Pat to buy it. Your father hated the idea of settling down." She had told him that a dozen times and he wondered what she was leading up to now. She broke a stick from a bush and walked for a while in silence, swishing at the long grass. "Are you ever going to settle down?"

"Some day," he said, hedging. "Why?"

"Why don't you ask this Sophie Bartell down here?"

"You've never asked me to bring any of the others home. When I did bring them home, you never seemed particularly interested in them."

"But this girl is different, isn't she?" She looked up at him, and when he smiled, she said, "I must be a better mother than I thought. I'm even intuitive as to when my son is in love."

"Is it as obvious as that?"

"Not to strangers, Ham. But I'm right, aren't I? What's she like?"

"She's a millionaire's daughter. I'm still trying to make up my mind whether that's a good or a bad thing. At least she doesn't appear to be spoiled by her father's money."

"Millionaires are no different from anyone else," said Janet. "They just have more money."

"Ah, Mum." He laughed, taking her arm, loving her as much as his father had done. "You can always reduce everything to such simplicities."

But two nights later he brought Sophie home for dinner. He didn't ask her about it, but she seemed to have taken particular care with herself, as if she placed some importance on this meeting with his mother. Of course, he told him-

111

self, silently admiring her as he drove her down from London, this goes on every day all over the world. I'm just a little later than most men in bringing home my first real girl.

He didn't know that his mother had also invited some others for dinner. Taz was there, with some new girl whose name Ham didn't catch, a brunette running pell-mell away from her adolescence, trying to look like an orchid while still smelling of pansies; and a young racing driver whom Ham knew, Peter Burghley, and his girl friend, Jackie someone-or-other. Ham wondered if his mother had invited the others for her own or Sophie's protection.

Taz was a little stiff with Ham, as if to let him know that the dinner party had been none of his arranging. "What happened to Pamela?" Ham asked, determined to be friendly and at ease with his brother. "She said she was dying to meet me again."

"I pushed her under a bus," said Taz. "It was all she deserved. I like your girl. But I have the feeling I've seen her before somewhere."

"Don't let it worry you. You'll be seeing a lot of her in the future. How's the Rugger going?"

Taz shrugged. "It fills in the winter. I saw Richie the other day. He said you'd had a bit of trouble at Silverstone, testing some tires. You must be getting case-hardened about crashes." He said it, looking obliquely at Ham, half jokingly, half in earnest. Is he hoping I might have to retire that way, Ham thought, compulsorily in a wreck? But before the thought could worry him any further, they were interrupted by Peter Burghley.

"I'm going to Sebring next March, Ham. You've driven there. What's it like?"

"Not too tough as a course," Ham said, glad of the interruption. "The glare is the worst thing, if it's hot. And it's pretty bloody on brakes. You're on the brakes almost as much as you're on the pedal. Who are you driving for?"

112

"Maserati are sending over two cars." Peter Burghley was one of the younger drivers who had suddenly come to prominence in the last couple of years, almost at the same time as the sport had begun to catch the imagination of the general public. He was the sort of boy who, back in the forties, would have been flying Spitfires in the Battle of Britain: small, thin, his blond hair too long, his voice that of the public schoolboy still unable to believe that school was behind him forever. He was nervous, unable to relax, questing for something that was more than just excitement but to which he could give no name, and on certain days he could drive a car with all the skill and fire of a dedicated artist.

"They were talking about you at the club the other night." He was an habitué of the Steering Wheel Club; he was still so unsure of the rest of the world that he had to cling only to his own. His only topics of conversation were racing cars and how the school Rugger team was doing this season. He read only motor magazines and the schools sporting column in *The Times*. He was aware that there was more to the world, but he was still afraid of it. "They were wondering if you were going to drive again next season. We'd heard that Bourne End have been angling for Taz."

There was another fortunate interruption. Janet called them all to dinner. As they went into the dining-room Ham said to Taz, "Thinking of pushing Peter under a bus, too?"

Ham sat between Sophie and Peter Burghley's girl friend, who said she was at present an out-of-work specialty dancer. She was a slim, dark girl with rapacious eyes; she looked on Ham and Taz as possible prey. Her eyelids were thickly blued, and she had twice as much mouth as she would wake up with in the morning. She was no older than Peter, but beside her he looked like a schoolboy out with Theda Bara.

"I hope you don't talk about cars all the time, Ham dear. Does he, Miss Bartell?" Leaning across Ham, letting him catch a whiff of her musky perfume and a sight of the hollow between her breasts. Not at the table, he thought; bare bosom is not a table dish.

"We never discuss cars," said Sophie, smiling across at her briefly before looking at Ham. "It's a taboo subject between us."

Taz's girl friend spoke from farther up the table; Ham wished he knew what her name was, Prue or Polly or something. "You're from New York, aren't you, Miss Bartell? Are you in the theatre?"

That places *her*, anyway, Ham thought. She's in the theatre, or hoping to be. She had the throaty voice common now with young British actresses who had just learned that sex was more than just a music-hall joke, and that throaty voices had something to do with sexiness. They began the night with these voices but by the third act they were back to their normal high-pitched anonymous tones.

"No," said Sophie. "I work on a magazine."

"I once knew a man who worked on an American magazine," said Jackie. "He took some art studies of me, in the nude. For their Art section, or perhaps it was Education, I can't remember. Anyhow, they sacked him."

"More soup, anyone?" said Janet.

"I had a reading for Larry Olivier yesterday," said the actress, eighteen and a friend of Larry Olivier. "He wants someone to play Vivy's sister in a new play."

"You're in the theatre then, Penny?" Sophie, anyway, had caught the girl's name.

"Well—" The girl had gone too far out on her limb; she swayed in the wind of her own conceit. "Actually, I'm studying at RADA."

"I don't know that they can teach you much acting at a school," said Jackie. "I think if you have it at all, it's all in here." She tapped her bare bosom, and Ham agreed with her: if she had it at all, it would certainly be there.

"I once knew an actress," said Janet, keeping the party

going. "I can't remember her name. She used to smoke cigars."

"Groucho Marx," said Ham, and a moment later everyone had stopped trying to impress everyone else. The rest of the dinner went off smoothly; Janet was a good cook and she had excelled herself tonight. She served the meal herself, but she had enlisted Mrs. Cudlipp, their charwoman, to come in and help her in the kitchen.

"Can you cook, Sophie?" she said, when dinner was over and the girls were helping her get out the coffee cups.

"I couldn't contribute to anyone's cookbook," Sophie said, "but I get by. Back in New York I have to feed myself occasionally. After all, I'm a working girl."

"Of course," said Janet, as if it had only just occurred to her that American working girls must eat, just like their English cousins.

The other two girls had gone through into the living-room and for a moment Sophie and Janet were alone. Sophie smiled at the older woman. "If ever I get the chance to cook for Ham, you won't have to worry about him."

"Even before I knew you could cook, dear," said Janet, smiling at her, "I knew I shouldn't have to worry for him."

"*Do* you worry?" Sophie said, not smiling now.

Janet hesitated and arranged a coffee cup carefully on its saucer. "You mean when he's driving?" Sophie nodded, and Janet looked at her for a moment without saying anything. Then: "You weren't old enough to have a boy friend during the war, were you?"

"No," Sophie said. "It's strange, but I didn't know anyone who went to the war. I was only a child then, and we—we didn't have many friends."

"You don't know what it's like just to wait, then, and be able to do nothing but just that. Wait, I mean. Being married to a racing driver—or in love with him, whatever way you're attached to him—is something like how it was during

115

the war. Ham was a pilot during the war, and I used to worry about him. There was no racing in those days, and I had his father home here with me. That was something."

"I was looking at the photograph of Mr. Rafferty in the living-room. He was handsome, wasn't he?"

Janet took the percolator from the stove. "I've never forgiven the cars for taking him from me. If you fall in love with Ham, my dear, that's one thing you must expect. The cars will always be your rival. Pat loved me, but he loved the cars just as much. And Ham is just like his father."

And, Sophie thought, I am just like my mother. I have fallen in love with a career man and there is nothing, absolutely nothing, that I can do about it. Nothing but surrender and hope for the best.

And going home to London in the Jensen with him later, she said, "Do you have to go back to Stoke Poges tonight?"

"No," Ham said.

"I've dug deep enough," she said, smiling at him, loving him with her eyes, loving him with her body while they were still miles from the bed, afraid of the future but knowing it had to be faced. "I can't go on being careful all my life."

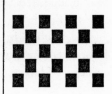

10

Early in the morning of Christmas Eve Richie rang Ham. "It's all ready, sport. We worked till two o'clock this morning on it, just to get it finished."

Ham went up to Chalfont St. Giles. The weather was cold and the sky had a yellow look to it on the horizon; already in the north there had been falls of snow. When Richie came out of the garage as the Jensen drew up in front of it, his breath hung in front of his mouth like little explosions of excitement. "We were gonna knock off about eight o'clock last night. But the boys said, 'Let's stay on and finish it.' They're as wrapped up in it as much as I am now. Come on in, sport. We got a car to show you."

They went through the garage and out to the shed at the back. The car stood there, unpainted, streaked with grease, the bodywork still showing the signs of the panel-beater's

117

hammer; it was unglamorous, rough, almost a little ram-shackle-looking. But Ham could see the beauty and speed in it.

"You're right, sport," he said, after he had walked round the car and peered into it. "You've got a car."

"It's a smasher, eh, Ham?" George Hayes looked as if he had slept in the shed; his hair was uncombed and sleep was still a thin veil on his face. "Richie's a flamin' genius."

"You don't have to tell him," said Richie, his face bright as a fat sun in the cold gloom of the shed; he was too excited to feel tired or the need of sleep. "He's known it for years. So have I."

"The body is still a bit rough." Charlie Carter was a tall sheaf of a man held together by the broad belt round his middle; his feet played out from beneath ragged-edged overalls and his wheat-coloured hair would only mock a comb. He always wore a cigarette stuck behind his ear, but Ham had never seen him smoking; it was as if he had one day given up smoking but kept the cigarette handy in case his will power suddenly left him. "I'll do better when I'm not so rushed."

"Bull," said Richie. "You wanted to finish the job just as much as George and I did. You bloody Pommies. Always trying to make out you don't get excited."

"I'll go back to Mulliner's," said Charlie, "if I'm going to be insulted."

"Righto," said Richie, dipping into his pocket, "how much do I owe you?"

"That's the worst of you bloody Aussies," said Charlie. "You can't take a joke."

The shed was full of good humour and camaraderie; these men had slaved together and produced something in which they had a common pride. Richie looked at Ham. "Well, do you wanna try her out?"

"Is she ready to go today?"

118

"I'd have been disappointed if you hadn't asked that," Richie said. "I've borrowed the Leyland and we're all set to go to Silverstone. I'd have driven the bloody thing myself if you hadn't come along."

They went up to Silverstone, Ham, Richie and Charlie riding in the cabin of the Leyland, and George, wrapped in some car covers, riding in the back with the car. Richie sang practically all the way, songs that he said an old bullock-driver had taught him back home: the words had a tender obscenity that must have moved many a bullock, and Richie sang them with feeling.

"Stone the crows, I'm happy! Did I tell you?"

Two hours later he was, if anything, even happier. Ham had taken the car round Silverstone and come back into the pits with his thumb and forefinger locked in the gesture of approval. He had got out of the car and, in turn, had slapped each of the men on the back.

"You can write to the Jaguar people and tell them you've given them a car to go with their engine. I touched a hundred and forty going down Hangar Straight and she sat there as if on a string."

"That was why we fitted the speedo," Richie said. "We were only gunna put in a rev counter, but I reckoned you'd wanna know what top you could touch."

"She was doing just fifty-five hundred at that speed. I could have gone higher, but I ran out of road. But she sounded sweet enough at that. And I shan't be doing a hundred and forty all the way round the Mille Miglia. What I want is an engine that can stand up to the thousand miles. This sounds all right to me."

"Any comments on the car?" Richie said.

"You've still got a few things to iron out, but that's to be expected. You can't expect a perfect job first time up, with a special gear-box, too. Your gears are a bit slow between first and second. And there's a tendency to understeer when

119

you're going into a corner. I think the trouble is you've got a better rear end than a front. You'll have to even that up. And the brakes judder a bit."

"All those can be fixed," Richie said. "What about comfort as far as driving?"

"Personally, I'd like the steering column sloped even a bit more. But then, not everyone drives the way I do. When it comes to the actual race, put in a three-spoke steering wheel, will you? You know how I like to hold the wheel, with my thumbs hooked over the spokes. And a shorter gear handle. I found that one a bit high. Couple of times I felt as if I was trying to scratch my armpit."

"Gee, I didn't know a driver had to be so fussy about small things," George said.

"They aren't small things and he's not being fussy," said Richie. "A thousand miles of scratching your armpit can be a bit tiring. Okay, Ham, we'll fix all those. We'll give it another go the first week of the new year." He looked up, his face suddenly sober. "I'm glad you like it, sport."

Ham nodded, all at once aware that Richie was an old and loved friend. "We'll show 'em, chum. We'll really show 'em."

They drove back to Chalfont, put the car away in the shed and Richie told Charlie and George to take the rest of the day off. "A happy Christmas to both of you. And this time next year I hope I'll be able to give a bonus to both of you. Paid outa profits from—" He stopped and looked around at the others. "What are we gunna call it?"

"The Launder?" suggested Ham.

"How about some Australian name?" George said. "Something like the Boomerang or the Kangaroo?"

"I think it ought to have some dignity," Charlie said. "That was what we always went for at Mulliner's. Dignity."

But Richie was staring down into the village, at the sign on the small green outside the pub. "The Merlin," he said.

"Merlin was a wizard. That's the name for it—the Wizard. What about it? A car with magic as well as speed."

"He's more than a genius," said George, admiration bursting his face apart. "He's a flamin' poet, too."

So Charlie and George went home, promised a bonus for next Christmas from the profits from the Wizard's sales, and Ham and Richie went down to the Merlin's Cave to drink to the car's success. And over their beers Richie said, "When this is all over, sport, what are you gunna do?"

"What do you mean, when it's all over?"

"This is just for one season. Once we've got this car started on the market and Bartell's introduced his tires, what happens then? He won't wanna go on financing a race team, and I won't be able to afford it. So what happens to you? Are you gunna sign up with a works team again?"

Ham tasted his beer. "I don't know, to tell you the truth. I've been thinking of retiring." Then, in a sudden burst of confidence, realising now that Richie was the closest friend he had ever had, glad of someone to talk to who would understand, he told Richie about the trouble with Taz. "The kid's right in a way, I suppose. I didn't have anyone to stand in my way when I took up the game. In fact, my dad encouraged me all he could. After this season I should have enough put aside to retire and go into something else. But what am I going to do? You know any old ladies who want a chauffeur?"

"That was what I was leading up to," Richie said and stroked the scar on his head. "How'd you like to come in as a partner with me on the—" He grinned to himself, as if amused or perhaps even embarrassed at being the maker of a car that deserved a name. "On the Wizard?"

Ham said nothing for a while. The bar was crowded; everyone had come in for an early Christmas drink. People were wishing each other Merry Christmas; the bar was full of good will. "It's not just the Christmas spirit, is it, Richie?"

Richie shook his head. "I don't have to wait on the calendar to ask you something like this, sport. I been thinking about it for some time. I was just waiting to see what you thought of the car."

"I'm tempted," Ham said. "And I appreciate your offer."

"But what?" Richie said.

Ham hesitated, then he said, "Did you do anything when you were young, back home in Australia? Play football or cricket?"

"I know what you mean." Richie was more sensitive than his rough-and-gruff exterior would have led a stranger to believe; he could catch another's mood as easily as he could read a blueprint. "I used to play Rugger. I was a pretty good scrum-half, believe it or not." He patted his stomach. "I gave it up the season before the war, and it almost broke my heart. I wondered what the hell I was gunna do in the winters. I thought I'd never be able to stand the sight of other blokes playing, and me just standing there on the sideline, watching. Yeah, I know." He drank from his glass, tasting the past as well as the beer; then he looked back at Ham. "Funny thing is, you find you can do it. Stand there and watch the other coves, I mean. Nobody likes to grow old, but when it comes to it, you can do it easier than you think."

"Well, then, can I think about it?" Ham said. "You don't want my answer right away, do you?"

"Take your time. Another grog?"

That night Ham went to see Sophie, as he had practically every night during the past month. She had not allowed their lovemaking to become a habit; and he was quite content to let her call the tune. Each had become part of the pattern of the other; they were linked by more than the joining of their hands and the fusion of their bodies.

They made love this night, with the electric fire glowing in the bedroom with a heat that could not match their own;

122

she was all passion and her body was an engulfing storm wilder than any of the race hurricanes he had ridden through. And later, for the first time, she asked him directly about the other women.

"Did you ever love any of them?"

"No." Which was the truth.

"In love with any of them?"

"What's the difference?"

"There is a difference," she said, younger and less experienced, but older and wiser than he in the divisions of the heart. "I was in love with you early in the piece. Now I love you."

"The others didn't mean anything. There just had to be someone there, that was all. At the end of a race and between the races. You needed someone to distract you, to take your mind off it. And the women were always available. Too available. On the Continent there are always plenty of available women about at the meetings. It's a little like the way it was during the war. There are women who look for excitement, just as there are men."

"There must have been dozens," she said; her hand moved gently over him, claiming him. "I don't want to know if there were. But you must have at least liked one or two," she said, torturing herself, being a woman in love.

"Of course I liked one or two of them," he said, but couldn't remember any of them, not one single one. "But as soon as I found myself liking them too much, that was the end of it. Don't you understand? It was better that way. I'd seen how some of the other drivers' wives suffered. I didn't want any girl suffering like that over me. It was enough to know that my mother worried about me."

"What about me now?" she said, and he realized he had said the wrong thing.

"One more race. Two at the most, if I drive at Le Mans."

"And what about all the practising? You'll be practising

more than you'll actually be racing. And drivers are killed in practice. Ascari was killed that way. And Castelotti."

"You're quite a little researcher, aren't you?" he said trying to make a joke of it.

"Don't joke, Ham," she said and dug nails into the bare flesh of his ribs.

"All right. But this will be the last season. I promise you," he said and wondered how many more promises he would have to make.

"I wonder how many times your father told your mother that?"

"Have you been talking with her?"

"Yes," she said and felt no shame about discussing him with his mother. "I'm not going to suffer the way she has, Ham." She waited for him to reply to that, but he said nothing. Then she went on: "If you do give up racing, what will you do?"

"Richie asked me that today," he said quietly, looking up at the glow from the electric fire on the ceiling. "I drove the new car today. It's good. He wants me to be a partner with him, if we do all right in the Mille Miglia. He's calling it the Wizard."

"Is that what you'd like to do? Make cars here in England?"

He noticed how the question had been phrased: *here in England?* And now he knew one of the reasons why he had asked Richie for time before making his decision. He got up and began to dress. "Come on," he said roughly, still making a joke of everything. "It's time we were getting back to Stoke Poges. We can't just turn up in the morning in time to collect our presents from under the tree."

She lay on the bed, unaware of her nakedness, angry at him for dodging the issues that meant so much to her. She wasn't hurt: that she could have taken: pain was part of the pleasure of love. But anger contributed nothing to love; and she was bitterly angry at him now. The cars *were* her rivals, and suddenly she was angry at them, too.

"You're not going to make a fool of me!" she burst out, and he stopped, with his shirt still hanging outside his trousers, his face blank with surprise.

"A fool of you? What on earth are you talking about?" Then abruptly he reached down and lifted her from the bed. She knelt on the bed and he held her there, his hands gripping her bare shoulders. "Sophie, I don't know what the hell you're talking about. But one thing I do know. I love you! You understand that? I love you, and I'll never make a fool of you nor hurt you in any way!"

Then he pulled her to him and kissed her harder than he had kissed her during their lovemaking. Her anger was still there in her, but there was nothing she could do about it. She knew now that it was the power of her own love, and not Ham, that would make a fool of her. And within her she wept again for her mother, who had had the same weakness.

11

It snowed during the night. Ham woke in the morning and looked out and saw the chalk scribbles that were frost on the windowpane; beyond it, as through a cracked eye, he saw the snow-furred branches of the oak tree. The snow was thick on the window sill; a robin splashed himself redly against it for a moment. Ham got out of bed and went to the window. The garden was a museum of white abstract sculpture; beyond, the countryside was an elephants' graveyard, littered with tusks of ice and skeletons of bushes. In the lee of a dark copse a cow bellowed; the sound literally seemed to break the silence as snow fell from the branches. Well, everything is in Sophie's favour, Ham thought. A white Christmas—what else, I wonder, does she need to make it perfect?

When he went downstairs Taz was arranging some presents

at the foot of a Christmas tree. In their pyjamas and dressing-gowns, both of which had been presents from their mother last Christmas, the two brothers now looked remarkably alike. Taz would never be as heavy as Ham, and there was more nervous energy in him; but otherwise he was just a fined-down and handsomer copy of Ham.

"Merry Christmas." They had seen each other several times since the night of the dinner party, but their remarks to each other had been stiff and studiedly casual. Ham had been staying up in town at the flat most of the time, and on those occasions when he had come down to stay at Stoke Poges, Taz had always found an excuse to have to go out.

"Merry Christmas," Ham said and put his own presents down beneath the tree. My God, he's a stranger, he thought; or he soon will be, if this keeps up. Last Christmas, he remembered, he and Taz had taken their mother to Mass, and then the three of them had gone over to Brigadier Allday's for Christmas dinner. Neither of the boys liked going to their grandfather's, but that day, somehow, they had both enjoyed it. And now Ham realised it was because both of them had been so close to each other, had enjoyed each other's company, laughed heartily at each other's jokes, and the warmth of their affection for each other had gradually worn the chill off their grandfather's presence. Brigadier Allday was coming to dinner today, but something else would be needed to counteract the chill of him today.

Taz said, "I took Mother a cup of tea. She said you had brought Sophie back with you last night." He hesitated, then he said, "You're going rather steady with her, aren't you?"

"Yes." He, too, hesitated, then he said, "Sophie is the first one I've ever been interested in."

"You always did have a sharp eye for a good-looking girl," Taz said, smiling.

"Your own's not so bad," said Ham.

The two brothers were searching for the frayed ends of

the cord that had once bound them. Then Janet came into the room, bringing her presents with her to put under the tree. "Isn't it wonderful it has snowed? Everything for a perfect Christmas. And, boys: Be nice to your grandfather, just for today. Ask him about his stocks and shares or something. Read up something about the Army and ask him about that."

They both kissed her, and Taz said, "We'll ask him about that Christmas at Poona. When the subalterns played musical pig sticking instead of musical chairs."

"You asked him about that last year," Ham said.

"And the year before," said Taz, laughing now, all his stiffness gone. "He'll always tell you the story, though."

Then Sophie came downstairs, her face radiant. "A white Christmas! Oh, what a hostess England is! I think you people must have been in the British Travel Association, just to get this turned on for me."

"Actually, it's just a film set," Ham said. "I went across to Denham early this morning and borrowed it."

Sophie had brought presents with her, even one for Taz. Ham had no idea why she had thought of Taz; then he remembered that Americans liked giving presents. On his only trip to the States, when he had driven at Sebring, his host had given him a pair of expensive hairbrushes; he had been puzzled by the reason for the gift at first, then he had realised it had given the American pleasure just to give him something. He had been touched by his host's generosity, but later had come to know it was a fairly general American characteristic. Other nations could be generous, including the English; but the Americans seemed to get the most enjoyment out of their gift giving.

Ham explained to Sophie that he and Taz always took their mother to Mass on Christmas Day, and she said, "I'll come, too, if I may. I'm a Catholic, you know." She looked at Janet. "But not a very good one, I'm afraid. I only go to church on special occasions. When I've got something to pray for."

"Most of us are praying for something when we go to church," said Janet. "Mrs. Cudlipp, our char, is a very good Baptist. But she says she prays every Sunday that she'll win the football pools. She wants to roll up to church in a car, instead of going on her bicycle."

They went to Mass in Slough and stood among the Irish workers from the neighbouring factories, the long-lipped, dark-haired expatriates who thought, moist-eyed, of the Ould Sod but wouldn't leave the good money here in England, not even if St. Patrick himself called them home. Then they drove back to Stoke Poges, and at midday Brigadier Allday, his hooked nose blue with cold and his bald head warmed by a balaclava, his Christian spirit polished by his annual visit to church, drove over from Iver.

"Merry Christmas, Miss Bartell," he said when he had been introduced to Sophie. She was wearing black tapering slacks and a scarlet sweater that made no secret of the shape of her bosom, but he kept his gaze rigidly on her face. The world had finally gone to the dogs the day women went into trousers, and he had never even partially accepted the fashion. He had even accepted George Eliot's other sins till he learned she had worn trousers, and then he had known why she was as she was. "I worked with an American during the war. Colonel Nevin. From Oshkosh."

"He was pulling your leg, Father," said Janet. "Oshkosh is in Russia."

"Oshkosh is in the State of Wisconsin," said her father. "Seventy-five miles north-north-west of Milwaukee and eight hundred and forty miles west of New York. I looked it up on the map. There is also an Oshkosh in Nebraska, but Colonel Nevin had never been there."

"I've never even been to Oshkosh, Wisconsin," said Sophie, smiling at Allday. "Ham tells me you spent a lot of time out

129

in India. I've always wanted to go there. I once had to research a story on what the British had done in India."

"What was your opinion?" said Allday, stroking his nose, ready for an argument.

"Oh, I thought you had done a fine job," said Sophie. "A better job than a lot of people, including us Americans, give you credit for."

Allday smiled and stopped rubbing his nose. "Miss Bartell, may I say that you are the first woman I have ever met who looks graceful and womanly in trousers?" He beamed at her, letting his gaze drop for the first time. Sophie had just been admitted to the British Empire. "Well, Janet, do we open our presents? What are we waiting for?"

Ham had bought Sophie a gold compact and a book of photographs of London; she gave him a gold wrist watch. "I noticed you never wear one. I'm surprised you're always so punctual."

"I had one, but it was smashed at Le Mans. I just never got round to buying another."

"Don't smash that one," she said softly and kissed him.

At half-past twelve the phone rang. "Hello, Rafferty," said Bartell. "Is Sophie there with you?"

Sophie took the phone from Ham. "Dad! Your voice is so clear. Where are you, New York or Akron?"

"I'm in London," said Bartell. "At the airport. I rang your apartment, but there was no answer. Then I guessed maybe you were spending Christmas with Rafferty. You wrote you've been seeing a lot of him."

Sophie turned to explain to Ham where her father was, and he took the phone. "I'll come up and get you, Mr. Bartell. You're coming here for Christmas dinner."

"That sounds like an order, son," said Bartell, and Ham noticed he had called him *son*.

"That's what it is. Today you're working for me."

130

Ham and Sophie drove up to London Airport. Driving back, Ham said, "How are the tires coming along?"

"I've brought two sets over with me. But we don't talk business today." Bartell had planned the trip to England so that he could spend Christmas with Sophie, but emotionally he was too awkward to be able to tell her so without embarrassing both of them. "I brought you a present, Sophie. I got yours just before I left Akron." He displayed the thick, dark overcoat he wore. "An English one, Rafferty. I'm the best-dressed man in Akron. One of the fellers in the Chamber of Commerce, he told me to buy a Homburg while I'm over here in London. He said he'd never seen me looking so distinguished." He laughed at himself; he was happy and mellow. "I brought you something to keep you warm, too."

He had been carrying a large cardboard box as well as his bag. Now, as they drove home, he handed the box to Sophie in the front seat. She opened it, filling the car with tissue paper. "Dad! A mink stole!"

"I went into Bergdorf-Goodman when I was in New York, and I said I wanted the best stole in the store. The clerk said they called that one Princess, and I said that was what I wanted it for, a princess." His bony, ugly face had almost crumbled with love and happiness. Watching him in the rear-vision mirror Ham thought: In a moment he's going to cry. "You like it, Sophie? You like your father's taste?"

"Do I! What girl doesn't like mink?" Sophie turned in her seat, rising up on her knees to lean over and kiss her father. Bartell tried not to show his relief; he had been afraid that she might have thought the present too showy and expensive. He had once heard someone say that expensive gifts were vulgar. He didn't care a damn who thought he was vulgar; just so long as his daughter was pleased.

Ham had never expected to see Bartell ill at ease and apprehensive about meeting anyone. But he was no longer the big tire magnate; he was his daughter's father. When they arrived at Stoke Poges he got out of the car and stood bareheaded in the snow, staring at the front door of the house like a boy on his first day at school. His hand went to his hearing aid, almost as if he were going to shut himself off from the introductions he had to go through. "I hope I'm not intruding on your mother," he said. "An extra one for Christmas dinner, right out of the blue—"

But Janet put him at ease at once and he warmed to her immediately. He shook hands heartily with Taz, and turned and did the same with Allday. Ham suddenly realised that Bartell was doing his best not to let his daughter down. He was a millionaire father who had just given his daughter a mink stole that must have set him back at least the equal of a British workingman's annual wage; but today he was more father than he was millionaire and he was anxious to prove it.

"It's a long time since I had a real home-cooked Christmas dinner, you know? Back home in Akron I usually have it at my club. It isn't the same, somehow."

"But a club has its advantages, don't you agree?" said Allday.

"Sure, if you are lonely and have nowhere else to go," said Bartell, and the Brigadier, who belonged to the Army and Navy and to the Carlton clubs, almost had a stroke.

But a little while later Bartell said he liked to hunt and shoot, and Allday looked at him with new respect.

"I didn't know you hunted, Dad," Sophie said.

"There are a few things you have to learn about me, Sophie," said Bartell, winking at her. "I took it up a couple of years ago. I go up to Wisconsin to shoot deer."

"I knew a colonel from Wisconsin," said Allday. "Colonel Nevin from Oshkosh."

"Oshkosh? Sure, I been through there plenty of times,"

said Bartell. "It's about seventy-five miles north of Milwaukee."

"That's correct," said Allday, and looked about for Janet, but she was out in the kitchen. He looked back at Bartell, all the chill gone from him. "What type of gun do you use?"

Dinner was a success, and Ham, full of turkey, pudding and contentment, looked at Sophie and tried to remember when he had felt as happy as today. After dinner they all went back to the living-room and sat about the fire. Allday sipped port and reminisced about Poona and the hill stations where he had spent his younger days; Bartell burped over soda water and told them about Mulberry Street and the time when he and his first six employees had had to picket the plant against the bailiffs. Each man listened to the other with interest and a respect that sat a little strangely on the shoulders of each of them; and Ham and the others just sat and listened to the stories and enjoyed them.

Then Taz went out to collect a new girl friend, a small redhead whose name was Jennifer; Ham wondered if any middle-class girls of her age group had been given plain names like Mary or Rose. Jennifer was quieter and seemed more intelligent than any of the others Taz had brought home; she was able to open her mouth and make a remark without spraying the room with superlatives. Later in the afternoon Richie and Kitty Launder, who had been invited by Ham, arrived with their two children.

"Ham tell you about the car?" Richie said to Bartell.

"We haven't talked about anything like that yet," Bartell said, sprawled out in his chair. He kept patting his stomach and nodding his head appreciatively at Janet. "You're a wonderful cook, Mrs. Rafferty. There's a slander, you know, that the British don't know how to cook." Then he looked back at Richie. "I brought you over some new tires. Maybe we can try them out tomorrow, eh?"

"Oh, Dad!" Sophie said. "Tomorrow is Boxing Day. It's a holiday here in England."

"Okay, so I'll pay 'em double time," Bartell said, winking at Ham. "I have to fly back home on Wednesday. Business is business. The world doesn't stop for it, eh, Brigadier?"

"I've never considered what my grandson does, as business," said Allday, who was replete but not so stupefied as to surrender all his opinions. "And now my younger grandson wants to take it up, too. It's the same as if I had taken up pig sticking as a career."

"That's a stupid thing to say," said Taz.

"Taz!" Janet's voice was sharp. "That's no way to speak to your grandfather."

"I'm sorry if I was rude," Taz said, but it was obvious that his apology was an empty one. "But to compare motor racing to pig sticking—ye gods! It's an insult to Dad. It's—" he didn't look at Ham at first, as if afraid that Ham would not back him up—"it's an insult to Ham. You might as well say that a test pilot is just an aerial acrobat."

"I made no comment on test pilots," said his grandfather. "And I meant no insult to your father or Hamilton. But everyone is entitled to an opinion."

Taz said nothing more, but Christmas had gone up the chimney with the smoke from the fire; it was just another cold day, and the room was full of unspoken hostile opinions. Ham looked at Sophie, aware of the fact that she had been looking at him from the moment Taz had first spoken. She is another one who compares it to pig sticking, he thought. He looked at his mother, at Jennifer, at Kitty Launder, his gaze travelling round over the women in the room. What would we do without them? he thought. And yet if the women of the world had had their way, how far would men have come from the cave? Did Columbus have a wife and did she ever try to talk him out of sailing into the West? Were there Mrs. Wrights struggling to keep the Wright Brothers

134

on the ground? He grinned, amused at putting himself in such company, and Sophie, not knowing why he smiled but liking it when he did smile, smiled back at him.

"Well, I hope what Richie is doing is business," Kitty Launder said, pouring oil on someone else's troubled waters. Out in the garden the two boys were throwing snowballs at each other. One of them is going to cry in a moment, I hope, she thought; and tried to will it, so that the interruption of her movement out of the room might break the unhappy tension. But the boys went on playing, maliciously untroubled. "He spends enough time in that darned garage of his."

"You better get a divorce," Richie said. "I'm gunna be there for the next three months. We gotta build another car, besides the one we're already working on. It's no use taking just one car to Italy."

"You're going to make me go broke," said Bartell. "Two cars."

"You wanna do the thing properly, don't you? Waddia think I ordered that second engine for? Don't be stingy, Joe."

"Okay, go ahead." Bartell waved a bony flag of a hand; he would have bought a fleet of cars today. "Build two cars. Maybe we can give the other one to Taz here to drive. Eh, Taz?"

"Thanks, Mr. Bartell. But I can't," Taz said, and Ham waited for him to explain about the promise that he had made to their mother. Don't say it, Taz, he thought suddenly; nobody else is interested in what is going on in this family. You've spoiled the day enough; don't spoil it any further.

Taz looked at Ham as if he had read Ham's thoughts, at his mother, then back at Bartell.

"I've signed with the Bourne End team," he said. "I'm going to Brescia with them, as reserve driver for them in the Mille Miglia."

135

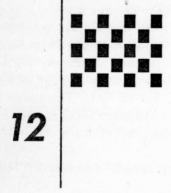

12

Next day, Boxing Day, Ham went up to Silverstone again to test the tires Bartell had brought over with him. Bartell, Sophie, Richie and George Hayes went with him. Richie had borrowed a Maserati that had been brought into his garage for servicing; he said he hadn't the cheek to ask again for a loan of the Jaguar in which Ham had crashed last time. The Jaguar had been repaired and was as good as new when they had handed it back to the owner; and the owner had understood about the crash, because accidents could happen even to the best of drivers and he knew Ham was a better driver than he would ever be. Even so, Richie said, you could wear out your welcome.

So today Ham was driving a Maserati. The countryside was still white, but the snow had begun to melt and black islands of trees showed up. A flight of birds, flying close together as if for warmth, did a figure-eight on the grey ice of the sky. In a field a piebald scarecrow, like an orator deserted by his audience, raised a frozen arm in declamation.

The track was dry and free of snow; Ham drove slowly round to check that there was no ice on it. Then he opened up the Maserati, but not right up. He had gone two laps before he found he was lifting his foot from the pedal long before he usually did when he went into a corner. He went round again, cursing himself for his caution, trying to tell himself that the day was to blame and that he was afraid of skidding on some ice he might have missed on his exploratory lap. But he knew there was no ice anywhere at all on the tarmac; if there had been he would have found it already. He had not been afraid when he had tried out the Wizard last week. But last week he had not been riding on Bartell tires, and it was Bartell tires that had caused the crash in the Jaguar.

On the fifth lap he forced himself to keep his foot down as he went into Copse Corner. He went round in a four-wheel drift; he reached the point where only power could pull him through the corner. At the corner of his eye the outside edge of the track was waiting for him, like a magnetic precipice; the car screamed like a living thing, shuddering at the strain put on it. He put his foot down, waiting for the tires to grip beneath him; he flexed his buttocks, as if trying to push the tires deeper into the track. A good driver drove by the seat of his pants. His brains were in his behind: every tremble, every shudder from the tires, wheels, suspension, chassis and seat cushion was a message. There was a split second when the car seemed to have no road at all beneath it; the precipice opened like a black flower of disaster. Then the tires gripped, moaned sharply, and the car had gone through the corner. He felt cold sweat break out on him; but he had made it. He went round three more laps, throwing out the challenge each time, then drew into the pits.

"Well?" Bartell said.

He could feel the sweat beneath his coveralls, turning cold on him now. But he could ignore it now. "They still don't hold as well on corners as I'd like them to."

"Here's another thing." Richie had gone round the tires and now straightened up. Ham turned his head quickly, stopping as he was about to climb out of the cockpit. "You've changed the valves since the last time, haven't you? These tires have lost air. That didn't happen on the last lot."

"Yes," said Bartell. "We tried out a new valve."

"It's no good, then," said Richie. "This one won't take high speed."

Ham climbed slowly out of the car, chewing steadily on the gum in his mouth. He had stopped just in time, then: a few more laps and the tires might have gone again. He took his overcoat from George and put it on, glad of its warmth. He looked at George and the latter winked admiringly. The boy, perhaps because he had no cause to look for them, was unable to recognise clay feet when he saw them.

"How can a valve be affected by high speed?" Sophie said. "All a valve does is hold in the air, doesn't it?"

"Centrifugal force does it," Bartell said, almost eagerly; he seemed glad that Sophie had asked the question. He seemed less disappointed in the failure of the new valve than glad that his daughter was interested in tires. "When a car gets to around one hundred and ten or one hundred and twenty miles an hour, the valve begins to open. Usually a valve cap is sufficient, but there must be something basically wrong with this valve. We'll go back to the other valve," he said to Richie. "Anything else?"

"I think we could do with a higher pressure than you've recommended. These tires are pretty hot, and they shouldn't be. Not after only eight laps." Richie saw Sophie looking enquiringly at him. "I won't go into the technical details, Sophie, but what it amounts to is this—if a tire is under-

138

inflated, its temperature goes up at high speeds. For instance, if you reduce a tire's pressure from forty to thirty-five pounds a square inch, you raise the tire's temperature by nearly fifteen degrees Centigrade. Once a tire gets too hot, the rubber compounds in it start to soften. It's only a matter of time then before the treads begin to fly off and the whole cover starts to disintegrate."

"That's right, make me nice and happy," said Sophie, and looked at Ham. "You see your tire pressures are absolutely right from now on."

"You haven't got to worry, girl," Bartell said. "By the time Ham has to race, I'll give him tires that are perfect. Leave it to me, Sophie. Ham's got confidence in me, haven't you, Ham?"

Ham could only nod: the lie might have been too apparent if he had spoken.

He drove Bartell and Sophie back to London. Bartell said he wanted to write a report for the benefit of his production manager and his technical men; he would get Ham to look it over and add his comments before he took it back to the States with him. So Ham drove him to the Dorchester, where he had checked in again for his stay in London. Then Ham and Sophie went for a walk in Hyde Park.

Snow was still on the grass; the summertime lovers had fled or been buried. "I wonder where the Hyde Park lovers go in the winter?"

"The same place Central Park lovers go," Sophie said. "Back to their furnished rooms, where they have to hold their breath while they make love, so their landladies won't hear them. Isn't it terrible how landladies never believe in love?"

"I think I'll start a rooming house for lovers. Not a brothel, but a house for real lovers who have nowhere to go in the wintertime. I believe in love."

"I'm a believer in love, too."

"Does your landlady back in New York believe in love?"

139

She smiled at him. "You're fishing, aren't you, to see if I ever had a lover back in New York? Well, I don't have a landlady. I have an apartment, just as I have here. Just off Washington Square. But when I go back I'll be moving from there. Dad has bought an apartment uptown. He told me about it last night." She walked in silence for a while, soft-footed in the snow. "He knows I don't want to go back to Akron. He said he wants to set up a home for us in New York, and he'll fly east every weekend."

"How do you feel about it?"

"I don't know." Her shoulders were hunched, her hands deep in her pockets; her feet were cold in her boots, and there was a chill in her heart. Her father, running down the years after her, had at last offered her a home; but now the home she wanted was with this man beside her. But he hadn't yet asked her to marry him, nor even talked of marriage. And if he ever did, she couldn't be sure that he would want to go and live in New York. "There are a lot of things to think about."

He knew one of the things that could be in her mind, but here in Hyde Park, in the silent snow and among the frozen ghosts of the summertime lovers, this wasn't the place to ask her to marry him. Because he, too, had a lot of things to think about. So he changed the subject. "I'll have to go down and see my mother tonight. She was pretty upset by Taz's decision to sign up with Bourne End. I don't think she ever expected him to break his promise to her. About driving in the big stuff before I gave it up, I mean."

"I think it was pretty darn mean of Taz," Sophie said, putting her father and the apartment in New York and marriage out of her mind; she realised that the subject had been changed deliberately and in a way she was grateful. If ever Ham did propose, she wanted it somewhere warm and dimly lighted, where they would be alone and she could say yes with her lips and her arms and her body. Hyde Park was accustomed to intimacy in the summertime, but somehow now, in the cold asperity of winter, it would seem indecent. "And I think he was pretty cruel, too."

"Maybe we're being a bit harsh on him. I can see his point. I *am* the lucky one. In being born first, I mean. If I'd been the younger of us, maybe I'd have felt the same way. In fact, I know I should have."

"But what about your mother? Why should she have to put up with all the worry and heartache? You men can be so damned thoughtless. Yes, and cruel."

"You're on her side, aren't you?"

"Of course," she said and looked up at him. "And I'm sure she is on mine."

He ignored that, looking straight ahead as they walked under the black filigree of the winter branches. "He's forcing me to retire now. I'll have to give it up, after Le Mans."

She said nothing, but her silence told him everything. She would have no regrets at all if he retired after Le Mans. They walked silently through the snow, turning out of the park and walking down through the narrow, frozen-faced streets of Mayfair. As if deliberately changing the subject, she looked up at the houses with forced brightness.

"I love this city, you know. I go for walks during the day. I pass the houses with those blue plaques on them, the ones that say So-and-So lived here, and I salute them. I've saluted Keats and Dickens and Elizabeth Barrett Browning and Dr. Johnson. Oh, I have so many to salute! It'll take me years. Wouldn't it be nice if some day they put up a plaque to you?" Then abruptly she stopped, clutching at his hand. "Oh no, it wouldn't! That would mean you were dead!"

"It would also mean they had got me confused with someone else," he said, smiling down at her.

She stared up at him, her face pale in the reflected light from the snow, then suddenly she smiled. "Oh darling, I do love you! Even when you make me worry so much."

141

"Worry? I haven't even begun racing yet."

"No. And I don't know how I'm going to bear it when you do. Oh, why couldn't I have fallen for a man in a grey flannel suit?"

A week later Taz's name was among those announced for the England Rugger team against Wales. Ham, who had been staying at the flat and had been home only once since Christmas, phoned him and congratulated him. He hadn't spoken to Taz since Christmas, but talking over the phone was no way of discussing with Taz his decision to start big-car racing next season. So they talked of the coming Rugger match and then hung up, each aware that the other had had something else to say but hadn't known how to broach the subject.

Bartell had gone back to the States, after asking Sophie when she would be coming home. She had hedged in her answer, but had hinted that she would like to stay on this side of the Atlantic till after the running of the Mille Miglia. Bartell had looked disappointed, but had said nothing.

"It was almost as if he felt we had wasted enough time without our having a home," she told Ham afterward. "But it seems silly to go back there for a month or so, then come all the way back here and then on to Italy. I told him I'd go home with him the day after the Mille Miglia."

All Ham said was, "That gives us just over three months."

"Yes," she said, smiling at him. "How long do you want?"

But that night she wrote to her father, saying she might go back with him next time he came over. She also made a request, the first time she had asked her father for anything since she was a child.

In the next week Ham took the Wizard up to Silverstone again, but there was still something wrong with the front suspension and the car had a tendency to understeer. He went into a corner too fast and when he tried to correct by oversteering, trying to provoke rear-wheel breakaway to

142

counteract the lost adhesion of the front wheels, he found himself getting nowhere fast, too fast for comfort. Only a sudden application of power got him out of the difficulty, but he knew that wouldn't be enough in the Mille Miglia. A thousand miles of corners was too much for a car in which you had to watch the steering all the way. The Wizard was taken back to the shed at Chalfont and Richie got to work again on the suspension.

Ham took his mother, Sophie and Taz's girl friend Jennifer to see the Rugger International. Taz played a brilliant game and scored the winning try. After the game Ham and the others went down to the door of the dressing-room. Taz, still in his football togs, flushed with his success, came out to meet them.

Strangers were coming up and congratulating Taz; four schoolboys thrust their autograph books under his nose. He was embarrassed by the adulation, but he was enjoying it; he scrawled his signature in the autograph books with a self-conscious flourish.

"That's him," Ham heard a man tell a girl. "Taz Rafferty."

"Isn't he good-looking!" said the girl. "Where does he come from?"

"I don't know," said her boy friend, peeved that his girl was only impressed by Taz's looks. "I'd never heard of him till this season."

"Rafferty," said the girl, as they moved away. "I've heard the name before somewhere."

Then one of the schoolboys turned away from Taz and pushed his book at Ham. "May I have your autograph, too, Mr. Rafferty? You are Ham Rafferty, the racing driver, aren't you, sir?"

"Yes," said Ham and had to restrain himself from patting the boy on the head. "Do you want me to sign on the same page as my brother?"

"Gosh, no, sir! A page for each of you." The boy watched as Ham signed his name. "Yours is worth something, you know, sir. And some day I think your brother's will be, too."

"I'm sure of it," said Ham and handed the book back to the boy. "In time it may be worth a great deal more than mine."

He watched the boy glide away through the crowd, and when he turned back Sophie was standing beside him and smiling. "I thought you were going to tip him. You looked so pleased when he asked you for your autograph."

"Was it as obvious as that?"

"Are you jealous of Taz?"

"No," he said and wasn't. "That will come later."

Taz was taking Jennifer out to a show in London, so Ham prepared to drive his mother back to Stoke Poges. She invited Sophie to stay the weekend, so first they drove up to South Kensington while Sophie picked up what things she needed. Ham and his mother sat in the car while Sophie went up to her flat.

"She's a nice girl, Ham. What's going to become of her?"

"What do you mean, what's going to become of her? You talk as if she's some destitute orphan."

She peered at him out of the furry depths of her coat; cold weather always made her look smaller. "Don't be dense, Ham. You know what I mean."

He tapped his gloved fingers gently on the wheel of the car. "I'd like to ask her to marry me. The fact that she's a millionaire's daughter doesn't worry me so much now. She's still more her mother's daughter than her father's." He had explained to Janet some of Sophie's background. "But I don't know whether she would want to settle down here in England. And what can I do if I go to America?"

"Perhaps you could go and work for her father?"

"And be known as the man who married the boss's daughter? No, thanks."

144

"You'll have to do something about her soon." The winter dusk came down the streets, feeling at the car with chilling fingers for entry. Janet shivered, suddenly weary. She looked at her elder son, hunched in the front seat of the car, big and restless and troubled, and tried to remember him as a boy. And couldn't. "It's not fair to her, Ham. And it's not fair to yourself."

"I'll wait a little longer. Till after the Mille Miglia."

"That was what your father said, when I asked him when he was going to retire. After the Mille Miglia."

And in that moment the cold of the dusk invaded the car. Or the cold of past grief, she wasn't sure which. Whatever it was, the fur coat was no protection against it. It cut like a knife into her, turned in her heart, scraped against her bones.

"Are you all right, Mum?"

"Yes," she lied, crying behind her eyes, crying because time was always so short, because there had never been enough time for her and Pat, because now her son couldn't read the signs and was wasting the time of his happiness.

Then Sophie got into the car and said, "There was a letter from my father. I stopped to read it."

"Any news?" Ham said, starting the car.

"Yes," said Sophie. "He said he had written to you, too."

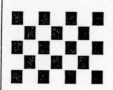

13

The letter for Ham from Bartell had come in the midday post, after Ham had called for Janet before the game. It was as blunt as Bartell's own speech, six lines and no more; he didn't overwork his stenographer. He said that Sophie was coming home to New York at the end of February and he thought it would be a good idea if Ham came across with her. Since Ham was, in effect, a salesman for Bartell tires, it might be a good idea if he had a look at the Bartell plant in Akron. Yours sincerely, Joseph Bartell.

Ham told his mother what was in the letter. "That will be a nice trip," said Janet, now out of her fur coat and almost sitting in the fire. "Especially the two of you going over there together. Will you fly?"

"I think so," Sophie said. "You'd like to fly, wouldn't you, Ham?"

"Well, I don't know if I'm going yet," he said.

"*What?*" said both women.

"I don't know how long your father wants me over there, but he seems to forget that I'm not only testing his tires. I'm testing Richie's car, too. We're not going to win the Mille Miglia on his tires alone."

"We'll only be over there a fortnight," said Sophie, and Ham looked at her; Bartell had evidently written a longer letter to his daughter.

"Well, I'll talk to Richie."

"Someone should talk to you," said Janet tartly, and got up to go and prepare supper. "Coming to help me, Sophie?"

Sophie followed Janet out of the room, and Ham was left with the impression that both of them were angry with him. They had also looked as if they thought him a little stupid.

Sunday morning Richie came down to see how the Rugger match had gone. "The boy did well," he said. "I was looking at the papers this morning. One of them called him another Obolensky, whoever he was. And another one pinned some Latin tag on him. Why do your Rugby and rowing reporters always have to use Latin quotations? Is that to show they are university chappies? Got time for a beer, sport?"

Sophie was helping Janet with the Sunday dinner, making a peach upside-down cake for dessert, something which Janet took to be an American working-girl's sweet. Ham went across with Richie to the Dog and Pot, the small pub nearby. The usual Sunday crowd hadn't yet appeared, and there were only a few drinkers in the small cosy bar. Light gleamed on the copper and brassware that the pub owner had collected; the walls were bright with small shields bearing shards of the regimental ties of the British Army. Ham ordered two beers and he and Richie sat on a couple of stools at the bar. A small, lean man in glasses was telling another blazer-clad man he was sick of winter and impatient for summer; they lifted their glasses and wished each other a succession of centuries when the cricket season began.

147

"I got a letter from Bartell yesterday," Ham said. "He wants me to go to the States for a couple of weeks. He wants me to have a look at the factory in Akron."

"It might be an idea," Richie said. "Tell you the truth, I think a word or two in the ear of his production men would be worth more than a year's reports to Bartell himself. The old bastard is a bit stubborn. He's never made racing tires before, but he thinks he knows all about them."

Ham looked at him. "Have you had some doubts about the tires?"

Richie sipped his beer. "Now you ask me, yes. Have you?"

"All he keeps talking about is how good they are in the wet. Maybe they are. But what happens if it's dry and stinking hot when I drive in the Mille Miglia? No matter how good a tire is in the wet, it's not going to be much help if the cover peels off it when it's hot. I've got no confidence in his tires. All the time I'm going round the track, I'm tensed up, as if I'm waiting for someone to kick me in the behind."

"It'll be a fine bloody thing," said Richie, "if I produce a car capable of winning the Mille Miglia and it goes out half-way round because the tires were no good. That's why I think you should go over to the States. They make good tires there, and they've made some good racing ones. Sidetrack Bartell if you can and find out who his top designer is. Then blow down his ear, hard. Two more beers."

"How's the car coming along?" Ham said.

"I'm still trying to iron out that suspension bug," Richie said. "I took it out myself yesterday morning, up along the road to Aylesbury. I didn't open her up, but I could feel the understeer still there. But I'll get rid of it, don't worry about my end of it, sport. The car had better be good. Everybody in the village knows about it now." He sat for a while, sipping his beer, then he said, "You given any more thought to that proposition I made the other day?"

Ham stared at the wall in front of him; an old pistol, the

brass on it highly polished, was pointed straight at his head. "When do you want my answer?"

"Well, I'd rather you didn't wait till your old age. If we do all right in the Mille Miglia, I'm gunna register as a company. I don't suppose you have to give me your answer till then, but it would be nice to know beforehand that you might come in." He looked at Ham. "You had any other propositions, Ham? One, maybe, that isn't such a risk?"

"Most propositions today are risks," Ham said. "Unless you're offered a directorship in I.C.I. or General Motors."

"Well, I can tell you, Wizard Motors will never be in their class," Richie said. "All I can promise you is that we should be able to pay our bills. We'll never make a million, like Old Man Bartell. But we'll be our own bosses and," he finished his beer, "be able to buy all the grog we want."

"I'll try to make up my mind as soon as I can," Ham said. "I'm trying to make up my mind about a lot of things just now."

"Including Sophie?"

Ham looked at him. "Is it obvious to you, too? My mother was giving me the needle about her last night."

"The girl herself will be the next one to ask you," Richie said. "I was like you, with Kitty. Couldn't make up my mind. Tried to tell myself no one should marry in wartime. You know, the usual bull about going out and never coming back, leaving your wife a widow before she's had time to get over being a bride. In the end Kitty asked me—no, she didn't ask me, she just told me we were gunna be married. And I've never regretted it." He looked out the window, at the black snarl of branches against the grey sky. "Except for your bloody climate."

Then Taz came into the bar. He had stayed the night at Jennifer's home in Esher and had brought her back to Stoke Poges for Sunday dinner. "She's helping Mother and Sophie," he said. "They told me you two were over here."

149

Richie congratulated him on the notices he had got in the Sunday papers. "You'll be a draw at Silverstone and Goodwood this year. All the Rugger crowds will be coming to watch you."

"They won't come to watch me if I don't win races," Taz said, taking the beer Richie handed him.

"Well, you've got a good coach in the family," Richie said. "That should be a help."

"Yes," said Taz, waiting for Ham to say something. Ham didn't know what their mother had said to Taz after Taz's announcement on Christmas Day that he had definitely signed with the Bourne End team; he himself had said nothing at all, because he had felt that whatever he did say would only provoke another row with Taz.

"There's not much I can teach you," Ham said. "You've been watching me long enough now."

He had offered Taz the opportunity to say more, to justify his decision not to wait any longer before taking up big-car racing, but Taz said nothing. It was as if, now he had made his decision, gone against both Ham's and their mother's wishes, he felt there was no need for justification. He had cut himself off and from now on he had to explain or justify himself to no one.

Richie slid off his stool. "Well, I better be getting home. Can you come up on Wednesday, Ham? We oughta be ready to try the car out again."

The cricketers looked after the three men as they went out of the bar. "That big one is Ham Rafferty, the racing driver," said the taller of the two cricketers. "He's probably looking forward to summer, too."

"I could think of better ways of spending it," said the man with glasses. "Driving a car! I wonder if he plays cricket?"

Richie drove away in his Standard, and Ham and Taz walked down the lane that led to their home. A pale sun had struggled through the clouds and was making a feeble effort to gild the day. Blackbirds sat in a long row along the telegraph lines, glinting like a necklace of blue metal. Frost beneath the bushes had begun to fade, like white shadows chased out by the thin light of the sun. Ham, feeling the cold after the warmth of the pub bar, suddenly longed for summer.

"I'll be glad when we leave for Italy," he said explosively, thinking of the valley of the Po, brown and hot under the sun, and the mountains shimmering in the noon glare till they seemed to quiver in the heat like sleeping animals.

But Taz, who wasn't feeling the cold, said, "You don't mind me now—I mean, perhaps racing against you in the Mille Miglia?"

Ham stopped for a moment, searching for words. He hadn't meant to talk about the Mille Miglia at all, nor even about racing; but he knew that Taz wasn't looking for an argument. He suddenly realised that, more than anything, Taz wanted his approval.

He put his hand on Taz's shoulder for a moment as he stepped aside to let Taz pass through the gate into the garden. "No," he forced himself to say. "But do you think you will get a chance to drive? Reserve drivers don't often get a go in the Mille Miglia. You know what regular team drivers are like about the big races. They'll only drop out if they've got a broken leg or some doctor holds a gun at their heads. I remember once Ferrari told one of his drivers at Monza that he couldn't drive. The cove swore for ten minutes without repeating himself, then burst into tears and wept for another half-hour. Yet he had a temperature of 104 and that night they carted him off to hospital with pleurisy. I hope you won't be too disappointed if you don't get a start."

"I shan't," Taz said. "They've said they'll let me take one of the practice cars round the course. So I'll know something about it for next year." He stopped as he was about to open the front door and looked back over his shoulder at Ham.

"I shan't be reserve driver next year. I've promised myself I'll be a regular driver in the Bourne End team or I'll be driving for someone else."

Ham couldn't resist it: "You've got it all mapped out?"

"Yes. That's the way it was with you and Dad, wasn't it?"

And Ham couldn't deny it. When he had come out of the RAF there had been no other thought in his mind but to take up motor racing and to get to the top, as Pat Rafferty had done. For the first year, with motor racing still trying to get back on its wheels, with petrol rationing in force, with very few circuits still intact after the bombing or the disuse of the war years, with no private money for new racing cars and none of the big firms prepared to back a team, with the public unable to get to what circuits there were because of lack of transport (Ham and his father had, in those days, gone everywhere by motorcycle and sidecar, wearing their racing gear because they had nowhere else to stow it), for the first year the going had been tough. Even Pat, who could command some sort of appearance money from those promotors who remembered him from before the war, had made no more than a bare living. But Ham, who had made less than three hundred pounds in that first full year of racing and after expenses had had less than two pounds a week to live on, had persevered. He had been convinced that motor racing would re-establish itself with the public, would find a new, more general public and some day would draw its hundred thousand spectators to the big events.

Before the war in England, motor racing had been a sport for the middle and upper classes, on a par with polo and rackets; the crowd that had gone to Brooklands and Donington had had none of the mixed-class air of an Epsom Downs or Wembley crowd. Pat Rafferty, born in an Irish bog, had pasted in his scrapbook the advertising motto that had been used to sell motor racing at Brooklands: The Right Crowd—and No Crowding. It hadn't been all snobbery that had prompted such a slogan; there were a good many who honestly believed that the sport should be kept only for those who really understood it. Such a slogan today would only arouse resentment or even derision; and a good section of today's crowds went only in search of sensation.

Ham, knowing that the old days of knowledgeable enthusiasts had gone forever but sure that in time the sensation seekers would be weeded out of the postwar crowds, had gone on. His determination had been even firmer after his father's death; he had even nominated to himself which races he would win. By 1950 his plan had been fulfilled; he was able to make his choice of team offers. Two years later he had planned to be World Champion, and he had almost succeeded in that, too.

"Yes," he said. "I had it all mapped out. There's just one thing, though."

Taz stopped, the door half-open. "What's that?"

"You can never map out when you'll hang up your helmet," he said. "Dad didn't choose his time to call it quits. And I don't know yet when I'll hang up mine."

That night, driving Sophie home to London, he said, "I'll write to your father tomorrow. Tell him I'm coming to New York with you."

"Oh, wonderful!" She pursed her lips, blowing him a kiss across the small space between their seats. "There's such a lot I want to show you. I love New York, too," she said, looking sideways at him from her slanting eyes, Oriental but not inscrutable.

"You planned this, didn't you?" he said.

"How do you mean, planned it?" she said, trying now to be inscrutable, realising she had given her game away.

"Did you write to your father and suggest this trip for me?"

She hesitated. "Yes," she said at last, because she didn't want to begin by lying to him. "Are you angry?"

"Why should I be angry about a free trip to America? But why?" he said, deliberately being dense, hoping she might be like Kitty Launder and take matters into her own hands. "Why did you want me to come to New York?"

But Sophie wasn't Kitty Launder; or perhaps American girls didn't propose to the men they loved. "Oh, I just thought I'd like to see how you looked in my background," she said lightly. "And you would like to go out to Akron, wouldn't you, and see the plant?"

"Yes," he said and dodged the issue again. "I'm very keen to go out to the plant. The tires that come out of there mean a great deal to me."

"You sound just like Dad," said Sophie; but didn't look in the slightest bit unhappy.

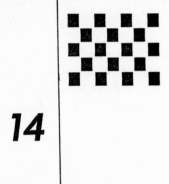

14

Bartell, wrapped in his English overcoat but still looking a long way from Savile Row, met them at Idlewild Airport in a shining cream Cadillac.

"I had it brought on from Akron. Give you some transport while you're here in New York. Let you experience some American comfort, stretch your legs without putting them into the damned engine. Hello, girl, how are you?" He kissed Sophie on her hair; he still did it as if she didn't belong to him. "I've got the apartment all fixed up for us. You'll like it. Even got us a maid. Coloured girl named Deanna. When I was a kid all the coloured girls had names like Pearl or Mary Lou. This one says she's named after Deanna Durbin. I think she's named herself. She's ten, twenty years older than Deanna Durbin." He ushered them into the car, talking all the time, like a maiden aunt who had just been favoured by a visit from a favourite nephew and niece. Sophie murmured something, and he looked around from where he'd taken his place behind the wheel of the car. "What's that? You say something, Sophie?"

"I was just testing," said Sophie with a smile. "Seeing if you had your hearing aid turned off."

Bartell stared at her for a moment, then suddenly he roared with laughter. "You mean I'm talking too much? Hell, girl, you don't come home every week!"

Bartell was not Ham's idea of a good driver. He drove fast and with only one eye on the road, talking to them all the time. He slammed the car to a stop at a red light. "I've got Ed Carlin up at the apartment. He flew in with me from Akron. I thought it would be a good thing for you to meet him, Ham, before we go out to the plant."

"Oh, Dad," Sophie said. "Have we got to talk business tonight? Ham's first night here? My first night home?"

Bartell saw he had made a mistake. "I'm sorry, girl. I just didn't think—" The light turned green, four cars behind them instantly hooted their horns like seals late for feeding time and he set the Cadillac rolling again. "Maybe I should have left it till tomorrow. But I just can't brush Ed off tonight. He isn't one of the boys I pay to butter me up. He's my production chief."

"I'd like to meet him," Ham said, pressing Sophie's hand, trying to tell her not to be too disappointed. "That's why I came across here."

"Is it?" Bartell turned round, and the Cadillac grazed the side of a bus, whose driver leaned out and said something about bums who owned Cadillacs and couldn't drive them, an abuse that sounded more communistic than capitalistic to Ham. "I thought the main reason you came across was to be with Sophie."

Ham felt Sophie's hand slacken in his, waiting for his

answer. "Yes," he said and felt the pressure of her hand again. "But I have to make a pretence of being here on business, haven't I?"

"Sure, sure." Bartell went back to driving the car. "But we have business planned for you, all right. I'll tell you more about it later, when we're with Ed Carlin."

The Bartells' apartment was in a tall new building on the corner of Fifth Avenue and one of the East Sixties. It was a penthouse apartment, and even Sophie was surprised at the sumptuousness of it. Like a man who had for so long had nobody to spend his money on but himself, Bartell had now splurged; Ham had no idea how much an apartment like this would cost to buy and furnish, but he knew he would only make himself unhappy even if he tried to guess. That the apartment as yet still had the cool, neat impersonality of a shop window didn't alter the fact that Bartell had made a beginning toward creating a home for his daughter.

He stood in the middle of it, his bony face fattened by pride and enthusiasm, owner of the Promised Land. "You like it, girl?"

Sophie went to him and kissed him. "It's wonderful, Dad. I never dreamed home was like this."

He caught her meaning, but he wasn't offended. He smiled down at her, holding her hands in his. "I wanted the best, girl. I have an awful lot of years to make up."

Then Ed Carlin, a stout, balding man with bright, merry eyes and a deep voice with a gurgle of laughter in it, came in from the terrace. He was introduced to Sophie and then to Ham, putting out a plump, strong hand to each of them.

"You're better-looking than your photo, Miss Bartell," he said. "Your father has it on his desk at the plant. We all find excuses to go in and look at it. Your father thinks we want to see him."

Bartell chuckled; even one of the butter-up men could

have insulted him this evening. "They all think I don't know it, too."

Then Deanna, the maid, came in. She was plump and full of laughter, a dark ray of sunshine. She came into the room, stroking the heavy silk curtains with her bright eyes, tramping on her bunions through the snowfall of carpet, looking as if she had worked for spendthrift millionaires all her life. She smiled at Sophie, a neon flash of white and gold, and Sophie returned the smile; the two women knew at once that they were going to like each other. Deanna looked at Ham, saw his green checked shirt, tomato bow tie, tomato waistcoat and yellow suède boots, and smiled welcomingly at him. Man, he was sharp! She'd always thought Englishmen wore only striped pants and derbies. Why, this man, he could strut his stuff on Lenox Avenue and send 'em crazy!

"We'll be eatin' out, Deanna," said Bartell, having trouble with her name. "When you have unpacked Miss Sophie's things, you can have the night off."

"You only got them two bags, Miss Sophie?" Deanna said.

"That's all," said Sophie. "We're only here for two weeks. I'll buy what else I need."

"Only two weeks?" Deanna said, and her plump face showed her disappointment and dismay.

Sophie smiled, but she was looking at her father. "I'll be back later, Deanna. To stay."

She hadn't looked at Ham, but she thought: I hope he got the message, too. Now that she had him in her own waters, she was determined to fix as many anchors to him as she could. In England, in his territory and environment, she knew she had been fighting a losing battle. Here, at least, she didn't have the cars as rivals.

They went to Twenty-One for dinner. Bartell wasn't known there, but Carlin, who was, had reserved a good table for them. He pointed out to Ham several celebrities who were sitting at other tables.

"Never mind about the other celebrities," said Bartell. "We've got our own, right here at this table."

"Not me," said Ham. "The waiters keep looking at me as if they're afraid I shan't be able to pay for what I eat."

"Well, you'll be a celebrity in a week or two," Carlin said. "Have you told him yet, Joe?"

"No," said Bartell and looked at Ham. "I was going to keep this till later, but I guess now's as good a time as any. We have entered you in the Sebring 12-Hour. You are going to win it, too, and be a celebrity like Ed says."

Ham waited till after the waiter had served them and had gone away. It gave him time to control his temper. Then he said quietly, "You don't think you should have asked me before you put my name down for it?"

"Hell, there wasn't time," said Bartell, beginning to eat as if he were starved. Round a mouthful of shrimp he said, "Why, what's the matter? We had to get you a car. By the time we got that fixed, it was time to send in your name before the entries closed. I guessed you wouldn't mind. You'll win this, Ham. We got you a Ferrari, one that belongs to a friend of Ed's. He was pleased as hell when we told him we could get you as driver. You were a celebrity to him, all right. Eh, Ed?"

"Sure." Carlin was quiet; he had sensed that Ham wasn't too pleased about what had been done. "Morrie Fishberg; he'd seen you drive in Europe."

"He was tinkled pink," Bartell said.

"I'm glad of that," said Ham. "And obviously you are, too."

He looked at Sophie, but she hurriedly said, "Darling, I had nothing to do with this! I'm on your side. I think the least Dad could have done was to ask you before he arranged it all."

"I told you, there wasn't time." Bartell cleared his mouth; he put down his fork. "What's the matter, Rafferty? Don't you want to drive at Sebring? You're working for me, remember? You didn't nominate what races you drove in when you drove for that works team, I bet."

"That's no way to put your case, Dad," Sophie said and pushed her plate away from her.

"Honey, let me handle this," Bartell said and missed the sudden sharp look that came into Sophie's eyes. "What's the matter, Rafferty? What have you got against driving at Sebring?"

"I've got nothing against driving there," Ham said slowly. "But you signed me for two races, remember? The Mille Miglia and the Le Mans. I'll drive at Sebring for you, but next time you want to enter me for a race, pay me the compliment of telling me about it first. I'm not a racehorse or a greyhound, just to be shoved into a race without being told about it. Nor am I one of your butter-up men. I'm working for you, Bartell, and on this side of the Atlantic I'm a nobody. Just a fairy in a fancy waistcoat, to the waiters. But I spent twelve years on the other side of the Atlantic building myself up to a position where I had some independence, where even the works teams I drove for paid me the compliment of taking me into their confidence."

It was a moment when he should have got up and stalked out; but he and Sophie were jammed against the wall. An exit, to be effective, had to be unhindered. So he sat tight, staring across the table at Bartell. If he had got up and gone out then, the break with Bartell might have been permanent. And it might have committed Sophie to a decision that, made in the heat of the moment, she might later have regretted.

The atmosphere at the table was like that at a wake where someone had just spat on the corpse; the corpse might have deserved the insult, but the other mourners wished they had been elsewhere when it had happened. Bartell had never been spoken to like this before; he had had it coming, pos-

160

sibly for years, but now all at once Sophie and Ed Carlin were sorry for him. The buttering-up Bartell had paid for, about which he joked but which he believed in with all the passion of a stubborn, egocentric man, hadn't prepared him for the insult of a rebellion.

Ed Carlin was concentrating on his food, chewing it as if it were expensive leather, unable to swallow but determined to clear his plate. Sophie had pushed her plate right away from her and was sitting back, as if she had finished dinner and was now only waiting to go. Even the waiter, who had been about to bring more food to the table, had recognised that something was wrong and was hovering discreetly in the background.

Bartell looked about the table and recognised the signs: they were all against him. For a moment it looked as if he were going to bluster it out: he was the boss, and by George, nobody, nobody at all, talked to him like that. Then he looked back at Sophie, saw the stiff disapproval in her face, and in that moment capitulated. She had never buttered him up, nor would he want her to. Yet he had begun to sense that she had some loyalty to him and he recognised now that what he saw on her face was an honest opinion.

"All right, Rafferty. Ham. I apologise. I didn't think you'd take it like this. I figured I was doing a good thing. We talked it all out, didn't we, Ed?" It had hurt him to admit he was wrong; he wasn't going to be left out on a limb on his own; he wasn't paying Ed Carlin just to sit there and lap up food. "We figured since you were coming over, we could get you some publicity. That's what we want. If you win the Mille Miglia, no one'll have heard of you on this side. Nobody here knows any race drivers. Oh sure," he was talking now to cover up the wrong he had done, listening to his own voice as if it were some sort of salve for the wounding of his ego, "everybody has heard of Mauri Rose and Wilbur Shaw. But who else? Sure, the hot-rod kids would hear of you and the people who go to the car meets over here. But race drivers aren't household words in this country like they are in England and Europe. Every snotty-nosed kid in England has heard of Stirling Moss and that guy Mike Hawthorn—yeah, and you, too. Over here the kids all over the country, they have only heard of Mickey Mantle, other baseballers, maybe one or two footballers."

"We had it figured." Carlin put down his fork. He knew when he had to earn his money. Joe was a hard man to get along with, but he was a good boss, and you owed him some loyalty. "If you win the Sebring, we can get you in the columns. And on Television. Maybe on the Ed Sullivan show, something like that."

"What will he do on the Ed Sullivan show?" Sophie said. "Drive a Mercury round the studio? Show the public how to do a four-wheel drift or whatever it's called?"

"They'll find something for him to do," Bartell said, waiting anxiously for the stiffness to go from his daughter's face. "They had a troupe of monkeys on there one night. All they did was eat goddam bananas."

"You like bananas?" Carlin said, and winked at Ham; the atmosphere had begun to ease.

"Maybe in that waistcoat, they'll put you on in colour," Bartell said, working hard, looking at Sophie more than at Ham.

Ham saw the anxiety in Bartell's face, and recognised where the man's real apology was directed. He felt no resentment, his anger all gone now, and he weakened. "All right. But what if I don't win the Sebring?"

"The bananas will have strychnine in them," said Carlin. "If you reckon during the race you can't win, don't trouble to cross the line. Just turn west somewhere along the track and keep driving. There are a lot of other fugitives in California. One more won't be noticed."

Ham flew out to Akron with Bartell and Carlin. He was shown over the plant by Bartell, and then managed to get himself closeted with Carlin for half an hour. He talked earnestly and lucidly, talking about something on which, by experience, he had become an expert, and at the end of it Ed Carlin said, "We should have had you over here three months ago, Ham. The Old Man is a stubborn bastard, though. Nobody can tell him anything in this plant. He knows tires, I'll give him that, but he knows nothing about racing tires."

"Will you be able to do something now?" Ham said. "I mean, without his getting stubborn about it?"

"I can handle him," Carlin said and rose from his chair. "Tell me something. Are you and Sophie engaged or anything?"

"Why do you ask?"

"I know it's none of my business," Carlin said. "But I've noticed a difference in Joe since he's had this reunion with Sophie. He's going to find it hard to forgive you if you take her away from him."

"We haven't talked about marriage yet," Ham said. "I've still got two races to drive in. Three," he said, remembering Sebring. "Sophie has given me enough hints about how she'd hate to be married to a racing driver."

"If she's anything like her old man," said Carlin, "she could be pretty stubborn about that. I wish you luck, Ham."

Ham went back to New York. A week later he and Sophie flew down to Florida. Bartell, who had gone direct from Akron, met them at Tampa with Morrie Fishberg, the owner of the Ferrari which Ham was to drive. Fishberg was a fat, smiling little man who had a Chrysler agency in Chicago. He wore big horn-rimmed glasses and his grey hair stuck up on either side of a bald scalp; he looked like an owl who considered it a wise thing to be happy. And he was most happy, he told Ham, when he was around automobiles.

"I'm too old to drive anything but a nice, big, comfortable car like this," he said, tapping the wheel of the Chrysler as they sped along between the bright ranks of the citrus plantations. "I'm sixty-eight, you know. I can remember as a kid—I was born in New York—going out to Long Island to see the Vanderbilt Cup. That was before your time, Mr. Rafferty. They ran the Cup at other places, Milwaukee, Savannah, Santa Monica out in California. But there was only one Vanderbilt Cup for real enthusiasts. The one when they'd run it on Long Island. Those were the days. They'd get half a million spectators out there, you know? Stand all over the course, just asking to be killed. The cars would come down on them at over a hundred miles an hour, and I'm talking about 1908 or 1909, when cars weren't as safe as they are today, and the crowd would stand right there in front of them till the very last minute. I remember once, I leaned out and touched Joe Tracy when he went past at well over ninety. It made my day."

"Nutty as a fruitcake," said Bartell, sitting in the back with Sophie.

Fishberg shook his head, smiling at Ham. "They'll never know, will they, Mr. Rafferty? Some people just aren't born to experience real happiness, are they?"

Ham's codriver in the race was to be Wally Heckberg, who had worked his way up from midget-car and stock-car meets and had driven for Fishberg at Indianapolis and Watkins Glen. He was one of the band of grease-stained, wind-weathered gypsies who, by luck, skill, perseverance and plain guts, make a living out of racing cars in the United States, working their way from track to track, from small hick town to small hick town, from state fair to state fair, always dreaming of the big time; and some of them, like Wally Heckberg, making it while they were still young enough to enjoy it. Wally was in his late twenties, a tall, thin-hipped man but with the shoulders of a middleweight wrestler. He had rather tired-looking

164

eyes, as if he had peered too long into the dust storms raised by other cars on the dirt tracks where he had begun his career; he had a habit of hesitating before he spoke, as if getting over an incipient stammer, and he chewed gum constantly. He looked on Ham as a soulmate when he found that the latter also chewed gum.

"Tell you the truth, Ham," he said, their first day out at the track, "I was wondering what you'd be like, kinda. You're big time to most of the boys here."

"You're only big time if your car's any good," Ham said. "How's this Ferrari of ours?"

"Like most Ferraris. Fast as hell."

Then Peter Burghley came up, his thin face pink with sunburn. "Ham, why didn't you stay home? I've been telling these Yanks how I was going to win this. Now I've got to beat you, too." Peter had already met Wally; he winked at him and looked back at Ham. "How's Sophie?"

"She's fine," Ham said. "How's Jackie?"

"Pining for me to get back to her. She's out of work again."

When Peter at last left them, Wally looked after him. "He's a nice kid," he said, from the eminence of five years' seniority and ten years' hand-to-mouth struggling. "How good is he, Ham? It's hard to tell under all that school-kid act of his."

"It's no act. That's all he is, really. A schoolboy. But one of these days he's going to be a great racing driver. He's the sort of kid who worries old coves like me stiff. Because they are the ones who, some day, are going to be good enough to make us veterans retire."

The night before the race Ham went to bed early, pleading that he would need the sleep. But sleep didn't come easily; he drove the race in his mind long before the flag fell. It had been agreed that he was to take first turn at the wheel, in the hope of building something of a lead; he was glad of that,

165

because he felt he could not have sat around waiting in the pits while Wally Heckberg was already lost in the heat and concentration of the race. He was, in effect, being baptised again and he wanted the baptism without too much delay.

As it happened, once he was in the Ferrari all his fear disappeared. But he wasn't consoled; he knew now that this was no real test. Unless a man took needless risks, the Sebring course, with its flat track and artifical bends that kept speeds well down, was as good as any for a man who had crashed to make his comeback on. It was nothing like the test that the Mille Miglia or Le Mans would be.

The morning was bright, and there was glare on the track, but even that didn't worry him. The race was due to start at ten o'clock, but there was a big crowd gathered an hour or more before that. Winter refugees from New York, in new gay shirts and new pink sunburns, had driven up from Miami; they were Americans, but they were as out of place here among the locals as if they were in Europe. A group of elderly retired people had driven over from St. Petersburg; the women sat under their big straw hats and gossiped, and the men went seeking their lost youth. Some cowhands had come up from the Kissimmee Valley ranches; they discussed the cars the way their ancestors in the West had discussed quarter horses. The locals, their clothes a little more faded by the sun than those of the visitors, their eyes a little more wrinkled, their speech a good deal slower, munched on pralines and discussed the cars and the visitors and thanked Gawd, yes sir, they didn't live in Miami. When the flag went down they all stopped talking and leaned forward in common interest and excitement.

Ham got the Ferrari away at the head of the field, using its tremendous acceleration to the fullest effect; but when he came out of the first corner he saw in his mirror that Peter Burghley was right behind him in his Maserati. As Wally had said, you had to drive the Ferrari all the way, but the farther he went, the more confident he became; the car had speed, it was too early to have to worry about the brakes wearing and he had tires beneath him that he knew and trusted. He settled down in his seat, chewing steadily, sitting back in his old relaxed style, driving with arms almost at full stretch; he had been glad to find that Wally also drove in the same long-armed style, because it meant that the seat didn't have to be altered for either of them at a change-over of drivers. He had never been known as The Master, as Fangio was, but he had been pointed out as a model to a lot of young drivers. Now, excited and pepped up by the knowledge that, for the time being at least, he had overcome his fear, he settled down to give Peter Burghley, one of the boys who would one day supplant him, a lesson in motor racing.

Peter accepted the challenge. He stuck close to Ham's tail; at times Ham felt he was pulling Peter along. Once, coming out of a corner, Peter tried to pass him on acceleration; but Ham, watching him in the mirror, used all of the road as he brought the Ferrari out of the bend, and Peter had to drop back. At the next bend Peter tried an old hand's trick: as they came out of the bend he brought the Maserati up and shunted the Ferrari in the rear. Ham grinned, and accelerated away. The boy was learning.

Ham and Wally had agreed to drive in three-hour stretches, to avoid fatigue from the heat and eyestrain from the glare. Ham still held his lead at the end of two and a half hours, and Peter was still running a close second. They had both lapped several of the slower cars, and the third man's only hope of winning was if both cars in front of him seized up or had to retire because of brake failure. The two leaders were professional drivers with cars built specially for this type of racing; the rest of the field were amateurs or part-time professionals whose cars just didn't have the power.

Ham glanced at his watch: twenty minutes to go. Now was the time to increase his lead, if he could, to give Wally something to get his teeth into as he came out for his first stretch of driving. Ham had no idea how good Peter's codriver was, and there was always the chance, too, that time could be lost at the pits during the change-over. Sebring was always a tough race on brakes and he knew the value of the extra few seconds for a quick look at the brakes when the wheels were being changed.

He began to take the corners a little faster, braking later, drifting more; coming out of the corners he used the maximum revs on each gear, getting everything he could out of the Ferrari's acceleration. And Peter tried to match him.

Coming down a straight, Peter found some extra power and brought the Maserati up alongside the Ferrari; they went down toward the bend together, with Peter on the outside. Ham left his braking till the last moment, then he began to tread on the pedal, pumping hard. He saw the Maserati go ahead of him, and he knew the worst before it happened. He saw Peter suddenly begin to brake, realising he had left it too late, and begin to fight the wheel. Ham went through on the inside, scraping the wheel of the Maserati as it slewed toward him; then he was having his own battle, taking the Ferrari through the corner. Then he was accelerating away again and there was no sign of the Maserati in his mirror.

Next time round he saw the crowd thick on the outside of the bend beyond the straw bales, hiding the car but unable to hide the black tree of smoke that bloomed to make an angry red eye of the sun. He wanted to vomit, but he was dry and empty inside.

15

Ham and Sophie flew back to England a week after Sebring. It had been a bad week for both of them, and when they stepped aboard the plane it was like leaving a land of nightmare. In Ham's baggage were some of Peter Burghley's personal belongings: a watch, a wallet, a small diary, to be taken back to his parents. There was nothing else of him to be taken back. His ashes had been among those of the burned-out car.

It was a quiet journey back for Ham and Sophie, of few words and fitful sleep. And then, as they crossed the coast, coming in from the grey Atlantic to the green countryside spread out below them, Ham said, "I think we should get married."

Sophie turned only her eyes toward him. "Are you serious, darling?"

"Dead serious," he said and regretted at once the choice of phrase.

She should have been excited, delirious with happiness; but all she could do was press his hand and smile weakly at him. "When?"

"As soon as you like."

"And where do we live?" she said, afraid of the cars, aware that the plane every moment was bringing her closer to them.

"You once said you liked England."

"Would you go on racing? I couldn't take that, Ham. I'd want you to go back to New York with me. I'd feel safer there. Feel *you* were safer."

"I don't *want* to go on racing," he said, admitting part of the truth for the first time. "But what do I do for a living if we go back to America? I'm not trained for anything." Then he told her about Richie's offer to go in with him as partner. "That, I could do. But what demand is there in the States for the handmade sports car? If our car did catch on, we'd soon find one of the big companies making offers to take us over. If we tried to stay independent, costs would beat us in the end. It's far cheaper to make the sort of car we want to make in England than it is here."

"Well, couldn't Dad find a job for you? You don't have to make cars, do you?"

"That's what I was afraid you'd say. No, darling. The last thing I want is to go to work for your father. If he had a job that I could fill, I mean not just a job for the boss's son-in-law but one where what little I know would be worth the money he'd pay me, then I'd have no false pride. I'd probably take it. But with the set-up at the plant as it is, he'd have to create a job for me. And one thing convinced me it would be a bad thing if ever I went to work for your father: That night at Twenty-One. If you hadn't been there, he'd have had me shot for talking back to him the way I did about Sebring.

He's never been used to having someone talk back to him. I couldn't work for a father-in-law like that, darling. I get along all right with him now, but I've still got a measure of independence. I'd have none if I went to work for him full time."

"Well, you'll have to do something. But what? Hadn't you ever made any plans or were you just going on till—" She stopped: she had almost said, *till you were killed on the track*.

"Oh, I'd thought about it long before I met you. Every man, unless he's a fool, thinks about it if he's in a job like mine. The racing driver, the matador, the professional cricketer, your baseballers, fighters. He has to start his life all over again, sometime when he gets into his thirties. If he hasn't made a lot of money, what can he do? I had a nightmare once in a while—I used to dream I was up in the Euston Road, trying to sell secondhand cars that no one wanted to buy. I wanted to go on for a few more years, put some money aside and look around for a business, a car agency or something like that. After I've driven the Mille Miglia and Le Mans for your father, I'll have enough to do that."

"I think I could get Dad to release you from your contract."

"And what would we use for money to get married on?" He turned away for a moment and looked out the window; there had been a momentary flash of sun but it was gone now as thick clouds swirled by. He looked back at her. "I shouldn't have asked you, darling. I'm sorry. Forget it."

"I won't forget it!" she said, and her hand was like a possessive claw on his; the tiredness dropped from her face, and her eyes blazed. "We're going to be married, you understand? I don't care how we work it out, we're going to be married!"

But even as she said it, she knew she was not just accepting him: she was defying the cars, trying to bury her fear in a fierce passion of love.

171

Taz met them at London airport in the Jensen. They drove Sophie up to her flat, Ham said he would see her the next day, then he and Taz drove back to Stoke Poges.

"We're engaged," he said, as they started off.

Taz congratulated him. "I never really expected you to marry. And yet the second time I saw you with Sophie, I somehow knew you'd finish up marrying her. When are you going to be married?"

"We haven't talked about that yet," Ham said, looking out at the cold paleness of the day, trying to remember the warm sunshine of Florida and unable to, because all he could remember of Florida was an angry sun and a black pall of smoke that had been the death of Peter Burghley. "We're talking about where we'll live."

Taz looked at him in surprise. "You're not thinking of going to live in America?"

"People do live there, you know. A hundred and sixty million of them. What I saw of them, they all looked reasonably happy, too."

"Oh, I know. I didn't mean it that way. What I meant was, look how far away you'll be from things. What racing do they have there? A few sports-car events and that round-and-round merry-go-round they have at Indianapolis."

"Don't ever quote that opinion to an American. They get half a million people to watch that round-and-round merry-go-round. It is certainly more of a test of a driver's endurance than it is of his skill, but it's still no picnic ride."

"I know," Taz said, wondering if he had been too critical of things American now that his brother was engaged to an American. He had never been to the United States nor met many Americans, and his outlook was still conditioned a lot by films and the jaundiced comments of British newspapermen, most of whom wrote as if it were their bounden duty to report only the blights in the American dream. "But still, it's held only once a year. What do you do the rest of the time?"

172

"If I'm retired," Ham said, looking straight ahead of them down the road, "what does it matter what I do the rest of the time?"

"Then you are retiring?" The Jensen's speed increased a little; Taz had put his foot down involuntarily.

"You're expecting me to, aren't you?"

"Look, Ham. Don't let's say I expect anything of you. I'm trying to stand on my own two feet now and I'm not expecting anything of anyone."

Ham said nothing for a while, then at last he said, "How's Mum?"

"She's all right. Still says she's frozen." Taz swung the car round another one that was being driven down the middle of the road. "Why do drivers in this country always have to straddle the dotted lines? You'd think they'd learned to drive on snakes-and-ladders boards. Follow the dotted line to Slough or wherever they're going." Then he said, and it was obvious he had been wanting to say it for some time, ever since Ham had got off the plane: "That was shattering about Peter. It upset Mother a lot."

"It upset me," Ham said, speaking a truth that was still sickening. "In a way I was responsible for his going off the track."

"That's bloody silly. Nobody is responsible for anyone else going off the track, not unless he deliberately pushes him. You're not that sort of driver. What did happen?"

Ham told him. "If he hadn't tried to beat me into that corner, he'd still be alive."

"Then it wasn't your fault. Peter had those lapses, you know that. He could drive as well as anyone for lap after lap, and then all of a sudden he'd have one of those mad moments of his. He'd have grown out of them eventually, I suppose." He was silent for a moment, then he said, "He was a nice cove, Peter. I liked him."

"How did Jackie take it?"

173

"I went up to see her. I was surprised. I thought she was a heartless bitch, but she was quite broken up about it. She was really fond of old Peter."

"I'd better go and see his people, I suppose. That's always the part I hate. I've had to do it twice before. It gets no easier each time," he said and then remembered: "No, three times. I had to come back to Brescia and tell Mum about Dad. She wanted to know every detail. It was bloody murder."

"She's already written to Peter's people. She always does that. I think she's written to the relatives of every driver who has been killed since Dad was. It's almost as if she feels she belongs to some club."

Ham could feel the extra warmth of his mother's welcome; it was almost as if he had come back from a war. She had seen every one of his races, except the previous Sebring in which he had driven; he tried to remember if her welcome home that time had been warmer than usual, but couldn't. When he told her about his engagement, she kissed him again and burst into tears. It was the first time he had seen her cry since his father's death.

"Look, this is supposed to be a happy occasion!"

"I am happy," she said. "Why didn't you bring Sophie back here with you so I could weep over her, too? You men. You've never got any appreciation of the wonderful moments in a woman's life. We could have had a nice big cry together." Then she smiled, wiping her eyes. "Of course I'm happy. When is the wedding?"

"That's the first thing everyone asks," he said and knew he sounded a little sharp. "Don't rush me. It's taken me years to get engaged. Give me time to get used to that."

"All the more reason you should be married soon," said Janet. "When does Sophie want to be married?"

"Right away," he admitted. "As soon as possible after we come back from Italy."

174

"A sensible girl," said Janet. "I'm on her side. I can't see the point in long engagements. If you're in love, you should be married."

"There you go, simplifying things again."

"What's simpler than being in love?" she asked, and he had no answer. Being in love had been simple for her; but for some people it was as complex as all life itself. He still had to find out where he stood, but he had little hope that it would prove as simple for him as it had for his mother. He could only wonder how his father had felt.

That night, while he and Taz were waiting for dinner, they sat in front of the fire while he told Taz about the trip to America. "Old Man Bartell got what he wanted for me. Publicity. After we came back from New York, after we'd won the Sebring, they had me on a Television show. One of those bright, happy announcers they have over there, like the ones we're getting here, too, kept laughing in my face all the time and asking me questions about cars that a ten-year-old kid wouldn't have asked. He got on my nerves, he was so bloody happy. He had the worst bloodshot eyes I've ever seen. But they told me afterward ten million people look at the program, so maybe one or two of them caught my name."

"They had me on the BBC last Saturday," Taz said. "You heard about the tries I got in the matches against France and Scotland. They had me on 'In Town Tonight.' With an Italian film star, a real dish, and the Champion of Champions from Cruft's Dog Show. The beggar tried to bite me just as I went on."

"You're getting your share of glory then."

"Who wants glory?" said Taz, with all the bitterness of youth. "That's not what I want."

"What do you want?"

Taz stared into the fire. "I don't know. It's hard to put it into words without sounding like a poet trying to write a pamphlet. I want—well, I want what you've had for the past ten or twelve years. What you had during the war. What Dad had."

"Excitement?"

"In a way, I suppose. But it's more than that." He looked up. "You should know what I'm getting at. I want what you feel when you get in behind a wheel, when you're waiting for the flag to come down. What Peter felt, and all the other coves feel. I don't know, perhaps it's what knights of old used to feel. Whatever it is, it's something that's dying out in this world. What I'm trying to say is, what I want is that feeling of being alone against whatever it is that's sent to test a man. You had it in Spitfires during the war. I think you get it behind the wheel of a racing car. Whatever it is, it's what makes you keep going back for more. Even when you know you're likely to get what Peter copped in the end."

Ham gazed into the fire. Behind him he knew its glow was reflected in the trophies arrayed there, making a silver fire of the wall. He turned and looked back at the green helmet that hung on the wall; then at the photograph on the nearby desk of the lean, laughing man who had been his father. There was dust on the glass—the charwoman had been careless today —but the dust couldn't veil the gaiety and love of living of the man.

But Pat Rafferty had not always been laughing. Ham remembered now how his father had always looked in the moment just before a race began. In that moment when the engines began to growl and then rise to a pitch of anger, when the air suddenly became blue and thick with the smell of racing fuel, when the starter with his flag raised looked like a man about to die as the cars strained to smash him into the track, in that moment Pat Rafferty had stopped laughing and a look of distance, of straining to see something that had no tangibility or meaning, had been there behind the glinting goggles. It was the look that was on the faces of nine out of ten drivers, the dedicated ones, the men who in other skins

176

were test pilots and matadors and mountaineers, the men who in other centuries had been explorers and knights and gladiators. It was the look of men who had found the world too small, who had been born to search for something to which they could give no name.

"Now you know why I haven't wanted to retire," he said, looking back at Taz.

"I know." Taz nodded his head. "And I don't blame you now. I just hope you understand how it is with me."

"What about Mum?"

"We haven't talked about it. But she manages to make me feel that I'm something of a traitor. It's no use trying to explain it to her. She wouldn't understand."

"I think she might," Ham said slowly. "If she would only let herself understand. But the trouble is, she can never forget that a woman always has to stand and wait. The races are always longer for them than they are for us."

"What about Sophie?"

"She feels the same as Mum. Worse, because at least Mum did understand something of how Dad felt. She doesn't even want me to race in the Mille Miglia. Not after seeing Peter killed."

"Will you race in it?"

Ham looked across at him. "I've got to. The time to retire is not right after you've seen someone, a friend, killed. The time to retire is when you decide it yourself, make your own decision. Not have it made for you by something that has happened on the track."

"Have you been able to explain that to Sophie?"

"I don't think you could explain it to any woman. She thinks I'm doing it to hurt her, as if it's some sort of cruelty a man has to let out of himself. She can't understand that I've *got* to do it. Otherwise I'll be the one who'll be hurt. She can't understand that a man has to live with himself. And he can't do that while he has doubts about himself. Or I can't."

177

Next morning Ham went up to see Richie. Work had now begun on the second car to be taken to Italy; another mechanic had been taken on and part of the front garage had been requisitioned as another workshop. "Kitty is beginning to complain," Richie said. "She reckons I only come home for breakfast. I've even had to give up going down to the pub for a grog."

"Don't work yourself into hospital," Ham said. "I'll need you in Italy. We haven't talked about a passenger for the Mille Miglia, but I'm hoping it will be you. I'll need someone to navigate for me."

"I just took it for granted that I'd be the bloke. Come on in and have a look at the car. I think we've solved that understeer bug. Can you try her out this afternoon?" Ham nodded. "How about the tires? You bring any new ones back with you?"

"No. But I think we might have some improvement now. I had a chance to talk to Bartell's production chief. He understood what I was talking about."

"When do we get them?"

Ham shook his head. "It looks as if we shan't get them till we get to Italy."

"That's a bugger. What happens if they turn out to be still no bloody good?"

Ham said nothing but turned away to speak to Charlie and George. There was hardly room to move in the shed now. Ham had already marked his trousers with grease as he had threaded his way through the clutter of tools, engine stands and the now completed body of the Wizard. A lathe hummed in one corner as the new mechanic worked on it, and Charlie had just stacked spare fenders against a wall. Ham grinned at the grease, dirt and cluttered confusion of the shed.

"Well, they say no birth is ever clean and easy," he said.

"Midwifery is not in my line," said Charlie. "Now at Mulliner's I was never as filthy as this. You couldn't tell me from the managing director."

"Nobody can tell you from the managing director here," said Richie. "I'm just as filthy as you are."

Charlie waved a huge hand that dismissed the managing director and looked at Ham. "Well, how does she look?" There was no mistaking the pride in his eyes as he nodded toward the car; the tiredness dropped away, and he looked almost refreshed. "I worked on the first Bentley Continental. I didn't feel any prouder than I do now."

The car had had all the roughness smoothed out of its bodywork. It had been painted British racing green; it had the sleekness of a green teardrop. Ham knew how difficult it was to combine good aesthetic design with good engineering design; the two things were not necessarily compatible. Some of the best racing cars, as far as road-holding and aerodynamic design had been concerned, had been utterly ugly. The Italians were much more advanced than anyone else in body design, but even they made elementary mistakes; they gave some of their cars exaggerated sloping roofs and big rear-vision windows that exposed the cars' back seat passengers to the risk of cricked necks and sunstroke. The Mercedes-Benz 300SL was one of the finest-looking cars ever put on a road, but the engineers had had trouble fitting the engine under the bonnet designed for it and had finally had to lay it on its side. The Jaguar XK models were one of the best combinations of aesthetic and engineering design; and Richie, without copying the XK, had at least equalled it. Ham knew that, when he first drove the car into the Piazza Vittoria in Brescia, he would feel as much pride in the Wizard as was now so plainly evident on Charlie Carter's big red face.

Ham had now taken to carrying his gear in the boot of the Jensen, so he suggested that they leave at once for Silverstone. Bartell had written Richie to buy and outfit a transporter truck, but delivery of it wasn't expected until just before they were to leave for Italy. So the old Leyland was borrowed again from the coal dealer, the Wizard was loaded aboard and they all set off for Silverstone.

Richie rode in the Jensen with Ham. "So you're engaged at last, eh? Good on you, sport. But that means, I suppose, you won't want to come in with me as partner?"

"It doesn't mean that at all. But you'll have to wait awhile for my answer. There are some other things I've got to find answers to. They're all tied up together."

"Look, sport, don't think I'll be offended if you turn me down. If you wanna go and live in America, I won't blame you. Frankly, I'd much rather go home and live in Australia than here. It's not just the bloody climate, either. But if I do, what'll I find to interest me? There's no car racing to speak of out there. There's not the interest in cars that there is in this country—most people out there just look on them as a means of getting from one place to another. I like the sunshine and the beaches and the way we live, without any bloody class consciousness. But after a while I'd find myself listening for the sound of a sweet-crackling engine. I'd find myself wanting to swap the smell of gum leaves for a good whiff of racing oil. I'd go looking for someone to talk to about Moss or Hawthorn or Fangio, about how good the Ferraris were for a while and whether the Vanwall will ever be as good as we hope, and all I'd find would be blokes wanting to talk about bloody racehorses or cricketers. I'll stay on in England, because—well, because it's close to everything. Everything that counts, I mean. But I could understand it if ever a bloke wanted to leave here and go and live somewhere else. Especially America. And especially if he was married to a millionaire's daughter. I wish Kitty's old man had been a pools owner or a City financier, instead of just a shire clerk."

They unloaded the Wizard at Silverstone, and Ham did ten laps. He didn't need any more; when he brought the car in he knew they had a good one. "She'll do. Just as she is. Don't touch her at all."

Richie, bundled up in a duffel coat against the March wind, his bald head hidden by a thick woollen skullcap, jumped up and down; whether from joy or to keep warm, Ham couldn't say. "It's up to you now, sport. When we come back to England at the end of April, we want the Mille Miglia under our belt."

"It's in the bag," said George Hayes, his nose a red beak in the wind.

"I'll have to find a bookie in Brescia," said Charlie, resting his hands on the bonnet of the car to warm them. "I'll invest a couple of shillings on the combination of the Wizard and Rafferty. I might even be rash and go as far as five bob."

For the first time he could remember in his racing career, Ham was embarrassed by the faith of the others in him. Then he realised that this was the first time when the reputation of a car, even its future and that of the men who had built it, had depended on him.

He had no words to answer their faith and hope in him. He turned away and walked slowly across to the Jensen, feeling the chill beginning in him that scraped the marrow of his bones more than the Siberian wind that was hurling its knives across the desolate landscape. He was afraid again, because he knew now there would be no safety limit for him on the whole thousand miles of the Italian roads. He would have to drive to the absolute limit, and these men, not knowing his secret, would be expecting no less of him.

He went back to Stoke Poges, bathed and changed and drove up to South Kensington. His mother followed him to the door as he was leaving the house.

"Bring Sophie back with you tonight. Now she's going to be my daughter-in-law, I want to give her a proper welcome into the family. I'm no good at talking to anyone over the telephone."

"I'll bring her down tomorrow. I'll stay at the flat tonight. We have to go and buy the ring in the morning."

"Is Sophie going to Italy with you?"

"I took it for granted that she was."

"Am I coming?" He realised with a shock that she had never asked him that before.

"Of course. You want to, don't you?"

"I should like to. After all, I'll have a double interest in it this time, if the Bourne End team decides to start Taz." She shivered a little, but it could have been because of the bite of the wind. "Perhaps Sophie and I can be of some comfort to each other. I mean, while you men are buried under the bonnets of your cars, talking technicalities."

He hesitated, then he said, "Have you reconciled yourself to Taz's driving?"

In the pale silver light of the late afternoon she looked suddenly old. "There's not much else I can do, is there?" she said, and her voice trembled as she shivered again.

He had never thought of it before, but it struck him now that there was sadness as well as humour in his mother's face. Perhaps it was in every woman's, in Sophie's, too, and he had never been aware of it.

"Give Sophie my love. I'm looking forward to seeing her again."

He drove up to London through the remnants of a day as depressing as the cold, tattered sky in the west behind him. People had chosen today to present him with their faith; but none of them had thought to ask him if he was worthy of it. It was as if he had been betrayed by someone else's trust in him.

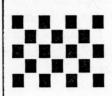

16

In the middle of April Bartell, Ed Carlin and another tire engineer, Bill Sitkin, arrived from the States with the new racing tires. There was no time for Ham to test them at Silverstone; and in any case a test of them now would have achieved little. The Mille Miglia was less than a fortnight away and if the tires did still have faults there would be no time to remedy them.

Ed Carlin took Ham aside when Ham went up to the Dorchester to see them. "I think they're okay, Ham. I had to work hard on the Old Man—he's a stubborn son of a bitch, if ever there was one—and I had to put ideas to him so he'd think they were his. I guess we could have made a straight racing tire, just like some of those you got ahold of for us. But that would have got us nothing. We had to put Joe's ideas into them, too. The nonskid tread—and I'll give him this, that is good, he's really got something there—and what the rest of us reckon is its best selling point, the amount of life in it. Joe's all for selling the nonskid tread, and that may be a good thing in this country. But the average American driver wants a tire that'll last as long as his automobile. I don't know that our tire will last that long, but we figure it will last twice as long as the average tire on the market now. Anyhow, what you want is a tire that'll last long enough to get you round the Mille Miglia. I think that's what we're giving you, Ham. I hope so, anyway."

"So do I," said Ham. "And thanks."

Ham and Carlin rejoined the others. Bartell looked up as they came in. He was holding Sophie's hand. "Funny how a ring on a woman's finger makes her look different. I should abuse you, Ham, for taking her away from me, just after I've found her again. But I can't. I can see how happy she is. And that's what I want most of all. For her to be happy. Right after you've won the Mille Miglia, we'll have the biggest damned wedding Brescia has ever seen."

Ham looked at Sophie, but almost deliberately she had turned away to speak to Sitkin. She had said no more about his driving in the Mille Miglia; the race was just no longer mentioned between them. They had gone through the motions of love for the past fortnight, but the engagement ring on her finger had been almost the only reminder that in a month or two they were to be married. Love hadn't even become habit for them; it was more like a distraction. Once they had gone to a cinema and there had been a newsreel of Castelotti winning the Turin Grand Prix. When Ham had looked sideways at Sophie to see how she was taking it, she was sitting with her head bent, her eyes closed, and her hands over her ears to shut out the whine and roar of the cars on the screen. When Ham and Janet had gone north to Oulton Park in Cheshire to see Taz drive for the Bourne End team in the British Empire Trophy, Sophie had pleaded a cold and had stayed in London that weekend. Taz had won the race and Sophie had phoned on the Sunday morning to congratulate him. But that afternoon, when Ham drove up to South Kensington to see her, she made a perfunctory remark about Taz's win and then, by a quick change of the subject, let him know that she wanted no more talk about motor racing.

Bartell, Carlin and Sitkin went up to Chalfont St. Giles to see the Wizard, and almost overwhelmed Richie with their enthusiasm for it. Even Bartell, who up to now had looked on it only as a vehicle to carry his tires, walked round and round it like a man seeing a car for the first time in his life.

"Say, this is really something! To look at you, Richie, nobody would have thought you had it in you to design something as pretty as this."

"Thanks," said Richie. "Looking at you for the first time, I wasn't impressed, either."

"You know," said Bartell, still admiring the car, "I might come in with you as a partner if you go into production on this. I told you once, I don't like to back failures. But I don't think this thing is going to be a failure."

Richie looked at Ham, then back at Bartell. "We'll talk about it after the race, Joe. I could do with a partner or two."

The new transporter had arrived, a giant closed van painted British racing green like the two Wizards. Richie would have liked a workshop van, too, but he had been afraid to ask Bartell for the money for it. But he had his contacts in Brescia and he had already written ahead and been promised the use of a small garage and its facilities on the outskirts of the town. He knew that, as a car manufacturer, he was still on the beggar level and he had to take what he could get. He was grateful that they had the new transporter, instead of having to ship the cars out to Italy in the back of the old Leyland or, worst of all, drive them out there. Plenty of drivers did drive their cars to Brescia for the Mille Miglia, but Richie was superstitious about driving a car a long distance over public roads before it had to race. Somehow it always seemed that something went wrong: a French farmer would barge out of a side road and put you into a ditch, or you'd have a blowout while cruising down Route Nationale 6 and finish up wrapped round the base of a poplar tree.

Richie, Charlie and George left two days later for Brescia. When the big transporter pulled out from the garage at Chalfont to drive down and stay overnight at Dover before catching the ferry for Boulogne, the drinkers came out of the Merlin's Cave and toasted its departure. It had begun to drizzle and Richie stood on the running-board of the transporter and thanked the drinkers for their good wishes, said he was bloody glad to be leaving the bloody English climate, and he would back with the Mille Miglia prize under his belt. Then he drove off to a mixture of cheers, laughs and good-natured boos. Three days later Ham flew out with Bartell, Carlin and Sitkin. The women, Sophie, Janet and Kitty Launder, were not flying out till the following Monday.

Taz had already gone. The Bourne End team had taken its cars to the Monza circuit north of Milan for some development tests before going on to Brescia. After his win at Oulton Park there had been talk that Taz might replace one of the other drivers in the Mille Miglia. It was a promotion at which Janet felt no joy. She had gone to Mass and, for the first time in her life, had prayed that one of her sons would not even be able to start.

Just before Ham left, Brigadier Allday drove over from Iver. "I've come to wish you luck, Hamilton. I hope I don't have to do it too many more times. A career that depends upon luck is not one that I should care to pursue myself."

"Thanks, Grandfather." Ham knew what an effort it had been for his grandfather to come over here and offer his best wishes; he looked with sudden affection on the tall old man whose outlook was frozen by inheritance. "Maybe this time next year I'll be a respectable businessman."

"If you have to drive in this race, I'm glad to see you're driving a British car. When you were driving for that Italian firm a few years back, I was ashamed to think I was related to you. I believe you drove an Italian car at that place in Florida recently?"

"Yes," said Ham. "And it was owned by an American."

Brigadier Allday managed not to shudder. "Still, there was some compensation in the fact that your brother won the British Empire Trophy in a British car. Well, good luck, Hamilton. If you can't win, be a sporting loser."

He got into the Rover, sitting stiff and straight behind the wheel as if mounted on a charger, and drove down the drive and out the gate. As the car went up the road Ham was sure that its radio was playing "Land of Hope and Glory." Brigadier Allday was a man of many virtues, but history had left him behind and he was not aware of it.

Ham and the others arrived in Brescia to a burst of beautiful weather. Swallows came north against a sky so bright that they were reduced to a thin black silhouette; cypresses threw shadows as dark and sharp as themselves on the glaring earth. It was not really hot, but after the cold drizzle of England it was almost like a heat wave. Richie, when he drove into Milan to meet them in a rented Fiat 1100, was wearing a loud checked shirt and a smile that was almost splitting his face apart.

"This is the climate. These bloody Italians know where to live."

"Another goddam kiddy car," said Bartell, folding his length into the Fiat.

"Stop laughing, Joe," Richie said. "How are you gunna sound if you come into partnership with me in the Wizard?"

"I'll never ride in the goddam things," said Bartell. "I like comfort. That's what cars are for." He looked out at

Sitkin. "There isn't going to be room in here for you, Bill. You look after our luggage and we'll send someone in to pick you up."

Sitkin smiled. "Sure, chief. What'll you send, a kiddy car or something comfortable? Just don't send in one of those little motorbikes I seen around here. I gotta have four wheels under me."

Bartell, Carlin and Sitkin, and the women when they were due, were booked in at a hotel in the centre of town. But Richie had booked himself and Ham into a small *pensione* just outside the town. Charlie and George had brought stretchers and were sleeping in the transporter.

"I thought it better if we stayed out of town," Richie said as he drove Ham out to the *pensione*. "We'll want some sleep the last few nights, and you don't get it right in town. This old codger, Lupi, knew your old man."

Giulio Lupi was a barrel of a man who reeked of wine, garlic and *bonhomie*. His teeth flashed like a sabre beneath the black scabbard of his huge moustache; he shouted aloud when he learned that Ham spoke Italian.

"I can talk to you! This little tub—" A fat hand spread like a starfish in the sun as he gestured at Richie, who smiled modestly, thinking he was being praised. "All he can say is *buon giorno*. It is a start, but it becomes monotonous. So you are the son of Rafferty, eh? What a driver! Only the Mantuan could be sure of beating him. Oh, we shall talk, we shall talk!"

Charlie and George came out late in the afternoon and had supper with them. "These Eyetalian birds," said George, rolling his eyes as a couple of girls, proud-bosomed and swing-hipped, went by. "Aw'll never be happy in Chalfont again. I got to know one, she comes around to the garage. All she can say is *si, si,* but be enough. Crikey, this's got Southend beaten a mile!"

188

Taz arrived just as they were finishing supper. He came into the dining-room and, when Ham introduced him to Lupi, was embraced with a bellow. "Two of them! Two sons of Rafferty, here in my house!"

"What's it all about?" Taz asked, after Lupi had gone off singing. His Italian was of the tourist variety and wasn't capable of keeping up with the volubility of Lupi.

"He knew Dad," Ham said. "We're chips off the old block."

"Have you been around the course yet?" Taz asked.

"We leave first thing tomorrow morning. About five-thirty, so we'll have a couple of clear hours on the road."

"I'm going round tomorrow, too."

"Does it look as if you'll be driving?"

Taz shook his head, disappointment plain on his face. "None of the other coves wants to move over to make room for Junior. You know what it's like in a racing team. Seniority counts all the time."

"In five or ten years' time, when you're the senior driver, you'll feel just the same." Ham had felt as Taz did now, when he had first started driving for a works team. He knew that in Grands Prix a lot of spectators, and even the junior drivers themselves, felt that there was some sort of injustice when they were pulled out of a race and their cars handed over to a senior driver who, for some reason or other, had lost his own car. But it was team discipline and it had its purpose. Senior drivers did not gain their seniority on their age and their length of service; they were the senior drivers because they were the best drivers. When a car was taken from a junior driver and handed over to a senior man, it was because the manager of the team considered the senior driver the better man. And since the team manager's job was to win races for his cars, not his drivers, he had no time to think about injustice or the bruises on a young driver's ego.

189

"I suppose so," Taz said. "But it's a bit frustrating. To come all this way and just sit around waiting for some other cove to break a leg or something."

"It will please Mum," Ham said quietly.

Taz nodded, not prepared to argue. "Well, I may see you tomorrow, somewhere round the course."

That night Ham went with Bartell to meet the Bartelli family. They welcomed him as if they had known him for years; there seemed to be hordes of them and he was clasped to countless bosoms and chests. They were the sort of family with whom a stranger could not long dodge adoption; even Bartell had taken off his coat and tie and looked as if he had lived in Brescia all his life. Wine glimmered rubily; cakes and fruit came, disappeared and came again; talk whirled and swooped in the room like a tireless flock of birds. All the talk was of the race, the race to come and all the races that had been. This was *la settimana di passione* for the Bresciani, and the Bartelli family had *passione* if nothing else. Papa Bartelli, thinner and more ungainly than Bartell and with an even sadder face, brought out a stack of yellowed newspapers that told the stories of the past Mille Miglia races. He pointed to a picture of Nuvolari, and silence dropped on the room for a moment: his like would never come again. He showed Ham pictures of Caracciola, Varzi, Arcangeli, Peri and Pat Rafferty. Then one of the younger Bartellis brought out today's copies of the Milan newspapers. Ham was featured; L'Aquila was back. And with the Italians' sense of both the romantic and the morbid, all the stories said that if an Italian couldn't win the race, it would be fitting and popular if L'Aquila won the race that had killed his father.

Ham left early and went back to the *pensione* and to bed. At five o'clock Richie woke him. "Righto, sport. We're going for a drive around Italy."

It was Sunday and people were already on their way to

early Mass. The sun had just come up over the mountains to the east and the shadows on the steep slopes had begun to retreat before the bright lava of its rays. A file of nuns walked along the road, their white faces looking for a moment like mute appeals in the black prison windows of their cowls; it took a second look to see that what one took for despair was peace. Cars were already on the roads, raising an incense of dust; the nuns turned aside and went in through the faded, dusty doorway of a church. People were up and about, as if no one in Brescia slept in Mille Miglia week; two groups met in the middle of a piazza in a violent clash of handshakes. A tinkling cart pulled by a sleepy donkey went past; a man leaned out and offered Ham and Richie ice cream for breakfast. A swish of golden swallows swept through a band of sunlight coming between two houses; two *carabinieri* got up from a darkened doorway, yawned and headed for the *stazione* to sign off. They saluted Ham and Richie as they went past and one stopped for a moment and patted the green shell of the Wizard.

"*Bella macchina.*" He stood for a moment looking at it, dreaming; then he heaved a sigh, smiled to himself, shook his head and turned and followed his companion.

Ham and Richie were using the spare car today. The new Bartell tires had been fitted, and the car had been prepared and checked the night before. Richie had equipped himself with a thick notebook and two fountain pens, an 8 m.m. cine camera and a dozen rolls of film.

"I'm leaving nothing to chance," he had told Bartell when the latter had enquired the reason for the notebook and camera. "I saw how the Mercedes team prepared for this race the first time they came down here after the war. Kling used over a thousand quids' worth of petrol just in practice. We can't afford that sorta thoroughness, but we'll get some sorta system. We'll get the films printed in Milan as soon as we get back, and we'll run 'em off as many times as Ham needs 'em to memorise whatever is on 'em. Blind corners, bridges, humps in the road. And the day of the race I expect to have the whole of the route typed out on rollers from notes I'll make in this notebook."

Ham and Richie got away a little after five-thirty. The roads had not been cleared for practice; the racing drivers had to take their chances today with the ordinary drivers, and vice versa. There were just over six hundred entrants for this year's Mille Miglia and it seemed that most of them had chosen today to make themselves familiar with the course. It also seemed that half the wheeled population of Italy had also decided to come out today for a jaunt on the Mille Miglia route. Several times Ham was challenged by middle-aged sports in tiny Fiat 600's; and every Vespa and Lambretta they passed was looking for a race. Beyond Ancona the driver of an ancient bus hogged the road ahead of them at fifty miles an hour, daring them to try to pass him. At last Ham slipped the Wizard through on a corner, grazing the side of the bus as he did so. The bus driver blared a clarion note on his horn and waved to them as they sped away; he had led a Mille Miglia competitor for five miles and he had had his moment of glory. When Richie looked back, the bus driver was turning the bus round to go back and deliver those passengers who had been overcarried.

The Italians, police and public alike, had an outlook all their own toward motor racing and the men who indulged in it. The roads had the usual Sunday traffic on them, but no one resented the drivers who came blazing down the middle of the road, blaring their horns and demanding right of way. Ham flicked the Wizard through the traffic at a speed that would have had him arrested in England or America; the Italians made way for him and cheered him on his way. He went into a village at eighty miles an hour; a policeman held up traffic coming out of a side street and saluted Ham as he went by. At seventy miles an hour the car was squeezed between two donkey-drawn carts; a glittering sea of cyclists opened before it and it went through with hardly a touch of the foot on the brake; it dropped to a crawl past a funeral but was hurriedly waved on by the undertaker.

Ham stopped the car several times, reversed it and went back to repeat a corner that looked particularly difficult or dangerous. One was a blind corner in a village; he made six attempts at it before he was satisfied at the line and the maximum speed at which he could take it. The whole village turned out to watch the performance, all standing suicidally close to the corner as Ham tore into it. When he was finally satisfied with what he could do on the corner and was on his way again, the villagers raced down the street after them cheering and waving. Then they turned round and raced back up the street again to the corner. Another car had arrived and was making its experiments.

"I love 'em!" Richie shouted. "Stone the crows, they know how to enjoy themselves!"

They stayed the night in Rome. While Richie remained at the hotel and tried to get some order into the notes he had taken, Ham went down to the Via Sistina to buy a present for Sophie. He walked through the soft Roman evening, seeing the couples strolling arm-in-arm in their own tiny worlds, and wished Sophie were here with him. He was tired and, after all this time, his leg had begun to ache again; it was a long time since he had driven so far in the one day. Yet next Sunday he would have to drive twice this distance and at considerably greater speed; by this time next Sunday evening his leg might be just a limb of fire and he would be wishing he had been driving a car that had no clutch. Only then did he realize that today was Sunday and that the shops were shut. He wandered on, trying to walk the stiffness out of his legs, but the lovers in the purple dusk, the silver weeping of

193

the fountains, only depressed him and made him miss Sophie more, and finally he turned round and went back to the hotel.

Richie was already in bed. "I had them send some food up. Cold *pizza* and some melted *geleti*. Very appetising."

"What do you expect, eating at this hour?" Ham said, but he was too tired to wait and go down to the dining-room. He nibbled at the *pizza*, swallowed two mouthfuls of the melted ice cream and ate a banana Richie had bought during the day. Then he undressed and fell into bed.

"How did the car feel today?" Richie said.

"Fine." The car had felt better than he did right now.

"What about the tires?"

Ham shrugged. "They were all right. But today was no test. I didn't touch over ninety-five all the way and most of the time I was doing only half-speed through the corners."

"How many more times do you reckon we'll need to go round?"

"At least once more, maybe twice. This is probably the toughest course in the whole of Europe. It's the one I know the least. I'd like a couple of weeks of just touring round it."

Richie was silent for a while. The room was in darkness, but the glow of a neon sign in the street outside flared and died on the walls. Ham, with his eyes half-shut in weariness, still feeling the sway and twist of the car beneath him, his brain seeming to lean sideways in his skull as he still spun and slid round corners and curves, was aware of the red glow beyond his lids like a throbbing pulse.

Then Richie said, "Bartell asked me again yesterday about coming in with me as partner. I put him off till we get back. I wanted your answer first."

Ham lay watching the red pulse beyond his half-opened lids. He was suddenly so tired that there was now a heavy ball of pain at the base of his spine: it was as if he were constipated with weariness. He was in no condition to give answers to anything; and yet Richie was, in a way, asking him to decide which way the rest of his life would go. It seemed that all at once his life had begun to gather pace; the end of his career, the end of something was racing toward him like the blind corners he had been confronted with all day. He shut his eyes tight, shutting out the pulse on the walls, and there in the darkness of his lids he saw the clear image of Sophie.

"You'd better forget about me," he said. "Take Joe in as your partner."

In the darkness he sensed Richie's disappointment, as clearly as on that night long ago he had sensed his mother's tears in the room in the hotel in Spa. But there was nothing he could do about it.

Though they had been to no altar, he was already wedded to Sophie.

17

Next morning Richie said nothing of the discussion of the previous night. But he looked tired, as if he hadn't slept well, and he was quiet. They left Rome at daybreak and headed north for Florence. Now there was weekday traffic on the roads; they had to blast their way past trucks. They went through the same routine again of stopping and going into a corner three or four times, getting to know its minimum margin of safety. Richie now had pages and pages of notes and, trying to write while they were speeding along, had broken the nibs of both fountain pens and had had to buy two more. He had already shot off ten reels of film and was beginning to wonder if he would need to buy more before they got back to Brescia.

They went through Florence, over the brown wound of the Arno and between the old buildings huddled tightly together as if afraid of the hills around them, and on toward the mountains. They went up the Futa Pass, Ham working hard on the wheel all the way as he pulled the car round the curves of the steep, winding road. Several times he looked at Richie and nodded appreciatively. This was the first opportunity they had had to test the car on actual mountain runs, and both yesterday and today it had gone well. If the tires held in the race, then it looked as if everything would depend only on the driver.

Then on the Raticosa Pass, Ham began to slow. "What's the matter?" Richie said and looked anxiously at the dials on the instrument panel. "She missing?"

Ham shook his head. "I'm looking for something."

Then just beyond a sharp curve, where the road seemed no more than an impertinent foolhardy slash in the steep fall of the mountain, he brought the Wizard to a halt. He got out and walked slowly back along the road and stood looking at something. Richie watched him for a moment, then he, too, got out of the car and walked back. They stood looking at the large whitewashed stone, like a headstone, dusty now but with its lettering still readable: Patrick Rafferty, 1899-1947. The final line was even simpler: *Un Campione.*

"A champion," Ham said.

"Someone thought a lot of him," Richie said quietly. "Who put that there?"

"One of the Italian drivers came back here and set it up. He was a nobody, all he ever drove in was the Mille Miglia, but his idols were Nuvolari and Dad. He wrote and told me what he had done. I never even met him to thank him. He was killed himself in the '48 Mille Miglia. And I don't even know where, so I could do the same for him."

A petrol wagon came labouring up the hill and went slowly past, its driver leaning out to wave and shout to them: everyone was their friend. The wagon went on, and silence came down the mountainside again like an invisible cloud.

197

Below them the slope was so steep that, from where they stood, the road seemed to be supported on its outer edge only by air. Far below, the valley lay in its own silence, its stone farmhouses looking like some long-forgotten ruins under their moss of grapevines. On the opposite side of the narrow valley terraces ringed the slopes, binding the flanks of the mountain. A hawk planed slowly down through the blue air, its silent flight only seeming to accentuate the silence of this high place.

Then they heard the car coming down the pass. A moment later the green Cooper-Bristol came slowly round the corner. It pulled up behind the Wizard and Taz got out. His passenger got out, also, but when he saw Ham and Richie he stayed beside the car. Taz had evidently told him why he was pulling up and, with an Englishman's inclination not to intrude on other people's private grief and memories, he now turned away and made a pretence of admiring the scenery. An Italian, Richie knew, would have come along to share the moment of grief and memory. On this occasion Richie felt that the Englishman's attitude was the better, and for a moment he wondered if he, too, should turn and walk away.

But then Taz had joined them. He stood looking at the simple memorial, then he said, "Mother might like to see this."

"She would," Ham said. "But I've never suggested bringing her here. It wouldn't do her any good. She'd only start again going through every little detail of how Dad was killed."

"Where did he go off?" Taz said. "Right here?"

"No," Ham said, and after so many years his memory was clear and correct. In his mind he came round the corner again, holding the old Aston-Martin on the road, and there was his father's car already going into its skid. The sweat broke on him, as it had then, and he turned away, looking down the road. "It was down there about another thirty or forty yards. He was trying not to go over the edge—" He

198

stopped again; the sweat was running on him now. He shut his eyes, but that was no help: the memory was only clearer. He opened them again, feeling the sweat and the pain and the fear that cloaked him, that he was sure he could no longer hide from his brother and Richie. I'm finished, he thought: I shan't even be able to drive in this race. He had made his pilgrimage, and he had been betrayed.

"We better be getting on," Richie said, as two more cars came down the pass and swung round the corner. He could see that Ham had been affected by the memory of what had occurred at this spot. But he hadn't recognised any fear.

Ham, still in the past, looked up and saw what appeared to be the black angel coming down from the mountain above them. He shut his eyes, more afraid than he had ever been, then opened them. The black angel materialised into an old man in a cape herding goats down a path so precipitous that at first it wasn't discernible. Somewhere a bird sang for a moment, stopping sharply: birdsong is not common in Italy, and perhaps this bird had remembered that: or perhaps its song had been stopped by death, by the plunge of a hawk or a thrown stone. Here on the mountain, with the dark rocks and the pungent wreaths of thyme and the utter silence, death was part of the landscape.

"Ham, we better be getting on," Richie repeated; and Ham shut his mind against the past.

"One feels one should do something," Taz said in a voice as cold and formal as a black-edged card; he was a stranger to death and its presence. "Flowers or something."

"Do nothing!" Ham's voice was almost savage; but if there was fury in him, he didn't understand it. "He didn't die to be remembered with flowers or services or words. If he's allowed any memories at all wherever he is, this would be one he'd want to forget. One thing he always hated was to lose. And, by Christ, he lost here!"

He turned and walked quickly away, nodding curtly at

Taz's passenger as he passed him but saying nothing, and got into the Wizard. As he sat down behind the wheel he could feel himself trembling and there were tears behind his eyes. What hurt was that he knew they were as much for himself as for his father.

Richie came along, got into the car, and they drove on. Richie said nothing, going back to his note taking and filming as if there had been no interruption, and in that same strained and unhappy silence they drove on to Bologna. For now Richie had recognised the fear, and wished that he had turned away and gone to join Taz's passenger in admiring the scenery.

At Bologna Richie said, "Let's stop for a beer."

They went into the dark cave of a small *trattoria* where old men sat over glasses of wine, their years pulled tight about them and their eyes already blank with the look of the grave. They looked up as the two foreigners in their dirty overalls came in through the beaded curtain, but these old men cared nothing for the Mille Miglia and were beyond the influence of heroes. They might have risen for d'Annunzio, but for no others.

Richie ordered beers and they sat down at a table by a narrow window. Richie said nothing till he had drunk half his beer. "Ham, would you rather call this race off?" he said at last.

Ham looked up, startled for the moment; then he put down his glass and looked out the window. On the walls of a house opposite there were the faded dusty remnants of a whitewashed sign: *Viva Coppi!* Fausto Coppi was a hero, the greatest road cyclist Italy had ever produced: every Italian urchin who straddled a bicycle wanted to grow up to be like Fausto Coppi: it was a dream that was more possible than that of being like Tazio Nuvolari, if only because bicycles were cheaper and easier to come by than racing cars.

200

Every year the whitewash was brought out and the signs went up all over Italy, silent cheers and humble monuments to a living legend: *Viva Coppi!* I wonder if Coppi is ever afraid, Ham wondered, coming down those mountain roads at sixty miles an hour? At least I have the solidity and protection of a car; all he has are his flimsy bike and his trust in his own skill. Maybe that is enough, if you haven't seen your father killed and haven't already gone once yourself to stare at death.

"It's as apparent as that, is it?"

"Look, sport, I'm not criticising you." Richie waved a fly away from his beer; he didn't look at Ham but at the old men huddled over their game of draughts. "I know what it's like. I've been scared myself. I've never told anyone this before, but I was glad the Jerries took me prisoner and shoved me into prison camp after I'd washed that time in Holland. I didn't want to fly a kite again, ever. I was just glad I didn't have to go back to England and look for excuses to be grounded. I've never been in a plane since, not even as a passenger. I'm telling you this because I want you to know that I understand how it can be."

"Thanks, Richie." Richie had offered him the chance of escape, but he knew he couldn't take it. He was in debt to Richie, even if only for his understanding, and he couldn't back out now. "I'll be all right when it comes to the race."

"You didn't mind me mentioning this?" Richie said, knowing that he and Ham had gone as deep as friendship could go, afraid that he might have gone too far. There was a point in every man's secret life beyond which even friendship couldn't go, where a man was alone with himself and no one else was trusted. Richie had never discovered that point in his own life, but he knew it existed. For a long time he had thought that it had been the point where someone would learn of his fear of planes and the effect his crash had had on him, but that point had just now been reached and passed and he felt better for it. "I don't want you to think I'm a bastard who can't mind his own business—"

"It's all right," Ham said and put his hand on Richie's shoulder as he stood up. "Sport."

Richie grinned, relieved and suddenly warm with affection. "Want another grog?"

"No, let's go."

They drove on to Brescia. The town seemed to have filled up even since their departure yesterday morning. The streets were thick with cars and trucks; in the dark, curdled streams of traffic you could hear the occasional angry rumble of a tuned-up sports car with open exhaust. Bunting had flowered overnight on the houses; flags made a carnival stall of a sober bank. Ham drove the dusty, travel-stained Wizard through the press of traffic and out along the road to Iseo, where the garage Richie had rented was situated. When they reached there, George Hayes came running out of the garage to meet them.

"Bad news," he blurted, but before they could ask him to explain, Bartell and the others came out of the garage.

"About goddam time," Bartell snapped at Richie. "I was going to wire you at Rome to fly back here, only they told me you'd have already left."

Richie climbed stiffly out of the car. "What's the matter?"

"The goddam race authorities—"

"Not the race authorities, Joe," Carlin said. "Don't blame them. It's the F.I.A."

The F.I.A. was the Fédération Internationale de l'Automobile, the controlling body for all such international motor events as this. Ham looked at Bartell, wondering what rules they had violated.

"They won't pass my tires," Bartell said and had to stop for a moment to swallow the spittle of anger that threatened to choke him. "They say they have never been tested in a race, they've never been raced at speeds they're likely to get in this race, and they reckon—" He stopped, speechless.

"They reckon," Ed Carlin finished for him, speaking quietly and without any show of anger, "it exposes you two to needless danger. They want us to switch over to proven tires."

"Oh, that's bloody ridiculous!" Richie said.

"That's what I told 'em," Bartell said, finding his voice again. "But I got nowhere. I was talking to some goddam Frenchman and he kept apologising all the time for not speaking good English. Who cares what he talks? That's why I wanted you back here."

"I can't speak French," Richie said.

"No, but you know more about this sort of thing than I do. You've been in the game long enough. There must be some way out of this!"

Richie sat on the side of the car, pulling at his lip. His face was sunburned and wind-burned brick red below the line where his cap had been; he looked almost comical with his pale bald head above his fat red face. A clown, but a worried clown. "This'll put the kybosh on the whole thing if they stick to their decision. You only see the one bloke?"

"There isn't anyone else to see," Bartell said. "So far he's the senior man here from this goddam F.I.A."

"Vici had this trouble when they first signed with Aston-Martin," Richie said. "The F.I.A. wouldn't let them use their tires till they had been proved in a race. It was a cow of a situation for a while, then Vici got smart. They asked how to race them? The F.I.A. had a conference on that and couldn't come up with any answer. So they gave Vici the go-ahead."

"Well, for Pete's sake, come on!" Bartell said. "Let's go see this guy and ask him the same question. I don't know why I didn't think of it myself!"

"You might have, Joe," said Carlin, "if you hadn't been so all-fired hot-tempered."

Richie turned his films over to Charlie. "Righto, Charlie, you know where these have to go in Milan. Tell the bloke we want 'em tonight if possible, but stay with him till he's finished 'em. We wanna run 'em off tomorrow. Ham and I are going around again on Wednesday." He looked at Bartell. "My wife and the other women arrive? Kitty has to type out these notes for me."

"They've arrived," Bartell said impatiently. "Come on, will you? What are you standing around for?"

"I'll take the notes in," Ham said. "Best of luck with the goddam F.I.A., sport."

"I'll just give him the facts," Richie said with a wink, but he still looked worried.

He went off with Bartell and Carlin to see the F.I.A. official. Charlie left for Milan in the second Fiat they had hired, and George wheeled the Wizard away to wash it down and prepare it for its second journey round the Mille Miglia route the day after tomorrow. Bill Sitkin offered Ham a lift into Brescia in the second of the Alfa-Romeos that Bartell had also hired.

"How'd the tires go?" Sitkin was a small man, stiff-backed as a tire lever and with a flat, mid-Western accent. He wore steel-rimmed spectacles and a wide-brimmed hat that made him look like a scholarly schoolboy playing at cowboys.

"It was no real test. They were all right, I suppose."

"You haven't much confidence in them, have you?" Sitkin said, driving the car with careful concentration, as if he had never been on a crowded road before. A bus came bustling down the middle of the road, its horn blaring for right of way, but Sitkin held his line and at the last moment the bus gave way and went past with a whirl of dust and a shout of abuse from the driver.

"I've had them blow out under me," Ham said. "Have you?"

Sitkin took his eyes from the road and smiled; it was a young smile and completely altered the set of his face. "You've got me there, Mr. Rafferty. I've never driven a car fast enough to blow a tire. Excuse me for sounding critical."

"It's all right," Ham said, warming to the little man. "Have you decided yet where to set up supply points in case we need them?"

"Pescara, Rome and Florence, at the control points. We are hoping that you'll get beyond Ravenna without meeting trouble. I think the idea is to have young Hayes at Pescara, I'll be at Rome with Ed Carlin and two mechanics we're hiring, and Charlie Carter will be in Florence. If all goes well we'll have a tire change only at Rome." He smiled again. "If our tires are as good as we think they are, you shouldn't need to change them even there."

Ham delivered the notebook to Kitty Launder, then went along to his mother's room in the hotel. Sophie was there, too, looking out of the window down into the Piazza Vittoria where the evening strollers had begun to circulate. Ham kissed them both, left them to have a bath and change into the clean clothes he had brought with him, and then took them both downstairs to the bar. The bar was crowded, but the headwaiter, recognising Ham, soon found them a table. Being a hero had its compensations.

"There's a hitch over the tires?" Janet said.

"Richie will iron it out. I hope so, for his sake."

"What happens if he doesn't iron it out?" Sophie said. "Does that mean you can't race?"

"Not necessarily," Ham said and saw the small hope that had been in her face suddenly die. "We can always race on other tires. But it will be a blow to your father. And Richie feels he has some debt to him. I don't think he'd be too happy racing on someone else's tires, not after your father has staked him the way he has."

205

"Dad can afford the money," Sophie said. "It's not as if it has all gone down the drain."

"I don't think that's the point," Ham said, trying not to argue with her, yet trying to make her understand that, having come this far, money now meant nothing to any of them in the venture. It had now become something more, a matter of pride and faith, a gamble on their genius and skill and, if you wanted to call it that way, his and Richie's courage during the actual race. Yet he knew that, when Bartell had first told them of the F.I.A. ban, there must have been a spark of hope showing in his own face; he remembered that he had turned away from Richie, and it must have been an involuntary hiding of the treachery that he harboured. But he could not tell her that. "Your father—and Richie—have put more than money into this thing."

"I know what you mean," said Janet, trying to help her son and yet recognising the oblique appeal that Sophie was making to him, recognising it and wishing she could help the girl, too, because her own inclinations were an echo of Sophie's. "Your father tried to explain it to me once about Ettore Bugatti."

Ham doubted that Richie or Bartell was in the class of Bugatti, but he was grateful for his mother's assistance. He sat hemmed in by the hum of the crowd about him. A radio was playing: a girl was singing "St. Louis Blues" in Italian: sadness was world-wide. At the next table six young men were arguing the merits of the Ferrari and the Maserati; none of them could have bought even a Fiat 600. Voluptuous Italian film stars smiled down from a row of photos hung behind the bar; beneath them a huge, flabby barman walked his beat like a guardian eunuch. Outside in the square a red car went past, its engine snarling, and the bar was hushed for a moment as everyone turned to look out through the big windows. One of the young men at the next table stood up and turned, his hand held out almost as if in appeal, a look of something akin to agony on his thin, handsome face. The Devil could have bought his soul at that moment for a racing car.

Ham said, speaking slowly, "You've done historical research, Sophie. You must have come across stories of men who got so far into things that there was no way back for them. I don't know his story too well, but Columbus must have been a man like that. If he'd turned back, who knows what America might be today?"

"There would still have been America," Sophie said quietly. "It was just one of those countries that had to be. Whether Columbus discovered it or not, it was going to be. It didn't grow out of one man."

"Maybe I put that wrongly. What I meant was, if Columbus had turned back, would others have gone on across the Atlantic? I suppose they would have," he conceded, for he had learned not to doubt the vision and spirit of adventure in men. "But someone had to be first. And it was Columbus. Or was it that other one, Amerigo—"

"Vespucci," said Sophie. "There was also Leif Ericson."

"Whoever it was, Columbus, Vespucci, Ericson, whoever got there first, there must have been dozens of others, maybe hundreds, who had had the same dream but never got started or else backed down because—well, because it didn't mean enough for them to go on." He had never had to plead for someone else before; he could plead for them better than he could plead for himself. "I'm not saying your father and Richie are brothers to Columbus. But they've started on a voyage, Sophie. They started on it the day they shook hands in the shed at Chalfont. If they turned back now, it would be more than just money down the drain. They'd be pulling the plug out of their lives. You can't measure what they've put into this in dollars and cents, pounds and pence. There's no currency for it, Sophie. It's just a man's life, the reason he works, the reason why the world has gone on rolling ever since man invented the first wheel."

He sat back, suddenly embarrassed by the words that had poured out of him; the Irish in him, the Pat Rafferty still alive in his skin and blood, had taken hold of him. Then he was aware that Sophie and his mother were looking at him not with amusement nor amazement, but with respect and, in Sophie's case at least, new understanding.

"There are some things in a man a woman can never touch," Janet said quietly. "Your father had it. I admired him for it and understood it. I was always sorry I could never share it, although God knows I tried." She stood up, looking at her watch. "I'd better go up and get a coat, in case it gets a little chilly. Taz will be calling for me soon. He's taking me out to dinner, to some place where he says I can slobber spaghetti all down my chin and not have people stare at me as they would back home. Good night, Ham. I'll see you at breakfast, Sophie." For a moment her hand rested on Sophie's shoulder, pressing it, then she turned and made her way through the crush of the bar, smiling at men as they made way for her, an Englishwoman whose dignity didn't freeze her charm.

When Janet had gone, Sophie said, "Is it going to be like that for me? Never being able to share completely with you whatever that feeling is?"

"I don't know," he said, listening to the sound of another car going past, softer and deeper this time, like the murmur in a tiger's throat. "It depends where we live. In New York, away from racing and everything that goes with it, I don't think you'll have to worry. I'll never have the feeling, just reading about it in the newspapers."

She was quiet for the rest of the evening. When he kissed her good night at the door of her room, it was almost as if they were back at the beginning of their relationship. She had become careful again.

Next morning Richie told him they had persuaded the F.I.A. man to reconsider his decision and now they were waiting on the arrival of other F.I.A. officials. "But it means that if the tires are passed, they'll have to be good and not let us down. Otherwise, they'll be barred for years."

"In the meantime we don't sit on our ass," said Bartell, who, now he was over his first hurdle, was impatient for the race to be run and his tires proved to the world. He was showing more nervous energy than any two of the other men, and his hearing aid hadn't been turned off since he had landed in Brescia. "We'll have a look at those movies Charlie brought back from Milan, and then you two can get on your way again tomorrow. Ed leaves for Rome tonight to get things fixed up down there. He'll stay there till next Sunday. How are the tires, George?"

George hesitated, indecision making his young face look even younger; he did not like having the onus of opinions thrown on him. "The tread had begun to loosen on one of the rear tires," he said. "Not much, but just a little."

"Let's look at it," Ed Carlin said and followed George to the back of the garage. He scrutinised the tire carefully, while the others watched him anxiously. At last he straightened up, puffing a little with the exertion of bending. "It's lifted, all right. But—"

"But nothing," Ham said abruptly. "That's the second bloody time that tread has lifted. Last time I nearly cracked my neck. What's the matter? Can't you fellers make a bloody tire that will stand up to some wear and tear?"

He was aware of Richie looking at him, but the words had spilled from him before he could control them. Then Carlin said, still speaking without raising his voice, "I can understand how you feel, Ham. But I think this tire is just one

209

that you might strike on any sort of make. Something had cut the tread, maybe you went over a broken bottle or something, and it had begun to lift back from there. That could happen to any sort of tire. Look for yourself."

Ham looked at the tire, then apologised. "I'm sorry. I guess I'm getting a bit on edge. It's always like this before a race, isn't it, Richie?"

He shouldn't have appealed to Richie, because Richie knew that it had not always been like this. But Richie said, "Too right. I'm a bundle of flutterguts myself. Let's have a look at those films. Maybe I can get a job with M-G-M."

They closed the doors of the garage, blocked up the windows and set up the projector Bartell had hired. Then they ran the films on a sheet stretched on the wall. They ran the reels through for the next hour. They came back again in the afternoon and ran them through again, and again that night. It was impossible to memorise the whole route of a thousand miles, but Ham and Richie now had a fair knowledge of the more dangerous parts of the course. It was as important for Richie to memorise the course as it was for Ham, for Richie would, for a good part of the journey, be nothing less than Ham's eyes.

Ham saw Sophie again that night, but left her early, since he and Richie were getting away again in the morning at five-thirty. Richie had come in with him to the hotel, and now he knocked on the door of Kitty Launder's room because he was depending on Richie for a lift back to the *pensione*.

Richie came to the door with his arm about Kitty. "Look at her sunburn, will you? She's beginning to appreciate a decent climate."

"We get sunburned in England," Kitty said, kissing the scar on his bald head; in her high heels she was a good two inches taller than Richie. "I remember once as a child I even got sunstroke."

"Must have been under a sun lamp," Richie said and slapped her rump. He kissed her. "Good night, love. If you're writing to the kids tomorrow, give 'em my love. Tell 'em to stay in outa the rain."

As they drove out of Brescia, past the garages and converted sheds where engines were being tested, past the whining and humming and growling and barking that sounded like a menagerie of savage animals, Richie said, "If we do win this race and things look like going all right for us, I think I might take her for a long holiday. Scandinavia, somewhere like that. They've got good beer up there. It hasn't been much of a life for her, me away every summer. And this past six months I've spent more time at the garage than I have at home. One night we had a barney and she threatened to divorce me. She wouldn't," he said, grinning ahead into the yellow glow of the headlights, fat, bald and as sure of his woman as any matinee idol, "but she'd have knocked my block off that night if she'd had something handy. I gotta make it up to her. She's been more patient than I had a right to ask her."

They left promptly at five-thirty next morning. They went faster this time; there was traffic on the road, but Ham knew something now of what lay ahead of him. Richie's notes had been typed out by Kitty and gummed together, so that they formed a long scroll mounted on rollers. He was using the notes now, giving Ham signals as they came to sections where Ham's length of vision was cut to no more than a rapidly decreasing number of yards. He was also adding to the notes as they sped along, his writing a jumbled, jagged scrawl between the lines of typing as his arm was jolted by the swaying, bumping motion of the car.

They stopped for an early lunch in a village halfway between Ancona and Pescara. They sat in the open, under a trellis strangled by a grapevine; beside the terrace an olive tree poked its arthritic arms toward them. While they ate,

211

other cars, easily identifiable by their open exhausts as Mille Miglia hopefuls, went roaring past. A Ferrari went by, and Richie stopped eating to listen to the fading crackle of its engine as it went racing on down out of sight, its sound lingering long after the dust it had disturbed had settled.

"That's music," he said, smiling to himself. "They can have all the other sounds they've invented. That's *my* music."

They stopped for only half an hour and then moved on again, intending to reach Siena and stay there for the night. On the long stretch down to Pescara Ham opened the car up a little, but still kept it under its maximum. There was a lot of normal everyday traffic on the road and though it was giving way to the practising Mille Miglia cars, you couldn't be sure that some driver might not turn right across the middle of the road in your path. They went through Pescara and headed for the mountains of Abruzzi.

They climbed swiftly, using the horn all the way as a warning on the bends. They went through Aquila, waving to a bunch of schoolchildren, and began the descent toward Rieti. It was quite hot now, especially in the cockpit of the car; above them the peaks had lost their sharpness in the haze of the sky. They went down through a series of fast bends, Ham taking the car wide when on the outside of the curve and hugging the corner when on the inside, blowing the horn all the time, making sure that he wasn't creating any danger for any driver coming up the mountain.

Then he came into a gentle S-bend that led into a sharp right-hand bend. He and Richie had stopped to look at this one on their previous trip round, and they had it marked for careful consideration. He felt Richie touch his sleeve, warning him of the sharpness of the right-hand bend, and he braked.

And the car began to slide. He felt it going from beneath him, no adhesion at all in any of the tires, and he worked frantically to keep the car on the road. But there was

212

nothing he could do; it was as if the road had turned to ice beneath them. With a shuddering crash and a tearing of metal, the car hit a low stone wall, swung back away from the wall, there was a moment of adhesion as the tires crossed the road again, then the car had gone through the retaining wall on the outside edge of the right-hand bend and was plunging down the slope. It hit a tree, swung broadside on, then rolled. Ham humped down in the cockpit, feeling Richie tucking himself in beside him; the car spun over them, obliterating the sky. Then there was another shuddering thump, a rending of metal, and the car had come to a halt, canted over at an extreme angle.

The horn was blowing loudly, like a long-drawn-out scream of pain. Ham, still dazed but instinctively afraid of fire, yelling to Richie to get out, tumbled out of the car. He rolled down the slope, clutching at bushes to stop himself, and finished up against a big rock. He lay there, stretched out as if crucified, staring down the steep slope that finished a hundred yards below in a boulder-strewn river bed. He said a prayer of thanks that the car had gone no further than it had. Then he got up on his knees, making sure he had broken no bones, and looked up the slope to see if Richie had yet got out of the car.

But Richie would never get out of the car again, not of his own volition. He was still humped in his seat, blood running from a cut on his cheek, one hand resting almost casually on the steering wheel. Somehow his helmet had been twisted off and had fallen outside the car; the scar on his bald head had turned almost white, the lizard gone from the rock. Before Ham touched him, he knew that Richie was dead, his neck broken in the single roll the car had made after striking the first tree.

The fat grease-stained left hand still clutched the scroll of notes, spotted with blood from the cut on his cheek. Ham saw the note: *Sharp right-hand corner, watch it;* and the

213

rest was a smear of blood. Ham leaned in and switched off the electric circuit, stopping the horn. In the sudden silence the car creaked and shuddered like a living thing, then it, too, had died and was silent.

A moment later a red flash went by on the road above, its tires squealing as the driver fought it through the bend, then it was accelerating as it went on down the road. The crackle of its engine died away down the mountainside, the music Richie would never hear again.

18

It was a large oil slick that had caused him to go off the road. A car or a truck, coming down the pass only minutes ahead of them, must have cracked its sump. The slick was long and broad, and Ham, drifting a little as he had braked to go round the right-hand bend, had slid all four wheels of the car across the treacherous surface. So that it was the cars, too, that had got Richie in the end; but a car he had never seen and one that might now be down in the village below, its driver unaware of the tragedy his vehicle had caused and cursing only because the cracked sump would delay him on his trip to Rome.

Ham had climbed back to the road and flagged down the next car to come down the pass. It had been a Triumph TR3 driven by a young Scot, with an older, dour Scot as passenger. The middle-aged man, who said his name was McKechnie, had got out of the TR3 and stayed with Ham while the driver had gone on down to Antrodoco, the village at the foot of the mountain. From there he had phoned through to Rieti, summoning a doctor and an ambulance. By this time a crowd had gathered, and there were cars and trucks parked dangerously on the steep slope of the pass. By the time the ambulance arrived, the road was black with people, and men had been posted farther up the pass to warn other cars as they came down. Ham, sitting with his back to one of the posts of the retaining wall, could hear a small group of women praying as they stared down at the wrecked car and the still shape under the old tarpaulin. It had been Mc-Kechnie and a passing truck driver who had lifted Richie's body from the car and covered it with the tarpaulin the driver had got from the truck. Ham, too sick and shocked even to stand, had sat with his back against the concrete post, not even looking at the two men as, gently but awkwardly, hampered by the steepness of the slope, they had lifted Richie's body from the car and brought it up onto the road.

When the ambulance had finally gone, McKechnie said, "Do you want us to send a message to anyone?"

There was no room for Ham in the TR3, and he had already been offered a lift to Rome by one of the Italian drivers of the various cars parked down the slope of the road. "I'll phone from Rome," he said. "I think it's better if I tell his wife, instead of a stranger."

"I don't envy you," said McKechnie, and he and the young Scot got into their car and drove off.

Ham took one last look down at the wrecked Wizard. He felt stronger now, and the shock had begun to wear off. On legs that were still unsteady he scrambled down to the car and looked it over: some of it would be salvageable but not much. He searched in the glove box for the few personal things he had brought with him; then he saw the blood-spattered scroll of notes on the floor of the cockpit. He brushed away the flies and reached in and picked it up. The sections of it wound round the rollers were clean and unstained; it was Richie's record of their journey and he had marked his death spot with his own blood. Ham went to throw it away, turned to hurl it far down the slope into the cold glitter of the river below; but it was almost as if he couldn't open his hand to let it go, and he stopped with his arm half-raised. Then abruptly, still with the scroll clutched tightly in his hand, he turned and climbed back up to the road. A few minutes later, stretched out but not relaxed in the back of a Lancia Aurelia, he was being carried on to Rome.

He phoned Kitty from Rome, chafing at the delay in getting the call through and yet in a way glad of it. He had had to call his mother in this way and tell her of his father's death; the fact that this was the second time he was to bring bad news over the phone made it no easier. When Kitty at last came to the phone she was laughing; behind her there was the sound of other laughter.

"Hello? They said it was Rome calling. Is that you, Richie? Ed Carlin has just been telling us one of his stories. Richie?"

"It's not Richie," Ham said, and then as gently as he could he told her the news. He heard her gasp, and the laughter behind her suddenly died.

There was silence on the line, and then the operator said, "Are you getting through?"

"Yes," Ham said.

Then Kitty's voice, light and hoarse, said, "What did you say?"

"The operator asked me if I was getting through. I— Kitty, is my mother there with you?" He had nothing else to say to Kitty Launder: for the moment words had no further meaning for them. There was silence again, then Janet came on the line. "Did she tell you the news, Mum?"

217

"Yes, son." Even in the distraction of the moment he remarked that she had never called him "son" before; she had now become old, and he wondered when it had happened. "Sophie has taken her up to her room. When are you coming back?"

"I'm catching the express in half an hour. Ask Charlie to come to Bologna and pick me up. And Mum—"

"Yes?"

"Don't worry. I got out of it all right."

"But you're still going to race?" But before he could answer, she had hung up. When he had slowly hung the receiver back on its hook, he knew that he had no answer. He hadn't given a thought to the race since the accident had occurred.

He caught the train to Bologna, riding slumped in one corner of the compartment. A fellow passenger, catching sight of the helmet and goggles he carried, tried to get into conversation with him, asking him if he was going to Brescia for the Mille Miglia, but Ham, curtly and a little rudely, shut the man up before he could get started. He turned away and stared out of the window at the brown countryside spinning backward past him. Italy had always been his mother's and father's favourite country. He wondered how his mother felt about it now.

He would have liked to talk to someone, but not to the man sitting in the corner opposite, not to a stranger. The ghost of Richie rode with him, and strangers couldn't talk about a ghost they had never met. He stared at the glass of the window, seeing his own ghost reflected there; then a shaft of sunlight struck across the glass and his own ghost was gone. He shut his eyes, to shut out the grief and fear mingled in him. He had become almost an intimate of death, but he still couldn't accept it.

Charlie met him at Bologna in the Fiat and they drove in a heavy, sad silence to Brescia. Charlie asked no questions

218

other than whether Richie had died instantly; he nodded his head when Ham said yes and seemed satisfied.

"His missus took it pretty badly at first. But when I left to come down here she was getting over it. Ham—" He turned his head stiffly to look at Ham; his big red face was closed up tight. "I don't know whether you're going to race next Sunday. But if you are, don't ask me to be your passenger. I— I'm not built for this sort of thing."

"Today, I couldn't even drive this little thing," Ham said, tapping the door of the Fiat. "I wouldn't ask anyone to risk his neck with me."

It was after midnight when they reached Brescia, but the town was still wide awake. Cars were still being tuned and tested; the night shook with jungle noises. Ham went straight to the hotel to see Kitty, but she had been given a sedative by a doctor and had gone to sleep. His mother and Sophie were sitting up, waiting for him, and so were Bartell and Ed Carlin. None of them asked him a leading question, they were all prepared to wait till he told them of the tragedy in his own time. He ate, the first food he had had since just before noon, and drank three cups of strong black coffee. He tasted none of the food or drink, but he knew he needed it.

Then he told them, broadly but not in detail, what had happened. At last Bartell said, "Was it the fault of the tires or something wrong with the car?"

"No," Ham said. "It was just that bloody oil slick."

"I'm glad of that," Bartell said slowly. "I wouldn't like to think Richie had died because of something faulty in my tires. I liked Richie. I'd give up making tires if I knew that one of mine killed him. I mean that."

"The tires were all right, Joe," Ham said. "If it did nothing else, the crash proved they were all right. We were smashed around enough to have blown every one of them. But they were all right."

219

"I'm glad of that," Bartell repeated, his fingers tapping the pocket where he carried his hearing-aid battery: he had not turned it off, even when there had been no one talking: it was as if now, all at once, he was afraid of silence.

Ham looked at Ed Carlin. "Are you going to Rome?"

"I was going tonight. But I decided to wait when—when you phoned with the news."

"What did the F.I.A. decide about the tires?"

"We can use them," said Carlin. "That is, if we still race."

Ham was aware of them all looking at him, not directly but in a way that he couldn't mistake; even Bartell, the millionaire, the man who paid others to butter him up, had left the decision to him. He felt suddenly constrained, knowing at last the limits of himself. He rose abruptly from the table, wanting to leave them, seeking someone else to make the decision for him. "I'm tired, worn out. Good night."

"I'll drive you out to the *pensione,*" Sophie said, rising and moving round to be near him, as if afraid of losing him; it was the first time she had spoken since she had kissed him as he had first come into the hotel.

They drove out to the *pensione* in one of the Alfa-Romeos. Lupi was still up, drinking at a table with two cronies; he knocked over his glass when Ham told him the news of Richie. He got up and went away deeper into the house, reeking of wine, his face collapsed behind the arrogance of his big black moustache. Sophie hadn't got out of the car, and Ham stood leaning with his arms on the door.

"Darling," she said, "I talked for quite a while tonight with Kitty and your mother. Or rather I listened." She sat for a moment, still listening, a young girl who had had opened up to her, the professional researcher, some of the life and reason for living of two older women, women who had lost their husbands, their major reasons for living. I always thought, from what Richie used to say, that it was Kitty who kept them there in England. But she'd have gone back to Australia with him. Gone anywhere with him. He was the one who wanted to stay in England. To be near cars and the racing. And she understood that. She said she'd had a quarrel with him about how much time he was spending at the garage, working on the car."

"He told me about that."

"She cried when she mentioned that. Said she hoped he hadn't died resenting her for begrudging him the time with the car. She said she knew how much it meant to him. She said she knew he didn't love her any the less, just because he had something else he loved, too." The car, its engine turned off, creaked as it cooled in the night air. A bat swept by overhead, dislodging a star; the star fell into the black mouth of a mountain to the east. She shuddered, as if reminded of some sin for which she had not yet been punished. "We'll live in England, if you like, darling. I'll even try to understand if you have to go on driving. I'll worry and I'll hate you every time you go out to race. But I'll try to understand."

Tenderness was there with love now; there was no need to touch her to know how her love was. "I love you," he said, with a gentleness he had never used before, even though he had loved her for months: love had been mouth against mouth and body in body and the part of him that hadn't been there when she was away from him, not loneliness nor sadness but an incompleteness: now for the first time love was words, a phrase that had become a cliché, a lie, a bribe, but which was still the best and only way of offering the heart.

Then a little later he stood in the middle of the road watching the cold red eye of the taillight lose itself beyond a bend in the road; they hadn't kissed good night, but neither had felt the need of it. They had begun the life together where the flesh was no longer a bond, only one of the many pleasures of being together.

In the morning Taz came to see him at the *pensione* while he was still having breakfast. "I heard this morning about Richie." His young face had suffered some sort of defeat; the searching look had gone from his eyes. "I went to see Mother. I tried to see Kitty, but I didn't have the guts. I wouldn't have known what to do if she had broken down while I was there."

"I have to go in and see her. She's leaving today, going home to the kids. Poor little devils."

"How will she get on? Financially, I mean."

"I don't know. You can't ask her at a time like this. She's probably not thinking even as far as tomorrow. But I shouldn't imagine Richie left her much. Everything he had has gone into the garage and the car."

"One car," said Taz. "It's not much."

"It's only the first car." Ham watched Lupi moving about in the sunlight outside, walking in the black barrel of his shadow; the gale had blown out of Lupi and he moved like a man stiff with arthritis. Ham knew how it was with some Italians: they felt everyone's death, even those of strangers. "There'll be others. Richie asked me to go in with him as his partner. I never gave him an answer. I wish he knew it now," he said and felt the presence of Richie: saw the lizard-like scar on the bald rock of his head, the merriness in the plump, boss-cheeked face, the characteristic hitch of the pants, heard the complaints in the gravelly voice about the weather, heard the request to have another grog. "I'll take over the car and garage. Bartell wanted to go in with Richie. If he's still agreeable, maybe he'll come in with me. Richie was never the sort to want a memorial, but I think there's nothing he'd like better than a couple of his cars passing each other on the Aylesbury road."

"Will you be able to sell them without a race to boost them?" Taz asked. "Back at the hotel Bartell was getting ready to cancel the entry. They're not expecting you to race."

222

"There's not much I can do," Ham said, trying not to show his relief. Richie had known his secret and Richie, involuntarily, had given him his way out. "I can't race without a navigator. I don't know the route well enough."

Then Charlie and George came into the dining-room, both looking as if they hadn't slept. "We'll drive you into town, Ham," Charlie said. "Or the Wizard is out there, if you want it."

They both stood looking at him, and Ham knew what they meant: the Wizard was there if he wanted to take it into town for the scrutineers to look at it. If he wanted it to be prepared for Sunday's race.

He stared back at them, and then he heard Taz say, "I'll come with you as navigator, if you want me. I asked Ainsworth this morning if he'd release me. I know the course a little. And Richie had his notes."

And in the faces of Charlie and George he saw something like hope start; for a moment the sadness lifted, and they looked like the men they had been before Richie's death. And then he knew that, if there was to be a memorial to Richie, it was not to be his cars on the Aylesbury road, no matter how many. It was to be one car on the roads of Italy, in the Mille Miglia, one car driven flat out for the whole thousand miles in the hope of coming in first.

"We'll take the Wizard in," he said, rising from the table, putting his hand on the arm of his brother. "Me and Taz."

19

Ham sat in the car, his foot on the pedal, waiting to ease it forward as the starter called him up onto the ramp. Beside him Taz sat checking the notes on the rollers; this was the carbon copy—the copy with Richie's blood on it had been burned. In front of Taz, on a wide shelf beneath the fascia board, there were two bottles of orange juice and a small box containing biscuits, fruit and chocolate; for almost the next eleven hours they would be continuously on the move and there would be no stops for meals. In the glove box there were two spare pairs of goggles, a spare pair of gloves for Ham, and some cleaning tissues. They both wore green helmets with short visors and goggles with green antiglare glass. They were dressed almost identically in green coveralls, wide waist belts and soft suède boots. Both of them had also liberally sprinkled the inside of their underpants with

224

talcum powder, a hint that Ham had had passed on to him by his father. They had done everything they could to ensure some sort of comfort, but were beginning the long journey with the knowledge that after the first hour there would be little, if any, comfort at all.

Friday morning they had brought the car into the Piazza Vittoria, easing it through the clamorous black throng that seemed to cover every inch of the big square. On the east and west sides of the square there were small islands of space partitioned off by wooden barriers. The crowd hung over the barriers, excitement like bright paint on their faces, dreams behind their eyes: some day they, too, would drive their glittering red Ferraris and Alfa-Romeos into those spaces to be inspected by the scrutineers. Somewhere beyond the crowd, driven up a side alley, a band was playing: cymbals clashed, and the drummer thumped at the hide in an ecstasy of joy and excitement. The faces of the buildings around were false: the buildings looked unsafe behind quivering walls of banners. Hordes of swallows challenged the flying flags; the pigeons had already surrendered the square and headed for Milan and the cathedral there; if there were any dogs or cats in Brescia they were not to be seen. The cars owned Brescia in this week before the Mille Miglia.

Two *carabinieri*, flashing their authority like muskets, had appeared out of the crowd and guided Ham and Taz through to one of the scrutineering enclosures. The crowd hushed for a moment, as the loud-speakers gave it the information it was waiting for.

"Before the scrutineers now we have the British Wizard of Hamilton Rafferty, competitor in the over 2000 c.c. class."

"Rafferty!" The crowd surged forward; those in front struggled for breath as they were crushed against the barriers. "L'Aquila!"

The number the Wizard would carry in the race, which was also the time at which it would start, was painted on the bonnet and side: 718. Then it was pushed forward for inspection by the officials seated at the tables. Seals were placed on certain sections of the engine and chassis, to ensure that no replacements were made before or during the race, and then Ham had got back into the car. He had gunned the motor for the benefit of the crowd, who had responded with an appreciative cheer, and then had taken the car out of the enclosure, pushing it at the crowd, which somehow found room to move back and make a path for it, and had driven it out of town and back to the garage.

Once committed to the race, Ham had felt easier. He still had doubts and was still afraid, but he had taken the first step and that had been the most difficult. Whatever followed now was at the whim of stronger forces than his own. He did not consciously think in terms of the workings of destiny; but whether he was conscious of it or not, destiny was now at the wheel of the Wizard. It was the force that became the shadow of every man when he committed himself to danger, the force that rode with the test pilot when he turned the nose of the plane down into the dive that would take him through the sound barrier; that stepped into the ring with the matador when the bull, wearing its goading pennants of *banderillas*, came at him with red death in its eyes; that went down with the diver into the depths where darkness and silence were absolute.

Now it was Sunday morning, thirty seconds to go and 7:18 was coming up on the clock.

The white-coated official flagged them forward up onto the bright yellow ramp. Behind them were five cars; 603 cars were ahead of them. The first car, a one-cylinder Isetta, had left at nine o'clock the previous night. At half-minute intervals for the next hour the cars had rolled down off the ramp and headed south for Rome, the turning point. From ten o'clock on, divided into different classes, the cars had gone off at minute intervals all through the night. Up to midnight the cars had been mere family cars, Fiats and Renaults, one or two Morris Minors, all specially tuned but driven by drivers whose one race in the year was the Mille Miglia. At midnight the first of the sports cars had begun to roll down off the ramp, but it was daylight before the first cars driven by the professional racing men had begun their long journey. As Ham took the Wizard up onto the ramp he knew that the leaders of the small cars were probably already on their way back from Rome. But they did not concern him. The winner of the Mille Miglia, as far as the general public was concerned, came from the big cars, the car that covered the thousand miles in the least time. Sitting there in the Wizard on the ramp, the centre of attraction for the thirty seconds that was given to each driver before he was flagged away and his place taken by the driver behind, Ham knew that the eventual outright winner was expected to come from the last dozen or so cars to get away. They were the big cars driven by the professionals and every professional wanted to win the Mille Miglia.

Ham saw the starter raise his flag. He raised the revs of the engine, easing his foot on the clutch; then the flag dropped and he moved the car forward and down the ramp. As soon as they hit the roadway he accelerated, going smoothly up through the gears, down the long narrow lane of the Viale Rebuffone, between the black hedges that were people; the people, bleary-eyed, weary-backed and hoarse-voiced, who had been here all night and would be back here again at midday to see the first of the cars as they returned. Then the road widened, the crowd thinned and the Wizard was racing at full speed for Verona, forty-two miles away.

This was different from when Ham had gone round with Richie in the other car. They were travelling almost twice as fast now; the engine and wind howl were deafening. All yesterday Ham and Taz had read and reread Richie's notes, looked at the films again and again, and devised signals by

227

which Taz could guide Ham. From now on, if they were to survive, they had to have complete confidence in each other. A wrongly read direction, a slackening of concentration at the wheel, and they could both go off the road to their probable death.

Ahead of them, after fifteen miles, they saw a green dot rapidly growing larger, becoming a Jaguar XK150. Ham brought the Wizard up behind it, and Taz reached for the horn button by his left hand. They went past the Jaguar with a long almost derisive blast of the horn, and then they were coming into a village. Taz made his signal, warning of an S-bend that could be taken flat out in top gear, and Ham chose his line and took the car through, going so close to a garden wall that dust seemed to fly from the masonry.

Beyond Verona, on the way to Vicenza, they were passing other cars rapidly; at 160 they went past an Austin-Healey that seemed to be in no more than second gear. Then they were through Vicenza and Padova was the next town. They went into Padova at 150, down the main street, braking hard, round the right-angled bend at the end of the street, scraping the straw bales as Ham took the car a little too wide. They roared through the town, aware of the black blur of the noiselessly cheering crowd, and headed for Ravenna, the first control point, a hundred miles further on.

They went into Ravenna with Ham braking hard as they approached the control point. Taz held up the route-card board when they were yards short of the control point. As they slowed, an official ran alongside the car, reached in and thumped a rubber stamp on the route-card, then fell back, waving them on their way. They had gone through the control point without actually stopping.

Beyond Ravenna was the winding road to Forli, then an abrupt turn south to Rimini. From here on to Pescara was the fastest stretch of the whole race. On their left the Adriatic, seen at intervals, was a vast sun-cobbled field on which

228

dark-sailed fishing boats sat like gorged crows. In the villages the fishing nets were hung out to dry, making latticework of the morning sun; on their right the olive trees marched away like gnarled old men in some army of veterans that had no destination. But Ham and Taz saw none of this; all they saw was the dusty blue road ahead of them. It spun toward them, bringing other cars with it; it was a ribbon, a thousand miles long, that the Wizard had to wind into itself.

They went over a humped bridge at 170, rising in the air like an airborne plane. Ham kept the wheels on line, confident Taz hadn't given him the wrong signal, and two hundred feet farther on the car landed back on the road, still on line and still doing 170.

Pescara was the second control point. Beyond the control, as they slowed, they saw George Hayes waving a green tablecloth tacked to a piece of bamboo. Their route-card was stamped, and they rolled onto the pit where George had established himself.

"You're second!" he yelled as he swung the arm of the petrol gravity tank over the rear of the car. "Twelve seconds behind the back-marker!"

A mechanic was cleaning the dead flies and insects from the windshield; another was checking the oil and water; a third had gone round the tires. Bartell hadn't spared any expense: these men had been hired for the day for thirty seconds' work. Ham munched on the peeled banana that had been handed to him; Taz was sucking an orange.

"Take her away!" George yelled. "See you in Brescia!"

Ham swallowed the last of the banana, popped a fresh piece of gum into his mouth, let in the gears and accelerated away with a whine of the engine and a scream of protest from the tires. If Rossano, the back-marker, had gained twelve seconds as far as Ravenna, which was where his time would have been taken and phoned through, he would

229

gain even more on the long stretch down to Pescara. Ham had to try to hold his own on this next stretch.

The next stop was Rome, 150 miles away, on the other side of the mountains.

This was the stretch where Richie had been killed.

As the last car had rolled down off the ramp and accelerated away down the Viale Rebuffone, Bartell, Sophie and Janet had turned away and begun to struggle back through the crowd toward their hotel.

"Nothing to do but wait now," Bartell said, trying to carve a way for the two women through the black, heaving throng. "I think I'll try to snatch a couple hours' sleep. I'm bug-eyed. Maybe I shouldn't have stayed up all night, but I had to see it, you know? Six hundred cars. Something like thirty thousand horsepower let loose on that road all at once. And every one of those drivers flogging those horses to the limit." He shook his head in wonder, and admiration, too. He had faced risks, all his life had been a risk, but he had never risked death. For a moment he was no longer the millionaire tire manufacturer, the man with three thousand buttering-up employees, the stubborn man with the belief in his own genius. He was one with the youngest boy in the anonymous crowd thick around him: for a moment he was pressed against a young man in his twenties, a stranger but his brother in excitement and admiration and secret envy. "A thousand miles. They are going to be tired when they get back. I think I'll go up and try for some sleep."

"I'm going to Mass," Janet said. "They always have High Mass at the cathedral as soon as the last car gets away."

"I'll come with you," Sophie said. "I'm worn out, too, like Dad. But I couldn't sleep, I know that. I'll come to Mass with you."

"Say a prayer for me," said Bartell jokingly, leaving them at the entrance to the hotel, switching his hearing aid off be-

230

fore he had even left them, summoning his silence; then he stopped and turned back. "No, not for me. For Ham and Taz."

"That's why I'm going," said Janet, but she was speaking to herself and the fact that Bartell was now deaf didn't matter to her.

The two women followed the crowd to the cathedral. They barely got inside the doors; there were no seats for them and they had to stand. There was not even room to kneel; those in the pews were eyed with frank envy. The priest's voice rose and fell in the chant: God was almost mocked by the lack of music in it. The incense smoke floated like breath in the stony chill of the cathedral; gradually the packed crowd gave its own warmth to the stone about it. High in the roof of the cathedral a nightmare of bats fluttered, like evil spirits that had been exorcised but were unable to escape. Janet stood with her head bowed, her sensible English hat pushed a little askew by the crush of arms and shoulders about her. The beads ran through her fingers; she wove a plea of prayer: Let them come back, Lord. Let them come back.

She had been standing at the window of her hotel room on Friday morning when she had seen Ham drive the green Wizard into the packed square. She had recognised the car and guessed who the driver was; she had had to put on her glasses to see who was riding with Ham. She had stared down at the car as it had inched its way through the crowd; then her eyes had blurred and she had turned giddy. She had moved away, to lie down on her bed till the giddiness had passed; but the window had drawn her like a magnet. She had drawn up a chair and sat there, half-hidden behind the cotton rosebush of the curtain, as if afraid of being caught spying. As she had stared down at the green car, now in the scrutineering enclosure, watching the numbers being painted on its green metal hide, her fingers had clutched at the curtain, crushing the roses that had no scent. There had been no resentment or anger at what her sons were doing to her; she had felt more disbelief than anything, even though she had known for years that what she was seeing had been inevitable. The disbelief arose, perhaps, from seeing them in the one car; she had known that some day, despite Taz's promise to her, she would see them in the same race. But she had never expected to see them in the one car. That was reducing the odds against her, tightening every screw in the rack.

Later they had both come to see her. They had come gently and cautiously into her room, like schoolboys who had broken a window instead of a promise.

"You don't have to tell me," she had said. "I saw you down there in the scrutineers' enclosure."

Taz had looked at Ham; it was he who had broken his promise, but he left it to his brother to speak for him. For the first time she felt angry at him; then she realised it was she who had asked for the promise, not he who had offered it. Her father, who had his faults and no tolerance, had taught her to be fair: she had gone through life being fair to everyone, friend and stranger alike, and she had arrived at the stage where fairness had defeated her: she had been left without defences. Anger, selfishness, conceit were defences: she had none of those. "Don't try to excuse yourselves," she said, trying to whip up some resentment, some authority, something to show she was their mother and they had let her down; but she might just as well have tried to strike them. She finished lamely, "I know how it is. I've expected it all along."

"It wouldn't have been this way," Ham said, sinking down on the bed; he looked old, old enough to be her brother and not her son. She put her hand to her head, as if to feel the grey in her hair; she caught a glimpse of herself in the ward-

robe mirror and was told the truth. "If Richie hadn't been—"
He stopped, not wanted to use the word *killed:* the pause
was effective enough. "He would have wanted us to race the
car, Mum. And there's Kitty to think of."

"Have you seen her?" she asked.

Ham shook his head. "Not yet. I've just seen Joe Bartell.
He and I are going to take over the Wizard, go on building
it."

"So you're really driving for yourself, not for Richie?" It
was her last flash of resentment, the last feeble effort with
the whip; instantly she was sorry and wanted to weep. "I
shouldn't have said that! I'm sorry. But—" She was left
to expressing herself with her hands, but they, too, were
mute. She clasped them together, each hand looking for
strength in the other.

"We'll be all right, Mother." Taz could only offer a young
man's comfort, the confidence of youth: he hadn't seen his
father killed, as Ham had, nor stood beside her when Ham
had telephoned the news through to her. There hadn't even
been time to have him flown out to the funeral; in those days
there hadn't been a daily service to Milan, nor had it been
easy to get on a plane.

"What happens after this?" she said. "Do you go on racing
this car? Till you have made its name?"

Ham rose slowly, almost painfully, from the bed; its
springs creaked, like an echo of his own effort. Pat never
looked as old as this, she thought, not even before the race in
which he was killed. Why does he look like this, she wondered; and felt that, somehow, she had failed him. Her son
had stopped being a boy, being a young man; and till now
she had never noticed how far down the years he had come
after her.

"We'll get this race over first," he said slowly. "That's the
way I've always driven. One race at a time."

233

And now here she was in the cathedral, among strangers but for the young American girl beside her, praying as she had been praying for over thirty years, as she had been praying from the afternoon of her wedding day.

Praying that she would not be left alone.

The day was now hot. Ahead of the speeding car the mountains climbed steeply to the cobalt blaze of the sky. The tops of the mountains were already scorched by the heat; the shadows of the houses on the mountainside looked like smudged ashes. Ham was bathed in sweat now; it made rivulets in the dust and fumes that had blackened his face and arms. His wrists and arms had begun to feel the strain of continually battling with the wheel; his left arm felt worse than the right, because of the extra work it had had on the gear lever. He could feel his left leg stiffening up from the continual effort on the clutch; he tried to straighten his leg out, to ease the ache.

They were on a straight stretch. He felt a touch on his thigh; he looked at Taz, not expecting any signals. Taz was shouting something, pointing down at his lap. He leaned his head sideways and Taz bellowed faintly in his ear: "Leak!"

He looked wildly about the cockpit, looking for the gush of oil or petrol; then abruptly he understood. He braked sharply, grinning to himself, and followed Taz out of the car as the latter leaped out to relieve himself. To race with a full bladder was dangerous; a bump could bring about serious internal injury. He unbuttoned his coveralls and looked up to see the long line of brown-robed monks standing on the bank above them. The monks, their shaven heads glistening like river stones, clapped their hands in encouragement; this was no time for false modesty or a slow pleasurable relief of the bladder, this was a time for urgency and pressure. The long line of monks and the two drivers stood there facing each other, laughing heartily, while the water ran streaming

234

between them and, on the road behind, other cars went by in hurricanes of sound and dust. Then Ham and Taz were finished, had waved to the monks and, still laughing, were back in the car and on their way.

Summer was coming early to Italy this year. As they climbed into the mountains the heat seemed to become more intense. They went through villages where the white walls of the houses were like a glare of ice; they raced through narrow streets where the shadows made them dark as tunnels. The race had begun to take its toll. They passed cars that had left the road; another car was jammed bonnet-first into the front doorway of a house; in a village square a car burned like a *festa* effigy. There was no way of knowing how they were faring in the race; at this stage it was a race against time more than anything else.

They were passing cars still in the race. As they climbed toward Aquila they came up behind a two-litre Ferrari whose driver looked as if he needed all the road if he was to stay on it. Rubber was being stripped off the Ferrari's rear tires, leaving ugly, frightening marks on the roadway; on every bend and corner the car finished in the gravel and dust on the edges of the road. Ham was no more than six feet behind the Ferrari as it went into and came out of each bend; gravel flung back by the car in front was pelting against the nose of the Wizard. Yet Ham knew he had to get past; he couldn't sit behind this slower car till they were down out of the mountains. Taz was blowing the horn and flicking the lights on and off, but the driver of the Ferrari was in a world of his own.

They went through Aquila, a tempest of two cars that blew people back against the houses, and began the descent toward Rieti. This was where Richie had been killed; but Ham shut his mind against the thought. The bends here were fast, and the Ferrari's driver took advantage of them. Here, his

235

car could compete with the bigger ones; extra power meant little; everyone was fast downhill. But this was where the drivers competed against each other.

Then they were coming down to the spot where Ham and Richie had gone off the road. Taz gave the signal, intimating the right-left S-bend and then the sharp right-hand bend; but Ham could see the whole road in his mind as clearly as if it were opened out for him. The Ferrari went through the first part of the S-bend already on its brakes; it went wide on the next section to take the right-hand bend. In that moment Ham brought the Wizard up on the inside of the Ferrari; for an instant the two cars were level as they braked for the right-hand bend. Then the Ferrari's driver's nerves gave; he trod even harder on his brakes. The bend was open before them now; Ham took his foot off the brake and accelerated. He was depending on the Wizard's power; the engine roared, he felt the tires grip and then they were through the bend and the Ferrari had been left behind. The gap in the retaining wall was still there, and the smashed tree against which the practice car had been flung; but Ham didn't see it, and Taz, admiring his brother's driving, forgot to look.

Then they were down out of the mountains, and on the way to Rome they touched 170. They came into Rome, over the cobbled streets on the outskirts, sliding on the corners as if the cobbles were blocks of ice; and now Taz was using the horn and the lights to warn, not cars, but spectators of their approach. The crowds, dedicated to suicide, had encroached on the road till there seemed only room enough for a bicycle to squeeze through. Taz continued to blast on the horn and Ham began to flick the car from side to side. The crowd fell back and the Wizard went through between the human walls at 130. Then they were at the control point.

Bartell had wanted them to make the entire journey on the one set of tires, claiming it would be a better advertisement for them if that feat could be achieved. But Ham, backed by Carlin and Sitkin, had objected. Ham felt that the main thing was to win the race; how far the tires had lasted was secondary. The ordinary Sunday driver would not be impressed by the fact that a car had covered a thousand miles in a race on one set of tires; he expected tires to last anything from ten to thirty thousand miles and he had little idea of how they were worn in a race. So it had been decided to change the rear tires here at Rome.

Ham clambered out of the car and walked up and down. Two mechanics were already at work on the rear wheels; a third had run a jack under the car and was waiting to lower it again. Petrol was being pressured into the tank, enough to get them to Florence; oil was pumped in and water sloshed into the radiator. Ham, moving up and down, trying to get the aching stiffness out of his leg, admired the way Ed Carlin had organised things here: this was almost like Mercedes-Benz efficiency.

Carlin gave him a glass of orange juice and a slab of chocolate. While Ham drank the orange juice Carlin was swabbing his face and neck with a wet sponge, like a second working on a boxer between rounds. "Rossano's your man to beat. He's still about ten seconds ahead of you—they just phoned through from Rieti. You picked up some on him coming through the mountains from Pescara. He's faster than you on the straights, so you got to hold him from now on and get ahead of him the other side of Florence. Okay, they've nearly finished. Good luck!"

Ham, his mouth still full of chocolate, swung into the seat of the car. The back wheels hit the roadway with a thump as the jack was jerked from beneath the car. Ham had already started the car and was in gear; the tires spun, gripped, and they were away. They had been on the road three and a half hours and now the toughest part of the journey was ahead of them.

237

On through Viterbo and up the Radicofani Pass, with spectators packed like suicide clubs on every bend. The sun was now high, beating down to make a furnace of the cramped cockpit. The heat, fumes, noise and dust were combining to form a torture that even the Chinese had never invented; the only escape was to shut the mind against it. Taz had already begun to feel sick; he welcomed the distraction of reading the notes, giving signals, blowing the horn and flashing the lights. They swept down out of the pass, passing a blue Gordini that went off the road into a wall at the moment they swept by it. They came down a long, straight slope, seeing the village ahead of them, and Taz gave the signal to brake and go into the village on a right-hand curve at half-throttle. Ham began to brake as the village shot nearer. He had seen the other car go into the village about three hundred yards ahead of them in a cloud of dust, and some instinct told him something was wrong.

They came round the corner of a house flush with the road and there was the red car right across the road in front of them. And it was surrounded by villagers all working furiously but lightheartedly to get it going again. A woman screamed, but Ham and Taz, deafened by the noise of their own car, didn't hear her. They just saw the faces turn toward them, white flashes of terror, and Taz suddenly cried out. Ham didn't brake any harder; he turned the wheel a little and let the car slide. The paralysed crowd swept nearer; Taz saw a child turn its face into its father's legs. The Wizard was now broadside on; the tail swung farther and now Ham braked again. The Wizard shot sideways, away from the crowd, and then it had stopped dead against the straw bales by the side of the road. There was a scream of relief from the crowd, but Ham was putting the car into first gear and pulling it away from the straw bales. The road was blocked and there was always the chance of another car coming round the corner. He slammed the car into reverse, got it straightened out, found a gap in the crowd and accelerated through. Taz, putting the safety catch back on the reverse position of the gear-gate, looked up and nodded in admiration. Ham grinned, pleased with himself and his brother's praise: he knew it was one of the best pieces of driving he had done in all his career.

The minutes and then the hours went by, and still they rode in their own burning, punishing world. They blazed through Siena, where for centuries there had been a horse race round the city square for the honour of winning a banner; the Wizard raced through the old city, a green metal horse striving for its own banner. Then they were coming down into Florence. The roads here were bad and the car bumped and fought like a wild thing; they skated down a long length of tramline that was like a strip of steel ice. They shot over a bridge, the Arno just a flash of brown seen at the edge of their eyes, through the narrow, winding streets at over a hundred, crossing a square in a long four-wheel drift, and then they were into the control point.

Their route-card was stamped and they kept rolling on to where Charlie, red-faced and his overalls dark with sweat, was waiting for them with the long arm of the gravity petrol tank ready for them.

"You'll have to go faster!" he shouted as he shoved the nozzle into their tank and nodded farther along the pits. "Rossano's just come in behind you!"

Ham spat out his gum and gobbled a new piece. He wiped his face with the wet sponge handed to him, then squeezed the rest of the water down the back of his neck. Charlie swung the petrol nozzle away, waving them on, and Ham crunched in the gears and shot the car away from the pits. Before he had to concentrate on the bend in the street ahead of him, he saw in his mirror the red 4.4-litre Ferrari just coming away from the pits behind him. That meant Rossano was a minute ahead of him on time. Where the four other backmarkers were, he could only guess. Since they hadn't been mentioned, he could only assume they were already out of the race. Which meant that Rossano, leading him by a minute and in a faster car, was the man he had to beat.

The mountains lay ahead, dark and suddenly grim under a bruised-looking sky. Heat had built up over the mountains, and already there were baleful grins of lightning beyond the farthest peaks. The road had now become doubly treacherous, and there was danger even on the simplest bends. Melted tar had mixed with oil and rubber from the hundreds of cars that had already gone through here, and in parts the road surface had now become just a deadly gamble. Ham was now having to work like a man bailing for his life in a sinking boat; his arms were in a continual whirl as he fought the wheel and flung the gear lever about in its gate. Occasional swift glances in his mirror showed that Rossano had not gained on this tricky stretch. But that was little consolation; he not only had to stop Rossano from gaining, but he had to gain on *him*. Somewhere in these mountains he had to regain the minute he had lost and gain a further minute or two to make up for the long stretches through Modena, Parma and Cremona, where the Ferrari's superior speed would tell.

They were at the summit of the Futa Pass when the storm broke.

After she and Janet had left the cathedral, Sophie went back to her room at the hotel. She lay down, but though she was tired to the point of exhaustion, sleep did not come easily. She had at least another nine hours to wait before Ham would be back here in Brescia, safe with her and all danger behind him; not till then would she be able to relax completely, so that now she sought sleep as she might a drug. When she finally did drop off, it was into slumber that was no rest at all; she tossed and turned and moaned to herself as if in the throes of nightmare. When she woke in mid-after-

240

noon she lay on the bed staring at the shuttered window, wondering where she was and why the window looked as if it were laced with bars of golden light. Then memory came back, and she looked at her watch in the dim light of the room. Two more hours before she could expect to see Ham again.

Almost eleven hours: an eternity of waiting. But if he survived this race (and she shuddered at the thought), there would be no more waiting after this. On Friday afternoon, a few hours after he had told her that he and Taz were going to race together in the Mille Miglia, he had called for her in one of the Alfa-Romeos and they had driven out to Lake Garda. And there he had given her his promise.

They had driven along the southern shore of the lake and turned north toward Bardolino. They had parked the car in the shade of three tall poplars and got out and gone down to the water's edge. Here, there was no beach, but a shelf of blindingly white stones: they walked across a cemetery of bleached skulls and when they reached the real edge of the lake, there were other skulls beneath the pale green, limpid water. On the far side of the lake a mountain reared itself almost fiercely into the sky, and behind it the sky had turned black with thunderclouds. But on this side of the lake there was still bright sunshine and, because of the whiteness of the rocks on which they sat and the dark threat of the mountain across the water from them, the sunshine had a brilliance that was like a pain against the eyes.

They took their shoes off and paddled their feet in the cool water. "I used to come out here with Dad before the war," Ham said. "In the thirties, when he would come here to drive in the Mille Miglia and I was just a kid. We'd hire a boat and just drift around in it. It's been my favourite piece of water ever since. But I'd never come back to it till to-day."

"It's beautiful." She looked around her, at the villas on the

241

other side of the road behind them, at the three poplars, like tall green dancers awaiting their cue, at the lone boat sailing far up the lake, its sail a sharp white splinter in the distant view. Far across the lake a pile driver of sunlight smashed down through the black clouds; a village was suddenly illuminated, falling apart into a burst of white cottages. Below it, on the very rim of the lake, a car raced along, a tiny red dot that disappeared into a tunnel and, as far as she knew, never appeared again. Then she looked behind her again. "I wonder if any of these villas are for rent?"

"Why?"

"I was thinking it would be nice to come here for our honeymoon."

He smiled and put his hand over hers as it lay on a rock skull. "I was hoping you'd say that. And if we could afford it, we might come back here each year for our holidays."

Both of them were wearing sunglasses, but the dark glasses couldn't hide the love in their eyes. "I wish we were married now," she said and dug her nails into his hands. "Oh, mister!"

"Easy," he said, still smiling, feeling his own desire rising in him and teasing her with it.

"It's the Italian in me," she said, trying to smile but sick with love for him. The sun and the storm across the lake and the skull-like stones around them suggesting death, had all suddenly became a turmoil in her: the wanting of him now was a physical pain. She stood up, pulling him up with her. "Let's go somewhere! Somewhere where no one can see us!"

He stood beside her. A car went slowly by on the road behind them, but they were oblivious of it. They stood ankle-deep in the water, their arms about each other, while the storm came down over the mountain and began to cross the lake. "There's one thing I brought you out here to tell you."

242

"Yes?" she said, not wanting to be told anything right now but that he loved her.

"Since we're going to settle down in England and make the Wizard, I don't have much to worry about as far as career goes. Your father is going to be my partner, not my boss. And I'm confident that it won't be too long before we're making money out of the Wizard. So," he looked down at her, "after Sunday I'm retiring."

"You mean that, darling?"

"It's a promise," he said. "My last race will be the Mille Miglia. I talked it over with your father this morning. If we do all right in Sunday's race, then we enter for Le Mans. But Taz will drive for us. And he'll drive for us, in sports-car events anyway, from now on. Happy?"

"Happy?" she cried, and pressed herself fiercely against him. "Oh, darling, darling!"

"Let's go and find that place where no one can see us," he said, and collecting their shoes, he picked her up and carried her back across the white shelf of rocks, now freckled with the first drops of rain, to the car.

And now, lying here in the dim room, with the crackle of cars coming up from the square below, those that had already been round the Mille Miglia, had come down the Viale Rebuffone and were now on their way back to their garages, their pride and glory and excitement behind them for another year, she was aware of the fact that the bars of light had gone from the shuttered window and the room had suddenly become darker.

She got up, crossed the room and flung open the shutters. In the square below, umbrellas were opening like black toadstools as the first drops of rain began to fall. Far to the south the sky was purple-black, and lightning leered and snarled behind the thick curtain of the storm.

And still another two hours to wait. Still another two hours in which she could lose out to the cars.

The rain hit the Wizard suddenly, like the spray of a huge wave, as it came round a corner on the Futa. One moment they were driving through dust, and the next moment the dust on the windshield had turned to mud. It turned to mud on Ham's goggles, too; and he snatched them down from his eyes. He gesticulated to Taz, and the latter dug in the glove box for a spare pair of goggles.

Steam was rising from the road and the surrounding rocks; they rode through thermal country. There had not been enough rain as yet to wash the mud from the roadway; the car slid on the greasy surface on every bend. Several cars had gone off the road as soon as they ran into the rain; one burned like a bright bush behind the silver stakes of rain. The Wizard began to slide as it came down a steep slope; it approached a corner almost side on. Ham, trying to see through the already smeared goggles he had just put on, felt a moment of chilling panic; his hands ceased to move on the wheel, as if something told him death was inevitable at this coming moment, and the car continued to slide. Then the urge for survival took hold of him; he couldn't die without fighting against it. He waited till the last moment, till they were almost at the corner, then he put power into the car. The Wizard slid a little further, the edge of the road rushing nearer, then the tires, Bartell's tires, took hold. Next moment they were round the corner.

The rain now was sheeting down. Cars ahead of them had begun to slow; they went past a train of five of them. The mirror now was distorted with water; it was impossible to see if Rossano was still close to them. They came up on a Mercedes 300SL; its driver was at least enclosed from the rain. He was in the middle of the road, determined to stay in the race, no matter where he finished or whom he held back. Spray was flying back from him in a dense mist; it was like riding in the wake of a storm wave. Taz was blowing the horn and flicking the lights, but the Mercedes' driver was lost to what was behind him. Then the road widened for a short stretch; Ham nosed the Wizard up alongside the Mercedes. The white car held the middle of the road for a moment; then abruptly it slowed. Its driver held up his hand in a gesture of genial defeat; he waved them on with his best wishes. Ham had survived two dangerous moments and now all at once he began to feel confident again.

He had always been one of the best wet-weather drivers. He had not gone off at Le Mans through any fault in his own driving; his skill was still there if only he had the confidence to use it. The rain had caused his father's death, but Pat Rafferty had never been a good driver in the wet; he had died because he was the sort of man who always took his chances, no matter what the conditions. The rain had never directly wrecked Ham, and now was his chance to prove he was still the master of it. It was also his chance to win the race, his one chance, because there was no one else in the running now, even including Rossano, who could compete against him in conditions like this. What he had told Richie months ago was true: in the Mille Miglia it was the driver and not the car who won the race.

They went through a village, crossing the icelike cobbles on a trailing throttle; they ploughed through mud at the end of the village and then they were on the open road again. They had a glimpse of cars stopped in the village, and villagers clustered like sheltering birds in doorways. On this open stretch Taz snatched a quick look backward. Rossano was nowhere in sight.

The sky above them now was black and lightning leaped along the tops of the mountains. They were driving with their headlights on, through gloom that pressed down on them like a solid curtain. The noise of the engine and the beat of the rain against the car made the thunder noiseless, but they could almost sense the trembling of the sky and the shudder of the earth beneath it. Right ahead of them lightning stabbed at a tree; they raced into a flare that turned the countryside to a moonscape. The world was dead, and they were the only living things in it. This was the frontier of the inferno land of Dante.

The cockpit now was awash with water, foaming about their feet. Their coveralls were supposed to be waterproof, but they hadn't been proofed against rain like this. Taz was trying to read his notes beneath a plastic covering; he began to grow scared that he would give Ham a wrong direction. They went down the Raticosa Pass, past the spot where their father had been killed, at a speed only a little below what they would have been doing in the dry. The stone memorial was dark with mud; but they went by without seeing it. And from that spot on, as if he had crossed some Rubicon of danger, Ham began to drive even faster, to drive as if he had been driving in rain all his life.

He went down the pass in a series of controlled slides that seemed to ignore the treacherous surface beneath them. Twice they scraped the stone parapet on the outside edge of the road; each time Ham brought the car away from it without slackening speed. Groups of spectators, like drowning black goats, huddled in the lee of small cliffs; their hands flashed like white horns as the Wizard went crackling past.

Then they were down out of the mountains and heading for Bologna. They went down the long tramlines into the city at well over 130, braking a long way ahead of the control point so that they wouldn't skid. Their route-card was stamped while they were still moving, the race official glad to get back into shelter again out of the pelting rain, and they were moving away and headed for the fast straights up through Modena and Parma to Piacenza.

Water had begun to have its effect on the car now. There was water in the brakes and in the kingpins, so that the steering had tightened till it was almost solid. Ham was steering now mostly by using the throttle and rear wheels, an art that Taz was forced to admire even while they rode the thin line that separated them from disaster. It was the art of a man with long experience and, now, supreme confidence in his own skill.

They raced through Modena and beyond it were touching 160, spray trailing behind them in a long, whirling veil. Ham, unable to see now through his goggles, had taken them off and was driving without them, his eyes slitted against the painful pelt of the rain. They were still passing cars, but none of them was challenging them now. It was as if everyone, even if he couldn't see the Wizard in his mirror, knew that the eventual winner was blazing up the road behind him.

Through Parma, Piacenza and through the rain all the way. Through Mantova, where the ghost of Nuvolari must have risen to salute them. And then they were on the long last stretch to Brescia.

Ham was driving now with confidence, skill, pleasure and a sweet agony of regret. This was his last race, and he had never driven a better one. He was soaked to the skin and he was cold and weary; his left leg burned with pain and the muscles of his arms had turned to lead. He had never been happier; and yet mixed with the happiness there was sadness. This time next year he would be in Brescia, one of those watching and waiting; at Le Mans, Silverstone, Spa, Nurburgring, he would only be able to watch and wait. While Taz, here beside him now, the young man with his racing life ahead of him, would be savouring this happiness. The envy of Taz had already begun.

He sat back, his arms at full stretch: for this day in all his career he was The Master. One with the great, with Nuvolari, Varzi, Caracciola, Fangio, one with his father. The Wizard's engine rose to a crescendo, the needle on the rev counter rose higher, spray thickened and was flung higher and farther back. They went down the long road at 170, racing through the last of the storm and into the thin sunlight that glistened on the town ahead of them.

Then they were coming into Brescia, coming up the Viale Rebuffone at a hundred miles an hour, the chequered flag ahead of them, and the roar of the crowd coming at them even above the roar of the engine. They crossed the line, the flag whipped down, and Ham began to slow.

They rolled to a stop in a patch of blazing sunshine. Steam was rising from the car; Ham lifted his feet out of three inches of water in the cockpit. Their clothes clung to them like other skins; their bodies were stiff with cold and fatigue. But they were both laughing.

Then Bartell, his thin, bony face splintered with the same happiness as they felt, was coming toward them. "You did it! You won! Rossano called it a day at Modena. Goddam, you did it!"

Ham turned and put his hand on Taz's knee. "It's all yours from now on, Taz. You lucky bastard."

Then he was clambering stiffly out of the car, walking away from the car without a backward glance, with Bartell jogging beside him, asking him how the tires had held, asking him didn't they have the best goddam tires and sports car in the world; walking down the steaming, shining road away from one life to another, walking and then running, stiff-legged and awkwardly, toward Sophie, coming to him with tears and laughter making a beautiful mess of her face. He clasped her in his arms, holding her to him, and then beyond her head he saw his mother.

Standing alone in the sunlight, she was staring past him at Taz, still sitting in the car.